Sea Devil Seven Seven

Sea Devil Seven Seven

A Vietnam Adventure

Dennis Wayne Ziniel

iUniverse, Inc.
New York Lincoln Shanghai

Sea Devil Seven Seven
A Vietnam Adventure

Copyright © 2006 by Dennis Wayne Ziniel

iUniverse books may be ordered through booksellers or by contacting:

iUniverse
2021 Pine Lake Road, Suite 100
Lincoln, NE 68512
www.iuniverse.com
1-800-Authors (1-800-288-4677)

ISBN-13: 978-0-595-38799-1 (pbk)
ISBN-13: 978-0-595-83180-7 (ebk)
ISBN-10: 0-595-38799-3 (pbk)
ISBN-10: 0-595-83180-X (ebk)

Printed in the United States of America

This book is dedicated to Petty Officer 3rd Class Scott Ferris Moore, Jr., who died in the crash of an SH-3A Sea King helicopter (BuNo 149908) offshore South Vietnam. His body was not recovered. Scott was assigned to Helicopter Combat Support Squadron Seven, which was serving aboard the USS Constellation at the time he made the ultimate sacrifice. Scott was born on the 28th of April 1949. His helicopter went down on the 20th of February 1970. His memory lives on in his family, his shipmates and his inscription on Panel 13W Line 037 of the Vietnam memorial in Washington D.C. Scotty you are a good man and you are missed.

Helicopter Combat Support Squadron Seven's primary mission off the coast of Viet Nam was Search and Rescue (SAR) and as it turns out, this squadron was one of the most highly decorated naval squadrons in the Vietnam Conflict. Since HC-7 was established on September 1, 1967 in Atsugi Japan, it has been awarded one Medal of Honor, four Navy Crosses, several Silver Stars and numerous Distinguished Flying Crosses. Helicopter Combat Support Squadron Seven was disbanded in August of 1975.

Foreword

This novel is based on events that actually happened. The story is being told as fiction since names have been changed as have some details to make the story flow more smoothly. The characters in this story are purely fictional and any resemblance to someone, living or deceased, is purely coincidental. This book has been written to preserve the memory of a generation divided by beliefs, yet united by culture. It is my intent to give the reader an insight into the times and events surrounding a squadron of sailors during the Viet Nam conflict, what they endured, how they felt, and how they reacted. I would like to recognize several people who were instrumental in seeing this work to completion. First and fore-most, this would not be a reality were it not for my, wife and best friend, Linda. I also need to thank Stacey Bornemann, Ardyce Ketterling, and Dale Toman for their input and comments. This book would not be the product it is without their help.

PROLOGUE

▼

The Sikorsky SH-3A helicopter flew one hundred feet above the choppy water as Keith peered towards the opening in the back of the helicopter, staring at sunlight shining through, where all should be darkness. He looked towards the first crewman, and although he mouthed words, nothing came. Not even the high pitch of the General Electric T-58 engines invaded the silence. When the crewman finally turned slowly towards him, his helmet visor was closed, so Keith had no idea who it was. Keith again stared toward the light, and felt the urge to investigate the lights' origin. There was more than one point of light emanating from the skin of the helicopter. He put his gloved finger on one point of light and felt a jagged edge. There were six holes with jagged edges…bullets. Panicked…he turned back toward the front of the helo. Lying on the floor were two still human forms covered with a blanket. Before he could lift the edge of the blanket, the helo went into a hover and a voice screamed at him. "Man your guns!" He looked out the side door and saw dark, thick foliage just as he heard bullets whining around him. He grabbed the grips of the mini-gun and fired in short bursts. He could see the tracer rounds racing toward the thick carpet of green below. As the helo landed, Keith could see human forms in dark uniforms running towards shadows hiding behind the foliage less than fifty feet from the helicopter. Someone screamed at him, "Cover me!" Keith covered the running sailors with his mini-gun spraying gun bursts to the left and to the right of them. They dropped to the ground. He continued firing. Suddenly the helo lifted off, and started forward flight. Keith was still laying a cover fire. It dawned on him that they were leaving and there were two shipmates still on the ground. Keith screamed towards the cockpit. "Stop! Turn around!"

The helo continued to head towards sea. He ran forward screaming at the pilot. "Go back!" But the cockpit was empty. The helo was flying itself. In the vacant pilot's seat someone had painted the numbers, "seven-seven", and on the copilot's seat the numbers, "seven-six".

CHAPTER 1

▼

As the cab swerved around the corner, Keith hit his head on the side of the roof, he was suddenly awake, going from one nightmare, to another, this one more real than the last. He bolted upright, and stared out the window at the mob of people, a thin layer of sweat glistened on his forehead. "Mobilize Against War Madness and Murder! Total Pullout Now!"

Men with beards and faded bell-bottom jeans and women looking more like young school girls with flowers woven through their long scraggly hair waved banners and chanted and screamed as vehicles carrying military personnel passed by them. "Baby burners! Baby killers!"

Keith Klein rode in one of those vehicles, a yellow taxi-cab, which drove past the protestors and through the main gate of Edwards Air Force Base. He glanced briefly at the protesters and then forced himself to keep his eyes straight ahead, although he felt a tightening in his throat and his stomach, he knew he had no choice in what lay ahead. He was under orders and he would do his duty.

The taxi stopped at the main boarding terminal where Keith checked in for his flight. He was in his dress blues, navy blue stovepipe pants and jumper with white tea-cup hat. His orders were in one hand, and his good friend Charlie Wood, or Woody as Keith called him, was at his side.

They walked outside the terminal building and boarded the waiting Boeing 707. Keith glanced at the thunderclouds rolling in heavily from the southwest, billowing and foreboding, and thought "Great, turbulence."

He found his assigned seat, in between Woody and a sergeant, who was already seated at the window. He strapped himself in, took a deep breath, and tried to relax.

Keith Klein was twenty years old and fresh off the farm from the mid-western state of North Dakota. Just one year prior to this flight he'd been eating hamburgers and sipping cokes at Jumbos Drive-In with his girlfriend, Patty. Then, thinking he wanted to go into architectural drafting, he had gone to Minnesota to attend Dunwoody Institute in Minneapolis. This lasted at least one quarter until he received a "Dear John" letter from Patty and raced home to reclaim his woman. Unfortunately, the only thing he accomplished was to lose his exempt draft status. Not wanting to get drafted into the Marine Corps or Army he opted to enlist in the United States Navy, and now here he was.

Keith contemplated the protestors, which now seemed to be an extension of his recurring dream. He didn't feel like a killer. He felt he was doing the right thing. Hell, did he even have a choice? Well, it didn't really matter anyway; he wasn't headed for Viet Nam. That was where all the problems were. Keith shrugged off the earlier events and looked around him.

Most of the passengers on the flight appeared to be military personnel, probably also bound for overseas assignments. Keith found himself checking out the stewardess as she flounced by, but found her a little too plump for his liking. He nudged Woody who was mooning over a photograph of a girl standing next to a corn field. "Nice corn." Woody grinned, but said nothing. "You're going to have to lighten up a bit, bud. It's going to be a long haul, and Iowa's a long way off." Woody stuck the picture back in his wallet. "Yeah, I know. Forgive me if I'm loyal at least until we get out of the States."

Woody ran his hand through straight brown hair in a comfortable manner that was familiar to Keith. It never did any good, as the hair would always pop back and he looked like he had never combed it. The motion was generally followed by a contagious laugh, which was sort of a chuckle hiccup. This, combined with a mutual sick sense of humor, had quickly pulled the two young men together during training and had made them inseparable.

Keith and Woody had been together since Memphis where they had received their aviation training. From there they had gone to San Diego for additional training on helicopters. Now they were headed to Helicopter Combat Support Squadron Seven, which was home based in Atsugi, Japan. Keith really felt lucky with his orders. It could have been much worse.

Keith leaned slightly towards the Army Sergeant on his left who was glumly staring out the window. "Where you from, Sarge?" Keith asked in an upbeat and friendly tone. The sergeant promptly answered without looking his way, "Kentucky." Silence again prevailed so Keith leaned over again and said, "Where you headed?" The young sergeant turned to look Keith right in the eye, "I'm headed for Nam, Dick Weed, so leave me alone."

Figuring the man wanted to be left to his personal thoughts; Keith turned his attention to a young woman coming down the aisle carrying an overnight bag with a sticker on the side that read "Make Love Not War." That struck Keith a little odd, considering this was a military flight. She was pretty, petite, with long ash-blond hair, and Keith gave her his best alluring smile when she glanced in his direction. She rolled her eyes and looked the other way, at which time Woody broke into laughter and nudged Keith, "I think she likes you," he teased. "Just my luck, another rich bitch with an attitude," Keith muttered under his breath as he scooted down in his seat. Thoughts of Patty flickered through his mind. This bad streak with women had to change. Woody wasn't ready to quit ribbing, "Any time you want to look at my picture, you just ask." Keith pretended to be looking in a different direction.

All passengers were finally seated and the plane began to roll. Woody chattered on about the girl back home, with Keith nodding once in a while, not really concentrating, and Woody not really caring if Keith was listening or not.

One by one, the 707's four Pratt & Whitney JT3D-7 turbofan-engines began to power up for takeoff. The jet taxied to the runway where they held position, waiting clearance for take off. When the control tower gave them the all clear, the pilot taxied onto the runway and then opened the throttles. The huge jet sped quickly down the runway and they were airborne in minutes, leaving behind the air force base, leaving behind the United States. Keith settled back in his seat, thinking he would get some sleep. He felt excited, yet slightly uneasy, and he didn't want to miss a thing once they got to Japan.

CHAPTER 2

▼

The 707 landed at Yokota Air Force Base, Japan, on September 14th, 1969, at 0200 hours. It was overcast when they arrived, damp and chilly. Keith and Woody stepped off the plane and carefully made their way down the steps and followed the rest of the passengers to the terminal.

Keith noted that the Japanese people seemed to be in a hurry, very polite and respectful-almost shy, but definitely in a hurry. Keith stopped short as a little slant-eyed man skidded in front of him, babbled something excitedly, bowed, and hurried on. At the same time as Keith made his abrupt halt, someone ran into the back of him almost knocking him off his feet. "Well excuse me, but could we keep this moving here?" Cynthia Croft tried to juggle another bag under her left arm so she could retrieve the one that had just fallen to the floor. She looked exasperated when the men turned slowly to look at her, obviously not in any hurry to get anywhere, "Well if it isn't Miss Make Love Not War." Keith smiled a slow lazy grin and picked up the bag off the floor, reading the side as if it were a great prophecy to mankind. "If you need anyone to accommodate you," he smiled and pointed at the words, "You just ask."

"Drop dead!" Cyndi grabbed the bag and tried to push past him. "Oh, a war greeting. How nice." Keith stood at attention, blocking her passage, and made a mock salute. "Really, Miss, Keith Klein, at your service, and this is my good friend, Charles Wood, or Woody as I call him." Woody nodded with a crooked grin as Keith continued. "How may I help you?"

Cyndi took a deep breath, and studied the man standing in front of her. He was about a head taller than she was, probably a couple inches less than six feet. He was dressed in typical Navy attire, with black curls spilling out the edges of his sailor cap. The eyes were dark brown and laughing at her. He seemed nice enough, but the quality that turned her off was that he was military. "You can get out of my way, Sailor Boy." She emphasized the word "boy." This time Cyndi put her shoulder into it, pushed past him and hurried into the terminal.

Woody, who had been observing from the sidelines, moved closer now and patted Keith on the back, "I can really see a romance budding there, friend." They looked at each other and grinned, "And you thought I had a problem."

Keith and Woody joined the other American serviceman at the check-in counter. After showing their orders and having them stamped, they were directed outside to a grey bus. The driver was Japanese and immediately started chattering and bobbing his head. "Hi, hi, Yokuska? Hi, hi, Yokuska?" Keith looked from Woody back to the driver.

"Hi to you too…uh, we have orders to go to our duty station at Atsugi." He showed the paper to the Japanese gentlemen, who promptly grabbed the paper and scampered for the door, "Hold it, guy! What's the problem?" Woody jogged after the nervous little man and grabbed him before he made it through the entry. The bus driver was really excited now. "Nonny deska, na. Yokuska? Atsugi?" Woody replied, "Yeah, that's it. Atsugi. We have to go to Atsugi."

The grateful man bowed politely. "Ah so, Atsugi." He continued to back away, bowing and bobbing and then got into the driver's seat. Keith let out a sigh of relief and boarded the bus to find that they had the whole thing to themselves.

The driver turned to them again, said "Atsugi moskosi," and floored it. Keith and Woody were thrown backwards in their seats. They again looked at each other doubtfully, "What the hell is moskosi?" Woody asked. "Be damned if I know," said Keith.

After a few moments in which they were jostled back and forth in their seats, Keith began to realize that everyone was actually driving on the wrong side of the road and the speed limit was definitely "fast" coupled with the fact that the roads were narrow with deep ditches on either side. They stopped at an intersection and walls blocked the view to see if there was traffic coming from the adjacent roadways. But Keith saw that the Japanese had solved this problem with concave mirrors mounted so the driver could view the oncoming and adjacent traffic. The ride with the winding roads, fast speed, and blind intersections made for an interesting and dizzying trip. Keith felt his stomach growl and remembered it had been awhile since they had eaten. He tried to distract his bodily functions by viewing the landscape. He couldn't see much of the countryside as it was about 0330 hours, but it was just as well, as he had all he could handle with swallowing hard and keeping an eye on the driver.

They arrived at Atsugi at 0430 hours and were dropped off at the main gate. The Marine sentry took their orders and called for transportation. They waited about ten minutes when they heard a loud noise coming from down the street. It sounded similar to the tractors Keith remembered from the farm. A few seconds later, an old, navy-grey Dodge pickup came speeding around the corner and down the street towards them. The driver stopped in front of Keith and Woody and stuck his head out the window.

"Aaauurragh. You the two pukes going to Seven?" The driver had long scraggly black hair, definitely not regulation, and was in dire need of a shave. His uniform, if it was a uniform, consisted of dungarees and a light blue shirt rolled up at the sleeves. "Well, what are you willy wackers waiting for? I ain't got all night. Christ, some people think just cause you got the duty, you got all the time in the world. Well, I ain't got all the time in the world, so get your asses into this here truck so's we can get you checked in and I can get some sleep, dozo."

Keith threw his sea bag into the back and quickly crawled into the pickup. Woody followed. Keith reached out his hand, "My name's Keith and this is Woody. What's yours?" The driver scratched the stubble on his chin, then gave Keith a quick firm hand shake and reached back to take Woody's hand as well, "They call me Rotor Blaster. That ain't my real name, of course. That's just what they call me." Rotor shifted the pickup into gear, let out the clutch, and pushed the pedal to the floor. The Dodge leapt forward with a lurch.

"Do you want to know why they call me that?" Rotor didn't wait for them to decide if they wanted to know why or not. "Cause I'm a legend in my own time, that's why." Rotor looked at himself in the rearview mirror. "Yeah, that's me, a legend. I'm probably the only guy in the whole damn Navy to shoot down his own helicopter, that's why." Woody looked over in awe, "You shot down your own helicopter?" Woody's mouth hung open.

Keith started to relax, feeling that Rotor may just be all talk and not such a bad guy.

Woody laughed, chuckled, hiccupped, and Rotor Blaster grabbed another gear and smiled broadly. "You mean you ain't heard of me?" Keith smiled slightly, "No, can't say that I have." Rotor sneered, "Yeah, well that's probably 'cause I was flying those damned helos when you was still shitting yellow." Rotor laughed loudly at his own joke, and Keith and Woody joined in half-heartedly.

They drove around the airstrip and finally arrived at the hanger. The hanger was a round-roofed metal building that had offices on the street side and two very large doors on the runway side. They walked in one of the doors on the street side and entered the duty office. The duty officer was not in, but the non-commissioned officer stamped their orders and told Rotor to give them a ride to the barracks. The NCO also issued Keith and Woody some clean sheets and a standard issue Navy grey blanket.

Rotor was getting impatient, "Do I have to run any more shit around this fine fucking night?" He leaned against the desk with one arm, holding the other behind his back. Keith noticed he had his middle finger extended and directed toward the senior NCO. "No," said the NCO, "You can hit the sack as soon as you deliver the two new guys."

The three sailors got back into the pickup, which finally fired after Rotor ground on the starter for about five minutes, and they sped off toward the barracks. "So, what's your real name, Rotor?" asked Woody. "The name is John P. Seymore from Franklin, Tennessee, population 6,612. But around here, you'd best be calling me Rotor. My old lady, she don't like this Rotor shit, so that's another good reason why you should be calling me that. You two willy wackers got that?"

Keith laughed and scratched his head, "I've got it, but I'm not a willy wacker, and neither is Woody." He hesitated a moment before adding, "What the hell is a willy wacker anyway?" Rotor slammed on the brakes and the pickup skidded to a halt. Keith and Woody braced themselves so they weren't thrown through the window, "Where the hell you two fairies from?" Keith was almost afraid to give him any information about himself. "Well, I'm from Mandan, North Dakota, and Woody here is from Carroll, Iowa." Rotor interjected, "What kind of women do they have back in them parts, anyway?"

"Well," Keith said, contemplating his answer carefully, "I figure they're pretty much built the same as anywhere else; all the same parts." Rotor said, "Well, if the women are like anywhere else, and you took them out, they sure as hell wouldn't put out on the first date, now would they?"

Keith contemplated the question and replied, "Well, with very few exceptions, that would probably be the case." Keith then waited for the punch line.

"So," Rotor said as he put the pickup back into gear once again, "What do you do when you get back home after she's got you all hornied up and wouldn't give you nothing?" Keith realized he had a lot of learning to do, not so much in the ways of nature, but he had to learn a whole new language. Rotor pulled up in front of a long grey, two-story building, the barracks. "Well, this is it Mr. and Mrs. Boot Camp. You can get out now, dozo."

Keith and Woody grabbed their C-bags and with their blankets and sheets tucked under their arms, walked up to the front door of the barracks. There was a sign taped to the door. It said "Wipe Your Feet, Dozo." Keith and Woody looked at each other, "What in the hell is dozo?" asked Woody. Keith shook his head. "I don't know, but don't ask." He was still reeling from the last answer. Keith assumed that everyone over here must hate it so bad that they were all being rude. The language barrier was going to be a real problem. "Maybe it's some takeoff from bozo." Woody laughed, "That sounds logical enough."

They entered the barracks and found the light switch. They flipped the switch and were immediately met with a barrage of greetings, "Fuck you! Shut off the fucking light you assholes. Were you dick heads born in a fucking barn? Have some Godamned respect for Christ sake." Keith cringed and looked around. Unlike the stateside barracks where there was an order to things and there was a duty office to check in, this was one big room. It was partitioned off into smaller cubicles using lockers, stereo boxes, and desks with one central lighting switch with a sign that said, "Lights Off At 2200 Hours, Dozo." Keith and Woody spied two empty racks at the far end and hit the light switch again, sending up a new round of insults. "Fucking pricks! About time, assholes."

Keith undressed in the dark and made his rack. He didn't say anymore to Woody that evening, fearing more verbal abuse. Keith lay down with his fingers clasped behind his head. Sleep didn't come easy. The war protestors kept coming back to him and he had a twinge of guilt. But after all he wasn't directly involved in the war, and if his number hadn't been up, he probably wouldn't have enlisted at all. Better yet, he could have copped out and gone to Canada. Having justified that point, and feeling a little better about himself, Keith turned over and went to sleep.

CHAPTER 3

▼

The barracks Master at Arms, or MAA, woke Keith and Woody at ten hundred hours. "The duty officer wants to see you boot camps at the hanger after lunch, so you best get up and go get some chow, dozo." Keith swallowed hard, feeling intimidated and unsure of himself. "What's dozo mean, anyway?" he asked.

The MAA smiled and walked away. "Okay…well thanks a lot," Keith put on his dungaree uniform and stowed the rest of his gear in the locker that was beside his rack. Woody met up with him at the door and after getting directions from the MAA, they proceeded toward the chow hall. The base was just like a stateside base, except the buildings were much older and huge by comparison.

Keith and Woody filled their trays in the chow hall and looked for a place to sit. They saw Rotor waving madly at them from a table towards the back. Keith wasn't sure he could handle the challenge of Rotor so early in the day. "Hey boot camps, get your asses over here. We got to get you guys some nick names, or you'll never fit in around here. I suppose Woody will work. That's not totally bass-ackwards. But you, Keith. Hmmmmm….Curly will do, until we can straighten it out." He slapped Keith on the back, "Get it? Until we can straighten it out?"

Rotor laughed loudly at his own humor and began hollowing out his hot dog with his knife. He grabbed some mayonnaise and spooned it into the hot dog and laid it on his lap. When one of the Japanese girls walked by to pick up empty trays, he stood up, grabbed the dog, held it to his crotch and squeezed, sending a stream of mayonnaise in the air, all the while yelling, "Aaauurragh, Aaauurragh!" The poor girl ran about ten feet and stopped, her eyes flashing, while she screamed, "Gaijin Buta" before she ran away.

Rotor roared while Woody stood with his mouth open again, and Keith just shook his head in wonder. "I bet she wasn't calling you sweetheart, right?" asked Keith. "More like American Pig. But she's slowly warming to me, I can tell. Yeah, it's not like the good old days." Rotor slapped the dog on a bun and took a bite, talking with his mouth full.

"A guy's really got to work to have some fun around here. Why, I remember when we first came to Nam…" Woody interrupted, "When were you over there?" thinking he was just making conversation. "Just got back last week." Keith looked up from his bean soup, "I thought you were stationed in this squadron." Woody chimed in, "Yeah," looking a little puzzled, "What were you doing in Nam if you're stationed here?"

Rotor looked at the two men in awe, thinking this was their way of making a joke. The two young men weren't laughing. "Jesus Christ, don't you know?" No one said anything. For the first time since they'd met Rotor, he spoke softly, calmly, like he was explaining something very serious to two children with serious learning disabilities. "Everyone in this squadron, with the exception of a few support personnel, goes to Nam. Hell guys, that's our mission, SAR, Search and Rescue. That's what we do." Rotor looked from Keith to Woody, who had stopped eating and were staring at him.

"Don't tell me you didn't know you'd be going to Nam?" No one spoke. Rotor laughed in disbelief. "Well, why da ya think ya got all that training, you willy wackers? Did ya think you'd be flying around Japan? Christ, we already won the war here. Why do you think they sent you to Capture and Survival School? What about all the swims? What about the combat training?" Keith and Woody looked pale, their color matching the off-white of the table. There was an acid taste in Keith's mouth and he could hear a pulse beating loudly at his temples. "You did stop and think about that, didn't you?" Rotor continued to look back and forth between Woody and Keith, totally amazed that these two young men had come all the way to Japan without a clue that they were smack dab in the middle of the war.

"Hell, you two better stick with me or you'll be dead in a week." Rotor rose to leave, slapping the guys on the back, "Come on you two, lighten up, we'll get you laid before you die." He headed out the door with Keith and Woody following slowly behind. Somehow Keith felt a little better when he followed Rotor out into the sunshine, but not much. Rotor, Keith, and Woody headed toward the cattle car stop. Rotor tried to make small talk, trying to lift the cloud that had suddenly fallen on the heads of the two new trainees.

The cattle car served as a base bus. It was like a semi-trailer except that it was low to the ground in order to allow people to get on and off easily. They all got on, took the trip around the runway and got off at the last stop, which was the HC-7 hanger. Above the door was a sign that said "Welcome to Helicopter Combat Support Squadron Seven. Home of the Big Mothers and Little Clem." Below the words on the sign was an emblem that looked like a three-headed wolf. Keith and Woody had not seen the sign the night before as it had been dark. Rotor pointed the way to the duty office and headed towards the maintenance area.

"Okay, guys," he scolded, "Stay out of trouble and don't do any dumb shit stuff." He watched them as they forlornly entered the office. He shook his head muttering under his breath, "You'd have thought someone would have told them...kids nowadays." The duty officer was in when Keith and Woody reported, "Airman Keith Klein reporting for duty Sir. Request permission to come aboard." Lt. Jamerson returned Keith's salute and said, "Permission granted, welcome aboard." He then took a deep breath and commenced with his canned speech specially prepared for new trainees.

"You are now part of the only helicopter combat support squadron in the United States Navy. In fact, this is the only naval helicopter squadron in the Vietnam War to be issued the "Medal of Honor" for bravery above and beyond the call of duty. Welcome aboard and please report to the personnel office next door, where they will process your orders and get you settled in. Good luck on your assignment."

Keith and Woody moved on to personnel where they met Ron Markel for the first time. Ron was nineteen years old, and stood about five foot two inches tall with brown eyes, dark hair and horn rimmed glasses. His blue uniform was Four-O, by the book, and his shoes were spit shined. He greeted Keith and Woody with a big smile and said "Welcome aboard guys," and began processing their orders. While he opened their orders they swapped stories. Ron told them that he was from Houston, Texas. He instantly took a liking to Keith when he learned that he was from North Dakota.

"Do you know Peggy Lee? You know that Peggy Lee is from North Dakota right? I think I have listened to just about every song she ever sang." All the while he handed them forms to sign, he chattered on about the voice of an angel as he threw in bits of information about HC-7.

They signed their travel vouchers and then reported to the training center. The Squadron Operations Officer was there to brief them. "The Squadron mission, gentlemen, is S.A.R., Search and Rescue, with secondary missions in VERTREP, Vertical Replenishment At Sea, and training. HC-7 has five separate detachments from our home base here in Atsugi. Detachment 110 is the Big Mother detachment and is stationed in the Tonkin Gulf with five SH-3 helicopters. Their sea rotation is ninety days at a time, and they rotate from carrier to carrier during that cycle. Detachment 111 is a vertical replenishment detachment, with two separate units. Detachment 111 uses CH-46 helicopters. Detachment 107 is south S.A.R. and has a crew of eight enlisted men and two officers. Detachment 104 is north S.A.R. Again they have the same crew complement as 107. Both Det 104 and Det 107 fly Clementines. There's also a detachment at Cubi Point in the Philippines for maintenance and training purposes." He took a deep breath, "Got all that?" When neither Keith nor Woody responded, he shrugged and continued.

"As we are short of crewmen on Det 110, both of you gents will be sent to temporary additional duty (T.A.D.) to Det 110, even though you were both trained on H-2 helicopters. Starting tomorrow, you will be training for plane captain and crewman on the H-3. After thirty days, you will be joining this detachment."

Keith felt that he was in some kind of a dream. Everything was moving so fast and nothing seemed real at the moment, except maybe Viet Nam, which was starting to loom like a large land mass somewhere in the watery recess of his nightmare. Ron, the yeoman they had met earlier, bounded into the room. "My turn," he spoke energetically. "If you're through with them, Sir, I would like to take these guys back to personnel."

As they walked across the hanger, Ron told them that he was a reservist from Texas and only had to serve a two-year tour compared to everyone else's four years. Keith looked around at all the helicopters and the work that was being performed on them. There were several helicopters setting outside the hanger as well. Ron continued with his informative conversation, "I've only got about three months left here, Boot Camps, so forgive me if I have a tendency to rub it in once in a while."

Ron gave them a tour of the hanger and all the maintenance spaces, took them to meet the Skipper, gave them a general rundown of squadron rules and regulations, and also gave them an indoctrination on the Japanese customs and laws. All in all it was a pleasant afternoon for Keith and Woody. Some of the earlier shock of the day was fading. Ron was friendly, easy to talk to, and suggested to Keith that some weekend they rent some bikes and tour the countryside, and maybe see some of the finer sights of the area.

Just before he got back on the cattle car to go back to the barracks, Keith finally asked Ron something that had been bugging him, "What does dozo mean?" Ron answered instantly, "Oh, that's the Japanese word for please." Keith smiled, and decided he was going to try to be a little more open minded about this place. How bad could it be? And yet the nightmare hovered close; he couldn't quite shake a foreboding feeling. When they got back to the barracks, Keith wrote a long letter home and lay down for a long restless night.

✳   ✳   ✳   ✳

There was total silence as the H-3 helo flew one hundred feet above the choppy water, an endless wave, lapping and washing as far as the horizon. Keith peered towards the opening in the back of the helicopter. Sunlight stared back through the opening, where there should have been nothing but darkness. He looked towards the first crewman, and moved his mouth to question, but nothing came out. He could feel the motion of the hovering helicopter blades, yet nothing invaded the silence. When the crewman finally turned slowly towards him, all Keith could see was his sun visor. Keith nodded in understanding. He'd been here before; he knew what he had to do. He felt as if he was in a trance and he slowly walked, zombie-like, to the rear of the helo where the points of light emanated from the skin of the helicopter. He put his gloved finger on one point of light and felt a jagged edge. There were six holes with jagged edges and on the opposite bulkhead there were six holes with smooth edges...Bullets...Panicked, now he remembered and turned around quickly. Toward the front of the helo, lying on the floor were two still human forms covered with a blanket. He knew there wouldn't be time to lift the edge of the blanket. The helo went into a hover and a voice screamed at him. "Man your guns!"

He looked out the side door and saw dark thick foliage and heard bullets whining around him. He grabbed the grips of the mini-gun and showered the jungle with five thousand rounds a minute. As the helo landed, Keith could see human forms in green uniforms running towards shadows hiding behind thick foliage less than fifty feet from the helicopter. Someone screamed at him. "Cover me!"

He showered the running soldiers with his mini-gun. They dropped to the ground. He continued firing. Suddenly the helo lifted off, and started forward flight. No, not yet, there were two shipmates still on the ground. He screamed towards the cockpit, "Stop! Turn around!" but the helo continued to head towards sea. He ran forward, screaming at the pilot. "Go back!"

But the cockpit was empty. On the pilot's seat someone had painted the number "77" and on the copilot's seat were the numbers "76". Keith did not have time to wonder. The helo was flying itself. Suddenly the helo was over water and it started to shake and vibrate. Keith jumped into the cockpit and grabbed the cyclic and the collective, but the helo would not respond. The helo hit the water and began to turn over. Keith found himself pinned behind the pilot's seat armor plating. Water rushed in the starboard door and window. Keith felt the water engulf him as it rushed over his head and into his lungs.

*   *   *   *

Keith sat up in bed, thinking he had screamed, yet the barracks was quiet. There was no sound except for the soft snoring of Woody coming from the next rack. Keith lay back, sweat glistening on his brow and he felt hot. He could feel the quick beats of his heart within his chest. Sleep eluded him for the next several hours as he lay awake analyzing his dream. He kept telling himself to get a grip, that it was only a dream, but it had seemed so real, and it had left him shaken and wondering what lay ahead.

CHAPTER 4

▼

The week slipped by quickly. Each day started pretty much the same with morning muster, inspection and announcements. Afterwards, Keith and Woody would go to the Training Center for orientation on the H-3 for plane captain and crewman training. A part of each day was spent studying the technical manuals on the H-3 helo's and learning how to do pre-flight and post-flight inspections on the helicopter. The H-3 was a big helo and carried up to five thousand pounds of cargo or personnel and flew at over one hundred and twenty knots, thus the name Big Mother, compared to the H-2 which was not designed to carry cargo and seated only two passengers plus its crew of four. The H-2, known in HC-7 as Clementine, flew at one hundred sixty five knots. Keith was told that although their primary mission was Search and Rescue, which meant to search out and rescue anyone who was in trouble or danger, they would also be carrying mail and transferring personnel.

Being a plane captain was only part of what was required to be a crewman. Both Keith and Woody had undergone strenuous swim tests back in the States. In addition to combat training and combat survival training, they had been instructed on rescue techniques for drowning victims and how to survive at sea and on land.

When Friday night finally rolled around, Keith and Woody were ready for something that didn't require much brainpower. They got into their civvies and headed for the taxi stand. Ron was going to be their guide and had decided that a weekend in Yokahama was just what the new boys needed.

Ron spoke to the Japanese taxi driver, "Train station, hiako."

The taxi driver nodded and pushed the gas pedal to the floor, taking the first corner on two wheels. When they stopped briefly for a light, Ron smiled. "Good word 'hiako.' Gets you where you're going fast." Keith tried to peel his body off the seat, composing himself by momentarily straightening his shirt. "And hiako means?" Ron grinned from ear to ear. "Emergency, probably not a good idea to use it a lot. If you have an accident, you have a lot of explaining to do. It sort of makes the passenger liable for damages." Keith struggled to keep himself upright, "Great, well at least you are the one who told him."

The light changed and Keith found himself once again plastered to the back of his seat, trying to keep his head from going through the back window. Nevertheless, he decided to tuck away that little word 'hiako' for safe keeping. A guy never knew when he'd have an emergency.

As they raced through the community, Keith absorbed the Japanese culture from the viewpoint of fast forward. Everything seemed to be pushed together, with no wasted space. The houses were smaller than your typical American home and most of them had red tiled roofs. Fences, high fences, were definitely, an, 'in' thing. There were no sidewalks, and people on bicycles shared the roads with the big trucks. All the vehicles had strange sounding names like Isuzu, Nissan, or Toyota. Everywhere you looked there was a buzzing of activity. They were moving fast. The Japanese society reminded Keith of an ant hill. There were many ants in a small area and all of them were very busy.

They arrived at the train station. Ron threw the cabbie some Yen and went to check on the train schedule. Keith was impressed by how Ron rattled off the language, "Pretty fluent there, guy." Ron shrugged his shoulders, "Nah, not really, just enough to survive. It's really a must, guys, if you don't want to be stranded on base or, worse yet, lose all your pay the first time out. You'll catch on fast."

The train came in twenty five minutes later and appeared to be full, which didn't seem to bother the mass of people who just kept getting on. Keith, Ron, and Woody joined the crowd pushing aboard the train. The train was standing room only, and even that consisted of bodies packed tightly together. The train headed out, pulling up at every stop to let people get off and on. Keith noted that even in the cramped conditions, everyone was polite and orderly.

After leaving the train, Ron guided them to a park in the heart of Yokahama. The park was immaculate and well taken care of, like everything else appeared to be in Japan. There were no signs of litter anywhere and all hedges and gardens were painfully manicured like fine art. Beautiful, large fragrant flowers in a rainbow of colors lined the walkways throughout the park. Neat little wooden benches were sporadically placed alongside the walkways for comfort of seating, but people were also lounging on the grass.

Woody suggested that they get some wine and get mellow. He remembered a liquor establishment they had passed and went back to see if he could get a bottle. Twenty minutes later Keith popped the cork on the first of two bottles of Akadama wine, took a healthy swallow and passed it on to Woody. Ron declined, saying he wasn't much of a drinker. They gave him a little friendly ribbing and continued to unwind, sitting on the grass, and staring up into the hazy blue sky. Ron looked like he was falling asleep and Woody wasn't far behind. Keith was surprised at how quickly the wine was going to his head. He figured they must have more powerful wine in Japan than back in the States. Off to his right he noticed a large water fountain with some ducks swimming on it and decided to meander over there to check it out.

*   *   *   *

Cynthia Croft sat by the edge of the fountain throwing pieces of bread to the ducks. She was in a foul mood. Her uncle, his majesty Admiral Edward Croft, had confined her to the base "for my own good" she mimicked as she tossed another piece of bread, bouncing it off the head of a startled duck who flapped quickly to the other side of the water. The Admiral didn't have a clue what was for her own good. It hadn't been for her good to pull her out of college at the most inconvenient of times. Not only was she losing credits, but losing touch with her friends. It's all she had left. Her friends and "The Cause," and they were fighting a good cause. Anything that would stop this fighting and killing was a good cause. All her uncle was concerned about was his damn reputation and this damn war.

She'd lost enough to wars, first her father in the Korean War, then her brother to this war. More recently her mother, when she took her own life. The insanity of it all, didn't they see that? All this loss of life and for what purpose, to save life, to save a cause, what if there were no one left to save?

Her thoughts were rudely interrupted when a familiar looking young man in civilian clothing walked up to the edge of the fountain, stood for a few minutes, and then fell face down in the water.

Cyndi stared at the man floating in the water, expecting him to get up. Seconds passed. When she suddenly realized that he wasn't going to bounce back up, she rose quickly and began frantically looking around her for help. No one seemed to be around now. Where had everyone suddenly gone off to? Cyndi found herself crawling into the fountain. "God, someone help me. Get up! Are you all right? What's your problem? Help us!"

Cyndi grabbed the back of a black curly head and pulled Keith's face out of the water, rolling his body over. The quick motion knocked Cyndi off her feet, putting her waist deep in the fountain with Keith's head in her lap. This movement was followed by the intake of breath as Keith filled his lungs with air. He opened sleepy drugged eyes to look into the frantic blue eyes of an angel, "God, this is good shit. Did you come with the bottle?"

"What the hell are you talking about? Are you nuts? You could have drowned!" Keith lay back, slurring his speech "I am downing, in the deep fools of your futeable blue eyes."

"I should have let you drown!" Cyndi pushed Keith off her lap and started crawling out of the fountain. Keith sunk below the surface and stared up at her with his eyes open, but unmoving. "Oh for Christ's sake!" Cyndi grabbed Keith's hair again and started pulling him towards the edge of the fountain. "What the hell's wrong with you anyway?" This time Keith didn't answer and Cyndi found herself hauling one hundred fifty pounds of wet dead weight over the cement edge of the fountain and dropping Keith unceremoniously on his head in the grass.

"Serves you right." She grabbed her purse and started to turn away, but again noted that Keith wasn't moving from his spot. She looked around her to see if any of his kind were in the area but only saw an old Japanese couple strolling by. "Oh, for Pete's sake! What am I supposed to do with you?" She rolled him over and Keith gave her a weak smile, through half closed eyes. "What was your name again? Kilroy something?"

"Keith…Keith Klein, at your serface, Ma'am," he said weakly. "Your wisk is my command." Cyndi looked around, "Where is your friend?" Keith tilted his head back, "I thought you were my friend?" Cyndi sneered, "Well, you were wrong. I should let you rot here." Keith reached out a hand and pulled Cyndi down on top of him. She struggled to rise, the wetness of their clothes making her feel much too close. He held her firmly, looking her squarely in the eyes, "These are rufff times. I could be died by tomorrow."

"You're going to be dead today, sailor, if you don't let go." Keith's eyes closed slowly and he relaxed his grip. Cyndi pulled herself from Keith's grasp and once again rose to leave. He looked so helpless and a little sad lying on the ground, a pool of water forming around his body. Cyndi sighed heavily and looked heavenward. "I suppose this is for my own good too." She half dragged, and sometimes with a little coaching and a little threatening got Keith to stumble along across the street to a hotel where she attempted to converse with the lady at the desk.

"Towels, I could use some towels." Keith lay at Cyndi's feet, while she searched through her purse looking for her Japanese/American dictionary. The Japanese woman looked from Cyndi to the man lying unconscious on the floor and tried once again to get her to sign the check-in log. "No, I don't want a room, just some towels and a taxi." In her desperate search, Cyndi ripped the handle off her purse. "God, you're going to pay for this, Sailor. Where the hell is that book?" Cyndi lay what was left of her purse on the counter and tried to calm her self by breathing in very slowly. "Okay." She reached for the log and spoke once again to the lady, enunciating carefully and loudly. "Fine, I'll take a room. I'll leave the idiot in the room, call a taxi to get myself back to the base and you don't have a clue what I'm talking about and could care less, right?"

The lady handed a key to Cyndi and motioned for a boy to help her carry Keith down the hall.

CHAPTER 5

▼

Keith woke slowly and found himself in his rack in the barracks. The first thing he noticed was that the window by his bunk was two feet high on the end closest to him and four feet high on the other end. Looking down, the floor was a good forty feet away. As he began to lower his feet to the floor an amazing thing happened. His foot started to grow as he lowered it and also extended forty feet to the floor. Keith decided that trying to get up just now was not a good idea, and that maybe he should get a little more sleep.

"Where the hell have you been? What happened to you?" Keith turned his head slowly toward the door. Someone was standing at the end of a long hall and screaming at him. Sounded like he was using a megaphone, "What?" The effort to talk hurt his teeth. "Where did you go?" Woody stood looking at Keith who didn't seem to be focusing very well. "Are you okay, pard?" Keith groaned, "Yeah, fine. Just need a little more sleep, I think. What time is it?" Keith spoke slowly with effort. The words sounded slightly slurred. "It's 1500 hours," said Woody. "I think maybe you'd better try eating something. Remember, you have a training flight first thing in the morning."

"Why would we fly on a Sunday?" Keith rolled over and pulled his pillow over his head, hoping Woody could take a hint. "Sunday? Boy, have you lost it, pard. Tomorrow's Monday." Keith rolled back over, the motion sending pains through his ears. He stared at Woody, "How could tomorrow be Monday?" Woody laughed, "Well, maybe it would only be Sunday if you hadn't insisted on drinking the whole second bottle of Akadama wine yourself. But being you hogged it alone, now it's going to be Monday."

"I did that?" Keith was feeling a heavy pounding at his temples. "Yeah, that's why we were so worried about you. We were walking down the street in Yoka-hama looking for an eating place and when we looked back you were gone." Woody lit a cigarette and handed it to Keith. When Keith shook his head he took a drag off it himself, "We didn't call the shore patrol, 'cause we didn't want to get you in trouble. We even enlisted the help of some other guys from HC-7, but we couldn't find you anywhere. Where the hell did you go?"

Keith tried to think, but the pain in his temples was spreading back across his head. Flashes of a fountain…water. Swimming? Woody continued. "I got pretty messed up on what I drank, but I only had a fraction of what you had. That wine really had a kick, didn't it?" Keith was starting to feel sick. "You know the strang-est thing about that wine? One of the guys who was helping us look for you said that Akadama wine is opium based. Can you believe it? Some shit, huh?"

Keith's head pounded. Well that ruled out sick bay. If they found drugs in his system, he would lose his flight status, maybe he'd even get kicked out of the ser-vice. "You sure you don't want to get a bite to eat?" Keith managed to shake his head. "Okay, bud. Well, I'm heading down to the chow hall if you change your mind. Later." Woody gave Keith one more concerned look, at which Keith waved him to leave. Woody shrugged and headed out the door leaving Keith sit-ting on the bed staring at his feet.

Keith felt the urge to puke. He looked at the floor, which appeared somewhat closer now. He slowly sat up. His head throbbed so badly now that he thought he was going to pass out. He managed to get out of his rack and at a snail's pace, Keith made his way to the head by running his hand along the wall. He tried to throw up but nothing came. No way was he going to be able to eat anything. Another trainee, Curt James, came in and leaned against the bulkhead. He stared at Keith for several minutes then finally spoke, "That was really some chick." Keith rolled his head to the side, "What chick?" Keith found if he held his breath, the pain would reside. Curt continued to lean on the bulkhead, and now crossed his arms, "The one that brought you back to the barracks Saturday morning. She's a real fox. Where'd you meet her anyway?" Keith stared at him stupidly, and Curt laughed and helped Keith back to his rack. "Boy, were you messed up! She asked if I would take care of you, so I got you into your rack." Keith said nothing, but was starting to remember long sandy hair and smoky blue eyes spit-ting fire.

"Not talking, eh? Well, I don't really blame you. I'd keep one like that to myself, too." Curt threw the grey blanket over the sick looking crewman and laughed again, "Sweet dreams." Keith moaned, rolled over, and went back to sleep.

CHAPTER 6

▼

Monday looked pretty much the way Keith felt—gloomy and threatening. Keith had not eaten breakfast. The last meal he could remember eating was at noon on Friday.

He arrived at the hanger a half hour before the flight was scheduled to take off and began the task of inspecting the helicopter. Keith checked the engine and transmission oil levels, hydraulic reservoir and the rotor blades. He was finishing up the rest of the preflight inspection when the pilots joined him.

"So, how's the bird look?" asked Lt. Jim Sloan as he zipped up his green flight suit. The lieutenant had been flying for ten years and always made a point to check out his crew carefully. Keith's pallor and slightly shaky hands were a dead give away of a rough night on the town. "She's up and ready to go, Sir."

Keith climbed aboard the helicopter and began his preflight checklist as well as checking his flight gear. He also checked over his wet suit and made sure that the first aid kit was on board. Satisfied, he strapped himself in for the trip. He had been assigned to take the second crewman position as he had the least amount of flight time. The pilot radioed the control tower. "This is Sea Devil 55 requesting permission to lift off." The pilot also radioed in the destination and vectored coordinates.

The tower responded. "This is Atsugi tower. Permission granted. Wind is out of the west at zero-eight knots. Have a good flight." The pilot pulled up on the collective, which lifted the helicopter, pushed slightly forward on the cyclic, which in turn caused the helicopter to nose down and start forward flight. The pilot set a course due south and headed out over the ocean.

As soon as lift-off had been achieved, Keith requested permission to check out the rescue hoist. Lt. Sloan radioed back to Keith. "Son, you look a little green around the gills. Have a little too much to drink last night, did we?" Keith replied, "I'm fine, Sir." Lt. Sloan clicked his mike, "Well, good, because I need to check this bird out for a gripe that was written up last flight on the rudder pedals and I didn't want to give you any unnecessary discomfort." He waited for a response, but none came.

"The last pilot said that when he tried to do a ninety degree roll, his pedal got sticky. Hang in there good buddies." Keith thought he heard chuckling coming over the radio before the lieutenant signed off.

Keith prepared for the roll by sticking his head out the aft door and hanging on, knowing that he would never maintain his stomach through the roll, and unfortunately he was right. The first crewman, Jonsey, laughed at Keith's predicament.

The pilot radioed back to Keith.

"Klein, could you check out a possible hydraulic leak starboard side just aft of where your head was hanging?" Keith could hear snickering through his head set, and thought he'd try to save a little face. "No hydraulic leak spotted, Sir, but we really should do something about the large amount of JP-5 that's running off the tail wheel."

The pilot immediately checked his fuel consumption, figured out how much fuel he should have on board this far into the flight and realized he had been suckered. The pilot radioed back, "Okay, Klein, my fuel consumption is normal. Say again about the leak?" Keith responded quickly, "Well, maybe it isn't JP-5. Could be we're getting pretty close to the water?" Lt. Sloan checked the altimeter and visually gauged his height. "Can't be water. We're still at one-hundred feet." Keith had to fess up, "Well, you got me Sir. Only thing it can be is part of my intestines that I lost about ten minutes back."

The Lieutenant radioed back, "Okay, High Roller, you'll be all right. But in the future, do not, I repeat, do not drink before my flight." Keith caught the seriousness in the pilot's voice. "You got it, Sir. I don't think I'll ever drink again." Lt. Sloan radioed back, "Right, Roller, I can almost believe that one."

The helo approached checkpoint Charlie, and the pilot radioed back, "Suit up, Roller. You'll feel better when you get wet." Keith put on his wet suit and flippers. He assumed a Navy dive position in the helicopter door, waiting for the ready signal. The pilot hovered at twenty feet and ten knots and gave him the okay. Keith breathed in slowly, trying to remain calm, breathed out slowly, then in again, held his breath, and jumped.

The ocean swells rose about two feet. Keith felt himself being swept up and down with the movement of the waves and the downdraft of the rotor blades from the helo shooting spray and mist all around him. Damn the rotor wash.

As pre-planned, it was Keith's task to rescue a drowning sea dummy bobbing in the water. He swam up behind the dummy's head and reached out to grab its hair. The hair came off in his hand. He reached for the dummy's shirt and found that the dummy was stuck to checkpoint Charlie's buoy. After struggling for twenty minutes, Keith finally got the reluctant victim into the rescue collar and since the dummy was supposed to be injured, Keith rode the collar up with him. When they reached the helo, Jonsey pulled them inside.

"Not too shabby, only about the second slowest rescue I've ever witnessed. Of course on the first one, Rotor had shot down his own helicopter, and still we got him out of there in twenty one minutes." Jonsey reached for the dummy, whose arm came off in his hand.

"Only difference is, Rotor lived," Jonsey laughed. "This guy is history; he doesn't even have any hair left." Keith thought if he could just die, he'd be okay. Lt. Sloan flew due north and when he got within range of Atsugi tower, requested permission to land. Permission was granted and Big Mother 055 landed and taxied to her hanger. While the crew was doing their post-flight inspection of the helo, Jonsey pulled up along side Keith.

"Look, I know you're new at this, and I know a hangover when I see one, but you've got to get with the program. People's lives depend on what we do up there." Keith's spirit sank to a new low. It was not in his nature to not hold up his end of the load and today he had let his crew down. "I know that. I don't plan on doing this number again, I assure you." Jonsey smiled and slapped Keith on the back, "Good, and don't take it too hard. Besides, I've got a real good cure for you. I think you're going to like this one, but you're going to have to skip chow." Keith signed off on his post flight check, "No problem, I don't much feel like eating anyway."

After completing their inspection, Jonsey and Keith walked to the front of the hanger and got in Jonsey's Datsun. They drove to a building near the front gate and went inside.

"You're going to love this. Just relax and enjoy, buddy." said Jonsey. They entered a locker room area. "Here, grab a towel and get undressed." Keith was in a trusting mood, and hoped Jonsey wasn't going to try and pull another one on him. He'd had all the test of wills he could handle for one day. From there they walked into an adjacent room and were greeted by a Japanese lady, who escorted them to a steam room. After Keith had been in the steam room for about fifteen minutes, he felt like a limp rag and if it were possible, even worse than before.

"Thanks, Jonsey, if I had a knife I'd do myself in. Are we having fun yet? This is your idea of a good time?" Jonsey leaned back against the wooden bench, "Relax, relax, it'll get better. Trust me." Keith was gasping for air, "Right!" Keith resigned himself to the fact that he probably would never reach old age.

Finally the Japanese lady returned and let them out of their hellhole. She now led them to a large tub where they were met by another Japanese lady. The two women proceeded to scrub Keith and Jonsey with soap and cloths, rinsed them off and then directed them to soak in the tub. Jonsey winked at Keith. "Better?" Keith nodded. Jonsey smiled as he thoroughly enjoyed what was happening, "Well, it's going to get even better."

After soaking in the tub, which was considerably more refreshing than the steam room, they were taken to another room with four tables lined up side by side. One of the ladies motioned for Keith to lay face down on the table and proceeded to rub and pummel the muscles on Keith's body, starting with the neck and working all the way down to his toes. She massaged muscles he never knew he had. The session ended with the masseuse walking on his back. Keith knew then that he was going to survive and that he owed Jonsey big time. By evening he finally sat down for a meal.

CHAPTER 7

▼

The rest of the week was very busy. Keith continued training on the H-3s. He finally managed to rescue the dummy in a record nine minutes flat, with hair still intact, and the whole crew cheering him on. Friday finally came and Keith and Woody decided to spend the evening at the enlisted club. They tried to talk Ron into joining them, but he attempted to decline. "No, that's okay guys, I'm not really much of a drinker. You go on ahead. I would just hold you back." Keith wasn't going to hear any of it. "Get your ass ready and let's go!" Keith grabbed his jacket and motioned for Woody to follow.

Again Ron tried to snivel out of going, "No leave me alone, I've got to write some letters home." Keith grabbed Ron under the arm, "Mama can wait. What you need is a real woman." Ron didn't say anything, and Keith and Woody exchanged looks. "You do like women, don't you Ron?" teased Woody. Ron, who had pulled free of Keith's grasp, pretended to be busy getting down pen and paper. "Well, I do believe, Keith, old buddy, that our friend Ron here needs to be introduced to the fine art of chasing women."

Keith and Woody both grabbed Ron under the arms, picked up his coat, and forcefully carried him out the door. They proceeded down the street to the enlisted club. When they arrived at the club, Keith ordered three beers. "You do drink beer, don't you Ron?" Ron was still not keen on the idea of being here, "Not usually, but I guess I don't have much of a choice, do I?" Ron slouched down in his chair with his arms crossed defiantly in front of him. "Not really," said Keith.

The men turned their attention to an American singer who was entertaining on the stage. She had endless legs, gorgeous blond hair, and a very short skirt.

"What do you think, Ron?" asked Keith, "Not bad, huh?" Ron finally looked up and became a little more interested. "Well, I guess she's not too bad."

"Well, when she takes a break," said Keith, "We should get you two together." Keith pretended to spruce up Ron by straightening his collar and licking down an imaginary hair. Ron pushed his hand away, starting to get in a more playful mood, but not willing to let Keith know quite yet that this could possibly be fun, "No, she's not my type." Keith barked back, "Why? Because she's a woman or because she's breathing?" Woody chimed in, "We're going to start worrying about you if you don't shape up pretty quick. Drink your beer. Relax."

Ron took the first sip of his beer, and decided it wasn't so bad after all. A group of loud Marines entered the bar and sat down at the table directly in front of the stage. Keith could tell they were Marines by the arrogant way they carried themselves and by their super short crew cuts. Woody also took this opportunity to go talk to some other guys from the squadron that had just come in.

Keith and Ron finished their beers and Keith ordered another round. While Ron ogled the singer, Keith attempted to make conversation. "Hear anything from your folks back home? Any good news, bad news?" Ron thought for a minute. "Yeah, I got a letter from my sister, Betty. She's still in school and all is well with her. She said that my other sister Sherry is supposed to be coming over to Japan too. Sherry is in the Air Force. Betty said there are a lot of anti-war protests on television." Keith sipped his beer, "So how do you feel about that?" Ron shrugged his shoulders, "Well, it stinks. The whole situation stinks, but there's nothing I can do about it. One thing I do feel good about is what you guys are doing. It takes a lot of the bite out of the war. You must really feel proud about what you're doing."

"Well, if you must know..." Keith wasn't sure he wanted to tell anyone what he really felt. But Ron seemed like such a sincere guy. Maybe he was a little too innocent and a little too naive. These were the exact traits that led Keith to believe he could be trusted so he opened up. "Well, to be honest with you, I'm scared." He finished off his beer and motioned for two more. "I'm too young to die. I'm afraid of getting hurt or crippled." He took a deep breath and figured he'd go for broke, "You know, my biggest fear is drowning." Ron looked at Keith seriously for a long minute, then burst out laughing.

"God, this is great! You're telling me that you joined the Navy and your biggest fear is drowning?" He laughed so hard, beer spilled out of his mouth and ran down his chin. Keith looked a little disgruntled, and tried to defend himself. "Well, I didn't know I couldn't swim when I went in." Tears were rolling down Ron's eyes. "This is serious."

"Okay, okay." Ron wiped his eyes and tried to compose himself. "I hear what you're saying about your fears and all," said Ron, "But there's still something here I don't want to miss. There are many times I wish I would have enlisted for four years rather than joining the Reserves. I would really like to see some action, save some lives, be a hero...see Nam."

"If you feel that strongly, maybe you should talk to the skipper. He may let you go. You never know until you try." Ron reached for his third beer, "You're right. I'm going to check into it first thing Monday."

The singer finished her break and returned to the stage. Ron watched her every move, "She's not so bad. Her legs are kind of nice." Keith punched Ron lightly in the arm, "All right, now you're catching on." Woody arrived back at the table with another round of beers. He immediately launched in to his stock of Marine Corp jokes, "Say, do you know how many handles there are on a Marine's coffin?" Ron looked baffled, "No, how many?" Woody beamed as he supplied the answer, "There are two, and do you know why? Because there's only two handles on a shit can."

"Ha, ha, ha. You might try that one again after we've had another beer, or better yet, go tell it to the Marines. I bet they'd get a real charge out of that one." After having had more than several beers themselves, the six Marines had started hooting at the singer who was trying without much success to ignore them. "Come on Legs, take it off. It ain't much to begin with. Come on, I want to see where those legs end."

Ron was taking all this in and was starting to get a little agitated. He spoke to Keith, "Those guys better cool it. Who do they think they are?"

"Ah, they're just some dumbass Marines." Said Woody. "She's probably used to it anyway." Ron was starting to get angry, and a little intoxicated, "No, she's not that kind of girl." Keith chuckled, "Yeah, right, like you'd really know."

The Marines were getting frustrated from getting no response from the singer. "Come on Bitch, at least take the top off. You don't have much up there anyway." Ron got up stumbling over his chair in the process, "That does it!" Keith grabbed his arm, "Sit down, Ron." Woody chimed in as well, "Take it easy. They're just having a little fun."

"Fun, my ass," said Ron. "I know a lady in need when I see one." Ron broke free of Keith's grasp and proceeded to walk unsteadily towards the table of Marines. "Oh, fuck, we don't need this shit," said Woody to Keith. "Now what are we going to do?" Keith looked over at Ron, "Leave him alone. Maybe he'll come to his senses."

Ron grabbed the nearest Marine by the collar and drug him to his feet. "Well, then again, maybe not," said Keith. By the time the Marine had made a fist, Keith was right behind Ron ready to pick up the pieces. Ron ducked and the fist caught Keith squarely in the chin sending him back over a table, out through the back door, and landing at the feet of none other than Cynthia Croft. "For Christ's sake, not you again! What is it with you that I'm always picking you up off the ground?" Cyndi stood with her hands on her hips surveying Keith as he rolled over, and sat up rubbing his chin. "Well if it isn't my angel of mercy." Cyndi, in true form responded, "Not your angel, Sailor. Not in this lifetime, not in any lifetime." From the bar came sounds of crashing bottles, tables tipping, breaking chairs, and smacks, groans, and swearing.

"Take that you son-of-a-bitch...dumb ass jar heads." Cyndi looked through the door than back at Keith, "Friends of yours?" Keith was still rubbing his jaw, "Well, some of them. Just a little Friday night gathering with a few acquaintances." Cyndi looked inside again, "You don't suppose you should go help out?" More screams and swearing erupted from the bar and the sounds of something being thrown against a wall. "No, it sounds like they're doing all right to me." Keith stood up and looked down into Cyndi's blue eyes.

"Say, I was going to thank you for the other night." Cyndi started walking away "No problem." Keith followed behind her, "No really, I could have gotten into a lot of trouble. You really helped me out." Cyndi stopped and turned, "Well, I couldn't just leave you lying there." Keith looked into Cyndi's sky blue eyes again, "I was that good, huh?" Cyndi started walking again, "You were comatose."

Just then a scream erupted behind them and they both turned. Ron came flying out the back door head first with Woody close behind. Woody's shirt was ripped and Ron had a cut lip, but both had grins on their faces. Woody was the first to speak, "That'll teach them jarheads to mess with us! Let's get the hell out of here before they come out here after us. Besides, the Shore Patrol's knocking on the front door."

Keith grabbed Cyndi by the hand and started dragging her down the street towards the taxicab. "What the..." Cyndi tried to pull free. "No, pretty lady, you're coming with us. Can't chance leaving you to that mob." Keith firmed his grip on Cyndi and pushed her into the cab. Woody got in on her other side and Ron crawled into the front and spoke to the cabbie, "Atsugi, hiako."

The cabbie floored it and the cab screamed around the corner. The sailors flashed their military identification cards to the Marine sentry as they went through the main gate. When Cyndi started to protest, Keith pushed her down behind him so the Marine guard couldn't see her. "You're going to get me in trouble, you asshole. Do you know who my uncle is?" Keith shrugged his shoulders, "Who really gives a shit about your uncle, sweet lips?" Cyndi crossed her arms and gave Keith a serious glare, "You really should give a shit. Especially, since he's the admiral of Far East forces."

"Shit!" Keith's mouth fell open and he loosened his grip on Cyndi, "You're putting me on, right?" Cyndi felt pretty good about his reaction. Served the bastard right for taking such liberties with her. "No luck, sailor," Cyndi now smiled sweetly. It felt good to finally be one up on the jerk. "Your ass is grass, and I'm the lawnmower." Keith recovered quickly and smiled back, "You know, that was almost worth it to see you smile. I wasn't sure you knew how." Cyndi resumed a serious face and feigned anger. "Okay, so where are you kidnappers taking me?"

"Train station, dozo," Woody said to the cabbie. Cyndi scowled, "The train station? You're taking me out of the country?" Woody scowled, "No, just far enough to get Ron laid. We promised him." He spoke in a matter of fact tone, much like a father who had promised his son an ice cream cone.

"Well, I am certainly not going to be the one to do that! What am I supposed to do while you perverts are getting your rocks off?" Keith quickly jumped in, "No, just Ron. Maybe you and I could find a coffee shop and find out all the things we have in common." Cyndi replied quickly, "So what are we going to do after that minute is up, or is Ron going to be really fast?" Keith shrugged his shoulders. "I'll improvise as we go along." Keith winked at Woody, which brought him a smack to the side of the head by Cyndi as they pulled up to the curb.

They all got out of the cab. "Well you two go along and have a good time," said Keith. Me and…Damn, I don't even know your name. Is it okay if I call you Angel?" Cyndi looked at Keith in total exasperation, "My name is Cyndi, Cynthia Croft actually, as in Admiral Croft, remember?" "Cynthia?" Keith stopped and did an elaborate inspection of the woman next to him. "No, not Cynthia. Cyn maybe. Yeah, Sin. Do you get it? Sin?" "Yeah, real original."

"Me and Cyn are going over to check out what looks like a restaurant over there." Woody waved, "No problem, see you tomorrow." Woody and Ron were already heading down the street in the opposite direction. Ron staggered a little, but had a flicker of hope in his eyes. Keith and Cyndi entered the restaurant and took a table near the door. The place was dark, but seemed clean enough from what you could see. Keith hated to ruin the start of a good drunk, but ordered a cup of tea for himself. Cyndi requested a cup of coffee.

"So what's your story, Cyn?" Keith asked as he took a sip of the strong tea and cringed. Cyndi seemed ill at ease but slowly sipped her coffee. "It's Cyndi. Not much to it really. Hate the military, hate the war, hate sailors. That sort of thing." Keith nodded, "Pretty generic, don't you think, Cyn?" Cyndi leaned back in her chair, "Makes it easy to understand. They all stand for murder and senseless killing." Keith looked Cyndi in the eye, "Maybe you need to look at it from the other side." Cyndi sat upright, "Oh, you mean like from your side? With a free license to kill innocent women and children with the blessing of God and your country, and all the women you can screw as a bonus? Sounds nice. I can see why you bought into it. Kind of exciting from that angle."

Keith was starting to get a little irritated with the direction the conversation was taking. It was not at all what he had hoped would develop from their little rendezvous. "It's not quite that simple, is it? I'm not here killing anyone. In fact I wouldn't be here at all except I would probably have been drafted." Cyndi mimicked Keith and replied, "Oh, I feel so bad. As if you didn't have any options." Keith jumped on that, "I also have responsibilities. We all have responsibilities. Or don't those count?"

Cyndi rose to leave. "Not for much, when you sacrifice your human dignity. You know, this is really a lot of fun, but I think it's time to get back." Keith rose and towered over Cyndi, "What are you afraid of Cyn? Maybe seeing someone else's perspective? Maybe afraid that you might find out that everything isn't always black and white? That would kind of throw off your little righteous cause, wouldn't it?"

Cyndi's faced turned a shade of red and Keith knew he had struck a nerve, "My cause, as you put it, speaks for itself. You, on the other hand, haven't convinced me of any grey areas." Keith did not seem the least bit flustered now, "Well, you're in the right environment to find out if there are any, now aren't you, babe? It might be a nice touch if you tried to be open-minded about it." Cyndi was not happy with the way the conversation was turning out. She was not used to someone standing up to her, "Don't lecture me, sailor. It's not becoming."

Keith opened the door for Cyndi and they walked out to the street. "Well, it's certainly comforting to know that you are comfortable enough around me to open up the way you are. I didn't think you cared at all." Cyndi walked slightly ahead of Keith, "I don't." Keith did not try to walk beside her, instead he took up a position just slightly behind her. "You did the other night." Cyndi continued on her brisk walk to the taxi stand, "I was afraid if I left you, you'd die. I, unlike other people, have a regard for human life." Keith kept his position, "Does this regard for human life involve brushing the hair off my forehead and kissing me on the lips?"

Cyndi stopped and spun around. She stood and stared at Keith, "I didn't do any such thing!" Keith smiled at her. "That's the way I remember it." She put her hands on her hips. "You were delirious. Talked almost all night. Just about drove me crazy. I tried to calm you down." She turned and headed toward the taxi stand again and Keith followed. "Ah," Keith waved for a cab. "So you did kiss me."

"I did not kiss you," said Cyndi her voice raising, looking around now, a little too desperately for a cab. "I merely brushed your hair out of your eyes, and maybe I rubbed your temple a little. Just to calm you. I was trying to get some sleep." Keith smiled, "Hmmm, seems strange that I would remember some of it, and not all of it."

A cab pulled up to the stand and Keith opened the door but blocked the entry for Cyndi was almost desperate to get around him. "I'm surprised that you remember anything at all! What the hell did you drink anyway?" Keith did not attempt to move, "Nothing major, a little wine, a little opium. The usual." Cyndi attempted to get around Keith, "God, what an idiot!" Keith held his ground, "Now, Cyn, you're just being a little hard on my ego. Another guy might start thinking that you didn't like him." Cyndi glared at Keith. "Another guy..." Before she could protest, Keith pulled Cyndi into his arms and lowered his mouth to hers for a firm quick kiss and then immediately released her.

It happened so quickly, Cyndi wasn't sure it was enough to slap Keith for or if she should continue chewing him out. But then she couldn't remember what she was about to say. "Great," Keith grinned broadly, noting that Cyndi was at a loss for a moment. "I've found the official button that turns off the authoritative mouth on life. And a pretty sweet button it is too." All Cyndi could think of as she finally climbed into the cab was, "Asshole."

Cyndi tried to collect her thoughts, and calm the beating that was going on inside her chest. It was not as if she had never been kissed before. She turned to look into the dark sparkling brown eyes of her former captor.

"Not very original, pretty lady," said Keith. "One might think that my one little kiss had a major effect on you." Cyndi looked up at Keith, "Dream on, Sailor." Cyndi needed some breathing room so she slammed the taxi door and soon the little white Toyota was racing down the street heading for the base. Keith grabbed the next cab and followed only seconds later.

CHAPTER 8

▼

"Who did he say he was?" Cyndi tried to clear the fog from her head and focus on the maid that had entered the room. She had been sleeping so soundly and wasn't at all sure she was happy about being interrupted. The maid spoke with a very broken English and made it even harder to follow.

"He say, Atsugi Welcome Wagon. Be here half hour. You get up now?" Cyndi had a pretty good idea who would come up with a lame idea like that one. "Welcome Wagon indeed." Cyndi looked at the maid, "Well, when the Welcome Wagon comes, tell him I already left on the train." Cyndi rolled over and pulled the pillow on top of her head. The maid persisted.

"He say going to take you for sights to open your mind." Cyndi sat up, "To open my mind?" This sailor was definitely an idiot. Okay, we'll play along with this. Maybe this could backfire on old Keith Klein. Cyndi rolled over in the bed, put her feet in her slippers and headed for the shower.

Thirty minutes later Cyndi stepped out in the sunshine and watched as Keith and a slightly hung over Ron pedaled up on bikes, pulling an extra one in between. In spite of herself, she smiled. In the middle of a war, these two doorknobs wanted to go for a bike ride. Cyndi called to them from the door, "It's against Uncle Admiral's rules for me to go anywhere with enlisted pukes." Even as she spoke she walked down to the road, looking straight into Keith's brown laughing eyes.

"We're Welcome Wagon enlisted pukes. Doesn't that make any difference?" Cyndi smiled, "Not much." Cyndi took the bike that Keith rolled towards her, "Then again, this could maybe get me sent back to the States. Might be worth it to put up with you for a few minutes." Keith followed her every move, "Pretty lady, a few minutes with me could change your whole life." Cyndi threw Keith a look that she hoped showed disgust. Keith responded with a large grin and a wink. "You make me sick," Cyndi looked past Keith to Ron who looked several shades of green to pale white around his mouth.

"Speaking of sick, your friend doesn't look too hot. Is he up for a bike ride?" Keith looked over at Ron and punched him lightly on the shoulder, "Oh, he's great. In fact…this was all his idea."

"Yeah, right." Ron woefully stepped on the pedal of his bike and started slowly forward down the road in front of the other two, weaving from side to side as he rode. "Actually," said Keith. "I told him if he didn't give me the tour he promised me, I would write his mother and tell her what he did last night." Cyndi laughed, "You're positively awful." Cyndi got on the bike, and started down the road after Ron, with Keith catching up to ride along side of her.

Keith and Cyndi were soon beside Ron who was already at the front gate showing his military identification card to the Marine guard. They showed their identification cards as well and headed off towards Atsugi Proper. They rounded the bend and turned onto the highway with Ron in the lead, Cyndi and Keith following close behind. They were forced to ride single file and to stay alert to the traffic as they competed for road space with the Isuzus, three-wheeled trucks, and other vehicles that were swerving and weaving crazily towards Atsugi.

After about ten minutes of riding in silence, the traffic thinned out and they found themselves in a more rural area. Houses were farther apart, and fields of rice spread out, intermingled with trees and wooded areas. They spotted a house being built, and Ron decided that this would be a good opportunity to pull over and rest his weary head for a minute.

"So," said Cyndi as she pulled up next to Ron, who was rubbing his temples and pretending to be interested in the process of constructing the building, "What exactly do you want us to put into the letter when we write home to Mom?" Ron glanced over at Cyndi and returned his eyes to the building, not responding. "I think it would be along the lines of…maybe a woman? And maybe…could it be…sex? And maybe…could it be…" Ron continued to rub his forehead, "Shut up you guys." Ron wished he could just lay down. "It wasn't even my idea to go out in the first place."

"Come on, Ron," said Keith. "We want details. Don't be shy now. Cyndi and I are adults. We can handle it." As they watched Ron, his ears slowly started to turn colors, first a very light pink, then a little darker and finally bright red. Ron finally spoke, "Well, there's not much really to say."

"Must have been something," said Keith tweaking Ron's cheek. "I think Woody had a pretty good time," said Ron trying to redirect the conversation. Cyndi chimed in, "Oh, so what did Woody do?" Ron was pleased that at least the focus was off of him. "We stopped at the first bar. And the hostesses…" Keith interrupted, "Oh! Do they call them hostesses now days?" Ron was becoming agitated, "Do you want to hear this or not?" Keith and Cyndi were enjoying this. "Yeah, go on. Go on." They spoke in unison. "Woody couldn't find any hostess that he liked at the first place, so he decided we should go to another bar." Keith could not let it pass, "Woody didn't like the hostesses?" Ron ignored Keith's question and continued with the story. "When we walked into the second bar, this gal came up to Woody, and wrapped her body around his body." Keith rubbed his chin. "So much for corn." Cyndi looked at Keith strangely, not catching the humor as Ron continued, "I think Woody was hooked from there. At least he bought her about four drinks before they left." Keith focused on Ron's eyes, "So you just went home after that, huh Ron?" Ron cleared his throat. "Well, not exactly." Ron started to push his bike back on the road, "I think I've said about enough. Let your imagination run wild. I was damn good." Ron grinned and started pedaling down the one-lane highway.

Keith reached over his bike to the ground, grabbed up a pebble and tossed it at Cyndi. Cyndi ducked and threw one back also missing. Keith laughed, "Well, I could have been damn good too, but I couldn't get any cooperation." Cyndi laughed, "Oh, was that a pass you were trying to make last night? I couldn't tell." Cyndi flipped her hair over her shoulder and started pedaling quickly, trying to catch up with Ron who was moving out about twenty yards ahead of them. She looked back to see if Keith was following. When Keith saw Cyndi watching him, he thought he'd take the opportunity to really impress her, put his hands behind his head and kept pedaling. "Look, no hands." Cyndi laughed, "Gee, aren't you special. What else can you do without your hands?" Keith put his hands back on the bars and started pedaling vigorously towards Cyndi, "Pretty lady, as soon as I catch up with you, I'll show you."

Cyndi squealed and started pedaling as fast as her legs could go. They passed Ron in a blur, and headed out into the traffic. Cyndi kept looking back to see if Keith was gaining on her. She didn't see the truck until it was almost in front of her. Keith saw it about the same time and started to shout a warning as he saw Cyndi swerve away from the oncoming truck and go over the edge of the deep binjo ditch. The bike stopped abruptly when it hit the embankment and Cyndi flew forward.

To Keith it all went in slow motion as he desperately tried to reach her as she slowly flew through the air. He was about five feet away when she hit her head on a concrete culvert and slid quietly down to the soft earth below. His shout finally surfaced, alerting Ron who was just coming up from behind. Keith raced over to where Cyndi was laying face down and gently rolled her over as he braced her head and neck in his hands. Ron was already at the roadside trying to flag down a car.

Cyndi looked pale and her skin felt cold to the touch. Her eyes were closed, and a trickle of blood ran down her forehead. Keith was panicked and reached for her wrist to take a pulse. He could feel a faint beating and was relieved.

"Cyn, are you all right? Talk to me hon." Ron ran back down the embankment and helped him carry Cyndi to a car and they headed back to the base. He cradled Cyndi's head in his lap. Grooves of worry lined his forehead. Ron stayed behind to take care of the bikes, but promised to meet them at the dispensary as soon as he could get there. Through the whole ride, Cyndi never regained consciousness and Keith continued to talk to her softly. "It's going to be okay, hon. I'm so sorry."

Keith felt desolate. He'd only just met this gal, yet he felt so attached to her. She was so contradictory to everything that he felt. She was so obstinate about the war, him, everything! He said a silent prayer hoping she was going to be okay.

The Marine guards assessed the situation and immediately waved the car through. Keith directed the Japanese driver to the dispensary, and ran in to retrieve some corpsmen, who followed Keith back out with a stretcher, transferred Cyndi to it, and carried her inside. Keith followed, holding her hand, but was stopped at the emergency room door, "We need some identification here," said the corpsman. "Are you related?"

"No, just friends," Keith spoke hesitantly, keeping a watchful eye on Cyndi. "Well, what's her name? Is she a military dependent?" Keith looked past the corpsman, "Yeah, her name's Cynthia Croft."

"As in Admiral Croft?" The corpsman looked at the girl with new respect, "God, buddy, what did you do to her? Sure wouldn't want to be in your shoes." Keith grimaced, "Biking accident. For Christ's sake are you going to take care of her, or not?" Keith was feeling agitated and angry. Everything was moving too slow. "Yeah, right. Biking accident." The corpsman rolled his eyes and wheeled Cyndi through the emergency room doors as Keith tried to follow, "You sit here. We'll take care of her from here."

Ron found Keith pacing the floor two hours later. Keith looked haggard and worried, a cup of untouched coffee in one hand. Ron put a hand on Keith's shoulder, "So how is she?" Keith continued to pace, "I don't know. They won't tell me anything." Keith ran a hand through his hair. "Has her uncle or anyone else come through here?" Keith shook his head. "No, I haven't seen anyone. I'm really worried. Do you think you could find out something?"

"Yeah, let me go check. I know a corpsman. Maybe he's on duty." Ron disappeared through the emergency room doors and was gone for about ten minutes. Keith thought he was going to lose it. He felt physically sick and angry. What could be taking so long?

"Okay," said Ron as he came back through the doors, "Brace yourself. This is the way it's going down." Keith backed up against the wall to listen. "All right, I'm ready. What's happening? She's okay isn't she?" Ron looked past Keith and out the window, "Well, actually, she's not here." Keith leaped away from the wall and came at Ron. "What do you mean she's not here? Where the hell is she? Fuck, she's not dead is she?"

"Idle back here, guy," Ron put his hands on Keith's shoulders to calm him. "As far as I know, she's fine. They transported her to the Yokuska Naval Hospital." Keith started pacing again, "Why'd they do that?" Ron shrugged his shoulders, "They have much better facilities there." Keith countered, "Then maybe she's not so fine. Didn't they tell you anything about her condition? Maybe I should go to Yokuska." Ron took a deep breath, "Okay, Keith, the other things is if you even try to see her now, you're going to make things worse. She's going to be in bigger trouble than she already is." Keith slammed his elbow against the wall, "So what exactly am I supposed to do? I feel responsible for this. They should at least have the decency to tell me what's going on."

Ron leaned against the wall, "Keith, you have got to remember that this is the Admiral's niece we are talking about. She told you early on who she was and that she was not supposed to be associated with enlisted personnel. The way I see it you are going to be lucky if you don't end up in trouble on some charge. They are definitely not going to give you any hints as to her condition or whereabouts. The smartest thing you can do is go back to the barracks and forget about it."

Keith squared off on Ron, "That's bullshit and you know it! I'm going to see her. One way or another I'm going to see her." Keith stormed out the door leaving Ron standing in the foyer shaking his head.

CHAPTER 9

▼

Monday arrived bright and sunny, a total contrast to the way Keith felt. He had spent the rest of Saturday and Sunday trying to find out something about Cyndi. In a last desperate effort to get some information, he had called to the Admiral's house and spoke with Cyndi's aunt. She informed him to stay away from Cyndi and if he pursued this avenue any further, he would find himself stationed in downtown Hanoi. He had even given Rotor a call, hoping by chance he would know somebody that could help him out. Now it was Monday, and he knew no more than he had when Cyndi had been admitted on Saturday, except that she was alive.

Keith reported for his test flight at 0600 hours. Helicopter 62 had a new starboard engine installed and the flight was to test this engine. They returned at 0730 hours just after morning muster. Keith was doing his post flight inspection when the plane captain told him that he should report to the personnel office. Keith immediately had a feeling of dread. As soon as Keith entered the personnel office, he saw Ron looking hesitantly at him. "What's up?" Keith threw his flight helmet on the counter. "This comes at a bad time, buddy, but you're leaving Wednesday," Ron handed a set of orders to Keith. "Where did this come from all of a sudden?" Keith said with suspicion creeping into his voice. Ron responded quickly, "Just got orders that you're being sent to Detachment 104. You will be flying out of Yokota to Clark Air Base in the Philippines. From there you are to go to Subic Bay Naval Air Station and catch a flight to Da Nang. The Big Mothers will pick you up in Da Nang and take you out to the carrier. You will probably have to stay on board the carrier overnight and then the Big Mothers should fly you up to north SAR." Keith was trying to follow all that Ron was saying and read the orders at the same time, "On the orders it's saying Cubi Point and you said Subic Bay." Ron could see the strain of the past few days written in lines across Keith's forehead. "Actually they're the same base. The aviation side of the base is called Cubi Point, and the black shoe side, or traditional Navy side, is called Subic Bay."

Keith caught sight of a familiar name and looked up. "Rotor's on these orders, too." Ron nodded, "Yeah, that's because you're being paired up for some reason or another. That's not all bad. It probably means that you'll keep rotating together." Keith was confused, "But why all of a sudden? What about all my H-3 training? What about this whole month? What about Det 110? What about the Big Mothers?" Keith was feeling apprehensive by the sudden change in agendas, "Is this because of what happened to Cyndi?" Ron shrugged his shoulders. "I just don't know," It pained Ron to see Keith looking so low, "I thought about that too." Ron handed Keith the rest of his travel itinerary, "Hey, big guy, there's three ways of doing things, the right way, the wrong way, and the Navy way. This is the Navy way." Keith felt a myriad of emotions ranging from disbelief to a rising feeling of foreboding.

Suddenly the door to the personnel office slammed open and Rotor charged in. "What the hell you mean I'm going back on Det? I just got back, for Christ's sake!" Rotor slammed his fist on the counter. He noticed Keith standing at the counter looking slightly pale and confused, "Oh, hi Mr. Boot Camp. What's your problem now? You look like you just got caught with the skipper's wife." He turned back to Ron before Keith could answer, "What is this bullshit? What kind of chicken shit operation is this anyway? You guys said I'd have at least sixty days in." Ron just nodded and let Rotor ramble on for a while. "Oh, you love it and you know it. You should be happy to get away from the old lady for a while." Rotor seemed satisfied that he had made an effort to show his displeasure. "Okay, so when do we leave?" Ron threw up his hands in a defensive manner. "Wednesday morning. Sorry guys, I don't give the orders, I just type them. You guys can go ahead and get ready to go. You're secured from all duties here. You are to be at Yokota Air Force Base no later than 0900 hours Wednesday morning."

Rotor grabbed the still dazed Keith and pulled him out the door. As Keith stood on the curb forlornly looking down at his orders, Rotor jumped into his broken down Datsun. "Okay, Boot Camp, this is what's going to happen. You head for the cattle car and catch a ride back to the barracks. I, on the other hand, have to head to Yokuska to say good-bye to the wife and kids. Okay?" Keith didn't respond. Rotor sighed, then answered for him, imitating a young boy's voice, "Okay, Mr. Rotor, sounds like a wonderful plan." Rotor jumped in the car and took off. He was half way around the end of the runway when he noticed that Keith had not moved an inch from the spot where he had left him. Rotor slammed on the brakes and spoke to himself, "Why do I get stuck with all the damn boot camps? Why?" Rotor turned around, drove back to where Keith was standing, reached across and opened the door for him. When he still didn't respond he grabbed him by the shirt and pulled him into the seat, "For Christ's sake. Pull your head out." Keith said nothing. "I know what you need." Rotor glanced over at Keith who looked haggard and unhappy. "Yeah, this is a good idea. You're in for a real treat now. Once the wife's snuggled you in between her huge, succulent breasts, you're going to forget all your problems." Keith smiled weakly. "Either that, or you're going to wish you were dead. I can't remember which right now." Rotor chuckled and headed for the barracks where they packed up Keith's C-Bag and flight gear. Form there they headed out the front gate.

CHAPTER 10

▼

They headed down the narrow paved streets competing for space with the big Isuzu trucks who were driving faster than Rotor was. On one side of the street were tiny white cottage-like houses surrounded by white stucco or rock fences. All the houses had gardens that enveloped the whole yard. The houses in most cases were little more than five feet apart. On the other side of the street were two story structures where business was conducted. All the store fronts were painted in Japanese lettering and Keith couldn't read the signs, but in his present state of misery, he didn't really care.

The hour's drive went pretty fast as Rotor tried to get Keith out of his doldrums by telling him jokes and stories and singing raunchy tunes. "I know a girl named Peggy Sue…Long, brown, hair and eyes of blue…She played doctor with the lads…Now she has no use for pads…Sound off…one, two…sound off…three, four. Good huh? Oh, for Christ's sake! Would be better if I'd have brought along one of the rescue dummies. At least once in a while their heads fall off and I could get a little action there. Arrraaaaagh." Keith tried to listen to Rotor once in a while, but it was too hard to concentrate. Mostly he stared off into the distance, looking at nothing in particular, thinking of Cyndi, his new orders, and Cyndi, and whether she was going to be okay.

An hour later they drove into the gate of Yokuska Naval Station and headed toward the dependent housing area. They drove past six identical rows of Navy grey houses. Rotor explained that the homes were set up in duplexes with two families to a house. Keith knew when they had come to Rotor's house. Aside from all the screaming kids racing across what appeared to be weeds or a poor excuse for a lawn, there was a menagerie of toys, tools and other indistinguishable items strewn throughout the yard. As they pulled up in front of the house, the door opened and there stood Blossom, all 268 pounds of her. When she saw Rotor, she let out a scream, ran toward the Datsun and pulled him bodily from the car and hugged him, lifting his lean 140 pounds clear of the vehicle. Rotor appeared to be in heaven. They exchanged ear nibbles and kisses and minutes went by before Rotor remembered his friend still sitting in the car. "Sweet Cheeks, this is my good friend, Keith Klein. Keith, I'd like you to meet my beautiful wife, Blossom."

Keith opened his door and slid his feet outside but remained seated. "Nice to meet you, Ma'am," He was about to stand and shake her hand but Blossom was laughing at one of her young ones. When Blossom laughed her whole body jiggled, and it was jiggling now as Keith found himself being drug from the car by the gargantuan woman and being crushed between her breasts. He could hear Rotor chuckling somewhere beyond the body mass. The evening passed peacefully. Blossom put on a feed that left Keith uncomfortable, sleepy, and almost contented. He watched Rotor as he played Monopoly with his kids on the floor. Finally, after the last rug rat was put to bed, Rotor pulled up a chair next to Keith and lit a cigarette. "Well, I guess it's just me and you partner." Keith nodded, "So how'd Blossom take it when you told her about going back on Det?" Rotor chuckled, "Ah, she's used to my comings and goings. As long as the check arrives on time, she don't much worry about where I hang my hat." Keith watched Rotor as he stretched like a cat and put his feet up on a foot stool, drawing in slowly and contentedly on the cigarette. "You have a really nice family," said Keith. Rotor lay his head back against the cushion, "Oh, don't go and get mushy on me now. After all, I'm not even sure if they're all mine." Keith looked at Rotor seriously and Rotor let out a hoot, "There you go again getting all heavy on me. You've got to lighten up, boy. We're going to be spending a lot of time together the next thirty days, so I want you to chill out right now. I've been there, so trust me."

Keith swallowed hard and took the cigarette Rotor offered him. He decided that maybe a little honesty might be a good thing. He spoke softly and hesitantly, "I'm a little nervous about this, Rotor. It's like my world is being ripped apart here. This thing with Cyndi is really eating on me, and now this transfer. I honestly never thought that I'd end up in the middle of a war." He sat forward, and took a deep breath, "What am I supposed to do? Cyndi is laying who knows where, and this war…that's why I joined the Navy in the first place. I thought that way I could avoid becoming another statistic on the six o'clock news. Now I find myself smack dab in the middle of the whole damn thing, coming from a different direction." Keith stood and started pacing the floor. He glanced at Rotor wondering how he would take it.

Rotor stood and looked steadily into the eyes of the younger man, trying to remember how he had felt so many years ago, "The first couple times I went out I was scared too. When I go out on a mission now, I'm still scared, but my training takes over." Rotor rubbed his chin and hunkered down in front of Keith, "If we get out on a mission, we just have to do our job and let the rest take care of itself. Some things in life you just can't control. Just do the best you can." Rotor slapped Keith on the knee, "And as for the other little problem, the car keys are on a hook behind the door, it's Room 203, the hospital is three blocks in that direction. If you put a dent in my car, you own it. Now, I'm going to bed for the night."

Keith looked at Rotor, eyes opening wide, realizing what he was offering him. Yokuska Naval Station. Of course! He hadn't made the connection until just now, "I really appreciate this." Rotor chuckled, "No problem, that's what partners are for." Rotor winked and headed up the stairs. "Here I come Sweet Cheeks, Big Elmo wants some sugar." Rotor laughed heartily at himself as he bounded the steps two at a time.

CHAPTER 11

▼

The hospital was easy to find, as it was well posted with signs and directions to the emergency entrances. Bright beaconed lights were mounted on all entry doors. Keith made a few loops around the premises to scope out the situation. It was not easy being inconspicuous with an old car that sputtered and groaned when you came to a stop. Keith finally parked a block away and walked toward the main entrance. As he entered the building he was met by a corpsman. "What can I do for you, Mate? Regular sick call hours are from 0700 to 0800." Keith put his hand on his chest, "I'm having trouble breathing. Can't seem to catch my breath." Keith leaned on the counter, coughing weakly.

The corpsman rushed forward and lay Keith back onto one of the benches in the lobby. "You wait right here, I'll call for the doctor." He looked around for assistance. Damn, where was anyone when you needed them? "I'll just be a minute, I am going upstairs to get the on duty doctor. Will you be all right by yourself?" "Yeah...I guess...that sounds good." Keith wheezed, "I'll be fine for a few moments, but hurry." As soon as the corpsman was out of sight, Keith jumped up and off of the bench. He ran down the hall looking for the staircase. He grabbed a physician's frock from a laundry cart setting in the passageway and put it on as he ran. Farther down he spied a clipboard laying on a table and tucked it under his arm and slowed his pace a little.

He located the stairs about midway down the hall and headed up the staircase. When he reached the top, he peered around the corner. The hallway looked empty and Keith frantically began searching for Room 203, staying as close to the wall as possible. He located it almost at the end of the hall and tapped on the door. A petite young wave opened the door and looked questioningly at Keith.

"It's time for Cynthia Croft's 2300 hour examination," said Keith from behind the clipboard. The young lady looked puzzled. "I don't recall hearing about any nighttime examination before." Keith hoped he sounded convincing, "This was a special examination requested by the Admiral himself. But if you want to call to verify, please go ahead." The wave stuttered and stammered for a moment, trying to think what she should do. She finally decided there should be no harm in an extra examination, especially if the Admiral had requested it. She stood aside to let Keith enter. Keith knew he had the upper hand now, "You'll have to wait outside, Miss. We wouldn't want to embarrass the young lady. Procedure, you know." The young wave immediately scooted out the door. "No, of course not, Doctor. I'll be right outside here if you should need me." Keith closed the door behind her.

The room was dark except for a single light from the adjoining bathroom. It cast a soft glow across the bed where Cyndi lay quietly resting. Keith approached slowly and stood at her side. The room was drab, grey, like everything else Navy. Not very cheerful surroundings to get well in, thought Keith. Cyndi was lying on her back, with one arm above her head. There was a bandage wrapped around her forehead, but Keith could see no other physical injuries. He couldn't keep from brushing a strand of hair off her face, and felt relieved to finally see for himself that she was okay. Her eyelashes fluttered and she opened her eyes to see Keith peering at her, worry written all over his face. "Hi, sailor," she said drowsily, "Am I dreaming or has the devil himself come for a visit?" Keith pulled up a chair close to her bed. He smiled gently down at Cyndi, "It's me, Pretty Lady, pitchfork and all." Cyndi looked around, "How'd you get in here? My uncle has got me under such tight wraps a flea couldn't get through, yet here you are." Keith reached over and took her hand in his, "I had to pay a few bribes, but I'm here. They couldn't keep me away." Cyndi smiled back, wincing and touching her bandage with her free hand. "Are you okay?" Keith squeezed her hand tighter inside of his. "Cyndi, I was so worried." Cyndi smiled again feeling sleepy and contented, "What is it with us, anyway? Either one or the other always ending up on our back." Keith laughed, "Yeah, but for always the wrong reason. I could think of a lot more pleasant things to do than ramming your head against an embankment."

Cyndi rolled her head and looked into Keith's eyes, "Well, it was the only thing I could think of on short notice." Keith chuckled softly, "I either need to get my hearing checked or you must be delirious. You're actually telling a joke." As they conversed, Keith played with Cyndi's fingers, and was slightly surprised and pleased that she hadn't pulled her hand away. She studied him now, "Well, actually, I'm on drugs. And it's not so bad either. But then you should know if anyone does." She watched Keith as he tenderly played with her fingers, "This is really a different side of you, sailor. A normal person would think you were worried about me." Keith looked into Cyndi's eyes. "Pretty Lady, you have no idea." He leaned towards Cyndi.

As their lips touched, they heard a commotion coming down the hall. People talked rapidly and loudly and doors opened and closed. Keith jerked backwards, "Well, that's my cue, Cyndi, I think I'd better get going. I just wanted to see for myself that you were okay." Cyndi sat up, "I'm going to be fine, but you'd better get the hell out of here before they catch you."

Keith turned Cyndi's hand over and softly kissed the palm, before he turned toward the window. "Well, I'm off to fight the war. They're sending me out on Det." He didn't know what else to say, "Take care." Keith opened up the window, swung his leg through, and disappeared over the edge. Cyndi heard a loud bang and a "Shit" as Keith struck the garbage cans below. She smiled, lay back down and rolled over as the young wave and the corpsman broke through the door, looking around the room. "Where is he?" Cyndi pretended like she had just woke up. "Where is who?" The corpsman was insistent, "The man who was in here. The fake doctor. Where is he?" Cyndi rolled her eyes, "My God, you mean to tell me you don't have real doctors here?" Cyndi's eyes opened wide in a look of exaggerated horror.

The corpsman was nervous and wringing his hands. The wave beside him began to sob, "We are in so much trouble!" The corpsman knew they were both in big trouble for letting the imposter into this room…the niece…of the Admiral, no less. He felt sick. "No," he said impatiently, "The guy that was here a minute ago." Cyndi smiled sweetly, "Didn't see a soul, but then again, I'm on drugs, I could have been hallucinating." She motioned towards the window. "Could you close that, please? It's getting kind of chilly in here." Cyndi grinned, holding her hand against her cheek as she rolled over and went back to sleep.

CHAPTER 12

▼

Keith and Rotor left the base at 0630 hours and slept aboard the bus going to Yokota. They arrived at Yokota two hours later and were deposited at the terminal where they waited for their flight. As was usual, their flight was delayed and they found themselves with a six-hour layover. Rotor looked at his watch, "Let's hit the NCO club. These Air Force pukes have got it made. You won't believe their clubs, Boot Camp. Or should I call you Roller?" Rotor grinned and Keith made a face. "Word get's around fast," Rotor slapped Keith on the back, "Especially when you're trying to break my old records...Roller." Keith nodded, "If it's all the same, I would prefer Keith." Rotor chuckled.

"Okay, Boot Camp. Sure no problem, Boot Camp." Rotor laughed loudly and slapped Keith on the back again, this time almost knocking him off balance. Keith didn't see any sense in arguing once Rotor had his mind made up. When they had all their gear stashed in a corner of the NCO club and were seated comfortably at a corner table, they each ordered a beer. "Boot Camp, I'm going to give you a little indoctrination to the Philippines. It's best I do this now as it may save your life later." Rotor looked at Keith like a father telling his son about sex for the first time. Keith let out a sigh, "Geez, is this going to be another one of your lectures?" Keith settled back with his feet on the next chair looking around the bar for a distraction. Rotor was not put off one little bit by Keith's comment, "First of all, I want you to carry this flare gun at all times." Keith sat up, shocked. He opened his mouth to speak, but Rotor held up a hand to silence him. "Second of all, I want you to carry these reloading cartridges. And third, I want you to know how to use this thing as a weapon."

Keith's mouth had fallen open as he saw the flare gun, knowing that it was standard issue in their survival gear. "How did you manage to get one of those off the base, and with the reloads too?" Rotor chuckled, "The same way I got these other three, and all these other reloads." Rotor pulled the others from his sock and handed a pair to Keith. Rotor looked the younger man in the eye, "It's not what you know, Boot Camp, it's who you know." Rotor chuckled at Keith's dumbfounded look. "Now listen carefully here, Boy Scout. If you aim the flare gun at a paved surface and slightly downward, like this, the flare will spread when it hits the pavement and make it look like the street is on fire." Keith looked dumbfounded, "What the hell am I going to need this for?" Rotor put the flare gun away. "Trust me, guy, you'll be glad you have it, and glad I told you what to do with it." Keith nodded, "Yeah, but I'm just a little concerned about carrying this stuff. We're not supposed to be carrying this kind of thing in a friendly country."

Rotor still had the fatherly tone in his voice, "Listen, my elementary school boy. There's no such thing as a totally friendly country. Come on, Boot Camp, join the real world here. I can't be around every minute to get your ass out of a jam. Listen, trust me on this one, I know what I am talking about. We are more of the ugly American over here than you think, friendly country or not. Many of the locals hate our guts." Keith sat stubbornly looking at Rotor. Rotor leaned back, "Just take the stuff." Keith reluctantly reached over to grab the flare gun. The mood was slightly spoiled for Keith. It seemed like things got scarier all the time. Even the streets of a friendly country weren't safe. He felt like he'd been placed in a second rate Western novel. Rotor took another sip of his beer, "Oh, come on, Boot Camp. Lighten up. Just want you to be prepared, that's all. You'll probably never have to use it even." Then under his breath he added, "Yeah, right. Dumb shit."

Keith ignored Rotor's last comment and finished his beer. They ordered several more beers and Rotor changed the subject to women and got a few laughs telling Keith about his sexual escapades. It was finally time to go so they gathered their gear, and trouped it back to the terminal.

They boarded the Air Force C130 cargo plane bound for Clark Air Force Base in the Philippines. The cargo bay looked like it could carry about six jeeps, but was loaded with boxes and crates of unknown contents, all bound for the base. Rotor and Keith entered by the ramp-type rear cargo door and proceeded forwarded until they found an open canvas seat, which was attached to the side of the fuselage.

They both had two pencil flares and reloads stuffed in their socks. Keith dozed off as soon as they were in the air. Rotor was gabbing away to some guy who looked like he was too long in the service without the benefit of gaining any experience. He had three hash marks and was still an E-3. Keith figured he must have been busted somewhere along the way.

Keith's first impression of Clark Air Base was "Damn, it's hot." The sun was scorching down on them as they stepped off the C130. He raised a hand to cover his eyes while waiting for the C130 crewman to give them the okay to unload their bags.

An Air Force sergeant arrived in a jeep with two German Shepherds and took the dogs aboard the airplane to sniff for drugs. As soon as the inspection was completed, Keith and Rotor claimed their bags and headed for a taxi stand. Rotor hailed a taxi, loaded his gear into the trunk, jumped in the back seat, and directed Keith to do the same. Rotor told the driver to take them to the front gate. "Why are we going to the front gate? Aren't we supposed to get our asses down to Subic?" asked Keith, "Shouldn't we be taking military transportation?" Rotor chuckled, "Yeah, we should, but we ain't going to, 'cause this way is a lot more fun." Keith was worried, "Well, what if we get in trouble?" Rotor was starting to give Keith ulcers. Rotor shook his head, "Oh Grandma, you worry too damn much. I'll get us to Subic in plenty of time, and it won't be so damn boring either." Being bored was not something that Keith was worried about, not when Rotor was around.

CHAPTER 13

▼

The taxi dropped them off at the front gate. They carried their gear through the gate and into Angeles City. Rotor started talking to one of the jeepney drivers who was standing there.

There were about five jeepneys lined up like taxis for hire. Rotor explained to Keith that a jeepney was a surplus World War II U.S. Army jeep. The United States left a whole bunch of jeeps here in the Philippines rather than ship them home. The Philippinos had stripped the jeeps down, lengthened them by as much as six to eight feet and rebuilt them from the frame up with local-flavored accessories. The front of the Jeepney was the only thing that let you know it was a jeep originally. The Philippinos then installed many lights, not unlike a Christmas tree. The jeep was painted with different scenes, usually religious. Tassels, like those found on bicycle handle bars were then placed in different places on the Jeepney. Some of the jeepneys had a great deal of chrome, while others were just painted with a multitude of colors ranging from whites to reds and blues with many shades thrown in. They were definitely bright and easy to see. There was the hood ornament, a chrome plated stallion, or an airplane of some sort. This almost-finished product was then fitted with antennas decorated with plastic streamers. There was almost always a portrait of the Virgin Mary on the dashboard, and a small wooden box where the driver kept his fares. There were two bench-like seats behind the driver along both sides of the vehicle. The passengers entered the vehicle from the rear. There was a roof but no windows along the sides or along the back. Rotor explained that when a new owner took possession of the jeepney the first thing he did was hang a flower garland over the rear view mirror for good luck.

Rotor then bowed gallantly to Keith. "Get in, old chap." Keith grumbled something under his breath, gave Rotor an impatient look and climbed into the Jeepney. Rotor chuckled and followed as he gave directions to the driver, "Oasis Hotel." Keith had a quizzical look on his face, "The Oasis Hotel?" Rotor smiled, "Cleanest place in town. Trust me. Besides, we can use the hotel bus in the morning to take us the rest of the way to Cubi Point."

As they drove, Keith took in the surroundings. He paid special attention to the little brown women who all had shiny black hair, which they wore down to their waists. They dressed in tight-fitting clothes that complimented their trim figures. "Boy," thought Keith," A fellow could really have some fun here." A fleeting thought of a longhaired blond with blue eyes brought a smile to Keith's lips and he thought that then again maybe the wait would be worth it.

They stopped at the hotel and a young boy grabbed their gear. Keith and Rotor checked in and went to their room. At first sight the room looked okay, nothing fancy, but livable. That was before Keith saw the cockroach crawling beside the bed, followed by his entire family including third cousins. Keith went to the bathroom to wash up, but could get no hot water from the tap, and only a trickle of cold water. The boy brought their bags into the room and held out his hand for a tip, "You want women, Joe?" Rotor looked at the boy who could not have been more than nine or ten years old, "How much?" The boy replied, "Porty fesos por one hour." Rotor chuckled, "For that price I could have half the women in the Philippines." The boy replied, "Por you Joe, I have one time sfecial good deal. Two women, two hours, thirty fesos." Rotor tipped the kid a peso and told him to shove off explaining to Keith that a peso still went a long way in this country.

Both Rotor and Keith got into their civvies, locked their gear into their rooms and headed downtown to the bar district. When the jeepney dropped them off, they went into the nearest bar and Keith thought he had died and gone to heaven. All those little brown girls in the bar were putting their arms around him, but had him confused with some guy named Joe. The ladies escorted Keith and Rotor to a table and Rotor ordered two San Miguel beers with two glasses of ice. "What's the ice for?" asked Keith. "No electricity buddy, and no electricity means no refrigeration. The ice man still does a booming business here. He makes his deliveries twice a day and since no Americans like to drink warm beer, he does a pretty good business." The thought of drinking beer with ice nauseated Keith, but then he really wanted to drink beer. A young hostess who sat beside Keith began to cozy closer. "What iss your name?" she asked. Keith could feel the warmth of her body, "Keith." He scoped out the lady. She smiled reveling several missing teeth, "Buy me drink Keet. Keet is nice name. You stationed Clark, Keet?" Keith decided he didn't care for the accent, "The name is Keith, and no I'm not stationed at Clark. Just passing through." Keith looked around, "How much is a drink anyway?" The young lady leaned in closer. "One time good deal just por you, Keet. One drink, ten fesos."

Keith looked at the lady with suspicion, "These two beers were only two pesos. What gives?" The young lady explained, "Hostess drink cost more but you good looking guy, special drink por you only, pive fesos." Keith thought about it, "Uh, no thanks." Keith looked at Rotor who was talking a mile a minute to another hostess in some strange language that had a lot of Bs and Gs in it. He was speaking it like he was a native. Keith interrupted, "What the hell you talking about, Rotor?" Rotor screamed back at him, "Quiet! I got some good shit going on here." Keith sipped his beer dejectedly and after a minute Rotor looked over at him. "Hey, Boot Camp, want to go to the cock fights?" Keith looked over at Rotor questioningly, "What the hell's a cock fight?"

Rotor leaned back in his chair, "You're pretty damn dumb aren't you, Boot Camp? Ya didn't get out in the world much I take it." He spoke it matter of factly, as if he'd finally had a great revelation and it was all clear to him now, "Didn't teach you much up in North Dakota, did they?" Keith shrugged, "Not about cock fights." Rotor sneered, "Or anything else, the way I see it. Let's go. I'll explain along the way." He good-naturedly put his arm around Keith's shoulder.

They left the bar and caught another jeepney. Rotor gave the driver instructions in the same strange dialect he had been speaking before, and they took off. "What kind of shit are you talking?" asked Keith. Rotor sighed, "Oh, it's called Tagalog. It's the Philippino national language. Keith nodded his head, "I'm impressed." Rotor smiled, "Don't be. It only took me a couple of years to get the hang of it. Some day I'll introduce you to my Philippino wife." Keith opened his mouth to speak but nothing came out. Rotor laughed, "Yeah, worst part is, I've got another one tucked away in Okinawa too." Rotor felt a need to defend his having three wives. "Hell, you never know where a guy's going to be. Always have to be prepared." He hooted at Keith, "You amaze me. You just got to get with the program, pard. Live a little before you die." Keith just shook his head and laughed. "Speaking of living, let me tell you about where we're going.

Cockfights are a favorite pastime around here. Each barrio…" He looked to see if Keith was following along. "That's like a village, you know." Keith didn't know, but be damned if he was going to admit to any more ignorance at that particular moment. Rotor continued, "Angeles City alone has about thirty barrios. Anyway…each barrio has its favorite cock. You do know what a cock is, don't you?" Rotor grinned and Keith flipped him off. "Now we're cooking. Anyway…they pit their cocks against the cocks of the other barrios and it's usually a fight to the death with lots of money being wagered. Good shit fun. You'll love it."

They arrived at a warehouse-looking building. It had unpainted siding and a corrugated tin roof. There were no windows except two small pigeon holes where the roof peaked. There was one main door at the front of the building, which Keith and Rotor headed for. They could hear the cheering before they entered the building. Rotor, trusting his instincts, gave Keith a warning, "Stick close. These places can get pretty hairy sometimes." The warehouse was packed with men of mostly Philippino persuasion. There was a small area in the center of the room that looked like a boxing arena. A cloud of smoke hung over the room, and a loud din could be heard as people cheered on the roosters. Several other locals wandered around with money stuck between their fingers, taking bets. "Tandang pusta. Tandang pusta."

Rotor told Keith that the two cocks waiting at the side of the arena would be next and that Keith should pick the winner. Keith picked the red one because it seemed to be more feisty than the black one. And even though Black looked spunky, he somehow lacked the winning qualities that Keith thought a fighting cock should have. Keith figured he should know his stock. After all, he did come from a farm.

There was a lot of chatter, and at last the two holders released their roosters and the fight began. The two cocks slowly circled the arena like two sumo wrestlers appraising their opponents. They bobbed their heads and made menacing gestures towards each other. After circling the arena twice, the black cock attacked. Using the sharp claws on its feet and its beak, it soon drew blood from the red cock, which drew screams and cheering from the crowd. The red cock was far from finished, however, and launched an attack of its own.

Keith was enthralled with the fight. Watching the crowd was almost as exciting as watching the roosters. Some people stared quietly and intently while others screamed frantically giving the roosters advice and encouragement. The battle lasted for about ten minutes with the black dominating the fight. Red came around near the end, but it wasn't enough. Black was on top and the match closed. "Well, you blew that one, buddy," said Rotor. "I hope you know you just blew twenty pesos on that brilliant error of judgment, Farm Boy," he added. Keith shrugged his shoulders. "Easy come, easy go."

The next match was about to begin with two big black roosters this time. Keith and Rotor elected not to bet on this one, but decided to observe instead.

"You're the expert here. Why don't you see if you can do any better," said Keith. "Na, let's get some air." They moved back towards the door.

There were small groups of men standing around talking in excited tones. Rotor tried to listen to some of the conversations as they passed. One group got really quiet as the two men approached, but after looking them over decided that the Americans would not be able to understand them anyway so they went on with their rousing conversation. Rotor pulled Keith off to the side. "These gentlemen are saying that there's a black cock fighting in the next match and they're sure that he's going to be the winner." Keith did not look at the men, "How sure?" Rotor made a point not to look in their direction either, "They seem to be very sure. How much money do you have, Roller?"

Keith got a gleam in his eye as they pooled their resources and went back inside to place the bet. The present match was not yet over, but they made their way to the front anyway. This match ended pretty much the same as the last one with one of the roosters down for the count. When the next pair of cocks came up, Rotor motioned to Keith that the black cock with the red head was supposed to be the winner. Keith and Rotor looked the cock over carefully and decided to bet the wad.

The match finally started and Keith became immediately concerned when the other cock started the attack on the black. It looked as if they had been suckered, until about two minutes into the match. Black seemed to get some air and when he finally got going, it was nothing but beak, feet, and feathers. The crowd went nuts. Black ended the match in less than five minutes and Rotor was already over collecting their winnings. From the wad of money Rotor held in his hand, it looked like they had made out pretty good. Rotor came over to Keith.

"My man, not too shabby. But I think we'd best be leaving." Rotor started briskly for the door, with Keith close behind.

They walked out of the warehouse planning on catching a Jeepney, but there were none in sight. "Let's walk," said Rotor, looking over his shoulder at the warehouse door. "We're carrying a sum of money equal to five years pay for most of the locals here, and we'd best be getting out of here quick."

They had gone only a short distance when again Rotor glanced behind them and noticed a group of about ten Philippinos forming to their rear. They were about fifty yards behind, but were moving out at a pretty good pace. Keith and Rotor automatically picked up their pace also, hoping to outrun the Philippinos, or catch a jeepney real soon. They were about a mile from the warehouse and still no jeepneys in sight. The crowd was now about twenty yards behind and closing. "Well, buddy, you got your flare guns?" asked Rotor. Keith glanced back, "Well,

I sure as hell didn't feel safe leaving them at the hotel. Of course, I've got 'em." Rotor was glancing back quickly now as the mob continued to close in. "This might be a good time to pull one out and put a load in it," suggested Rotor as he pulled a flare gun from his sock and inserted a load. Keith was now paying very close attention to Rotor's instructions.

It was just getting dark and the area was covered with trees. There were no street lights which added to the sailors uneasiness. The shadows added depth to the ominous situation they suddenly found themselves in. "When I give the word," said Rotor, "I want you to turn and fire your flare gun at the blacktop on your side of the road. Aim the gun to hit about fifteen feet behind you. I will do the same over here. Okay?" He looked to see if Keith was with him on this one, and whether he could be counted on. Keith looked Rotor steadily in the eye, "I'm with you, Rotor. Let's do it."

When the Philippinos were about twenty-five feet behind, Rotor acted. "Now!" Keith and Rotor both turned simultaneously and fired their flare guns at the road surface. The flares hit the blacktop and spread out like a wall of fire covering the entire highway. Keith could see the Philippinos' eyes get wide as they turned and ran from the advancing flame. Rotor and Keith ran too, but in the opposite direction. After about ten minutes of jogging in silence, they spotted a jeepney, hailed it down, and directed the driver to take them back to their hotel. They were laughing and patting themselves on the back the whole ride.

Keith laid his hand on Rotor's shoulder as they got out of the jeepney, "You're okay, buddy." Rotor smiled, "You're not so bad yourself, Dick Weed." Rotor punched Keith in the arm, "We're one hell of a team." Keith liked the sound of that, "Yeah, a team." Keith wasn't sure if that was good or bad but right now he didn't care. He felt great after their near encounter that could have ended up with less than favorable results had it not been for Rotor's foresight. Keith suddenly had a weird thought, "Was he turning into another Rotor?" He shuddered involuntarily. Rotor appeared to have read his thoughts. He puffed up like a proud father.

"Yeah, someday boy, you can say that you learned the ropes from the legend himself. Rotor." Keith looked at him uncertainly, and Rotor slapped him again on the back, "Don't think about it too hard, child. Let's get some sleep. Lots more adventures where that one came from. This is only the beginning." When Keith still hesitated, Rotor laughed and walked on ahead. Get some sleep? How could a person sleep after an incident like that? They could have been killed. Or worse yet, tortured. Keith followed slowly behind. Sleep would be slow in coming tonight.

*   *   *   *

Keith immediately knew where he was, and knew that he had to act quickly. He had to get to the cockpit to ensure that both pilots were flying the helo. He saw their flight suits from the back. Their heads nodded as they checked the instruments. Keith tried to communicate with the pilot, but there was no response. He tapped his helmet, but there appeared to be complete radio silence. Keith's eyes were drawn to the rear of the helo where the rest of the drama was to be played. He could feel the motion of the hovering helicopter blades, yet nothing invaded the silence. The first crewman worked silently, his back to Keith, and he knew it would be futile to try to communicate with him. The stage was set to start, but at least they had pilots. What else did he have to do? He surveyed the now familiar scenario. The pinpoints of light shined through the bullet holes, yet he didn't remember when the battle had occurred. Keith remembered something else. He turned slowly to see the two figures that lay covered with blankets towards the front of the helo. The helo went into a hover. "Man your guns!"

The silence was broken as bullets whined around him. Keith grabbed the grips of the mini-gun and sprayed the jungle. He saw the enemy running for cover in the thick foliage. The helicopter landed with a soft thud and someone screamed, "Cover me!"

He could see two shipmates on the ground. The silent crewman grabbed the gun from Keith's hand and motioned him towards the cockpit. He had to stop the pilots. Too late. The helo lifted off, and started forward flight. No, not yet, there were men still on the ground. He screamed towards the cockpit, "Stop! Turn around!"

The helo continued to head towards sea. He ran forward screaming at the pilot, as he pulled off his helmet. "Go back!" As he raced passed the lifeless bodies, a hand reached out and grabbed him by the ankle. He went down landing on top of one of the bodies. The blanket had fallen off and he was staring into a familiar face, the eyes wide, the mouth open in a silent scream. Keith's mouth opened to match the scream of the dead man. On the dead man's forehead some one had written the numbers "seven six".

CHAPTER 14

▼

The morning greeted them as every morning in the Philippines did this time of year - humid and hot. Keith and Rotor grabbed their gear and stowed it aboard the hotel bus to begin their trip to Subic Bay Naval Base.

"So what do you think about that cool five thousand pesos we made yesterday, buddy?" asked Rotor. He stretched his arms over his head, feeling content and lazy in the bus. The air hung thick and humid.

"Not a bad way to double your money," Keith patted his pocket. Today he was feeling pretty good. The terror of the night before was fading into only a memory of a daring adventure. "What are you going to do with your half?"

"Well, that's about seven hundred dollars. That should almost be enough material to make Blossom a dress. Ha," he laughed, "Maybe I'll do that." Rotor scratched the stubble on his chin and contemplated for a few minutes.

"Then again, that could get me one hell of a month out in the barrio, away from these damn sailor towns. A woman, booze, and chow to boot. Yeah, that sounds more like it. What about you?" Keith was enjoying the ride, "No plans. Going to tuck it away and see what comes down. Rainy day and all that." Rotor smiled at Keith, "Grandma, I give you three days out in the local towns with these little brown bodied ladies and it'll all be gone." Keith retorted quickly, "Yeah well at least I'm not a bigamist."

Rotor smiled as if someone had paid him a compliment, pulled his cap over his eyes, and slid down in his seat for a snooze. Keith studied Rotor for a few minutes. Rotor really knew how to take the edge off. In the last twenty-four hours, Keith hadn't worried once about being killed in Viet Nam. Maybe he thought for a moment he was going to die in the Philippines, but Rotor had a way of making you look at life a little differently. He'd had a little fun. No one had gotten hurt. Yeah, things were looking up.

It was about a three-hour ride to the base, of which Keith slept the last two hours. The driver dropped them off at Magsaysay Drive on the Olongapo side of the bridge leading to the Naval Base. It was about 0400 hours and getting hotter. "God, what's that awful smell?" Keith had barely put a foot to the ground before the pungent aroma of something dead or dying reached his nose. "Shit River," responded Rotor, looking around, like he hadn't really noticed. "No kidding," Keith looked around, almost expecting to see a sign. "What do they really call it?" Rotor was grabbing his bags, "They reeaaallly call it Shit River. Kind of fitting, don't you think?" replied Rotor, sniffing the air. "Actually it's a sewage ditch. One of the main local attractions." Keith felt if this was one of the main attractions, he didn't think he'd be doing much sight-seeing.

They grabbed their bags and headed across the bridge. Keith set his bags down and looked back to see what Olongapo City looked like, since he'd slept during the ride through town. All he saw was a wide main street. On both sides of the street, as far as you could see, there were two story buildings and every building seemed to show signs of a bar or night club. Rotor had stopped also, following Keith's gaze, "What we have here, my man, is the most damned efficient whore-house in the world. There are ten thousand registered whores in this town and they are all ready, willing, and able to service the Seventh Fleet when it arrives." Keith looked back at Rotor, "What do you mean, registered?" Okay, so he was setting himself up for another one of Rotor's jokes, but he had to ask, Only this time Rotor was serious, "I mean they're really registered." Keith smiled slightly, "Yeah, right." Rotor carried an astonished expression that could have led one to believe he was giving the Sunday sermon, "Honest. They carry cards saying they've been checked out at the clinic and they're VD free whores." Keith looked back at Olongapo, "Wow. I'm impressed." Keith surveyed the area like a little boy looking in a candy store window. Rotor felt really important for having delivered this vital piece of information and once again resumed his fatherly duties, "This is about the calmest you'll see this town. You should see it after lunch. It really starts to pick up then and doesn't shut down until about 0one-zero-four0, which is curfew and then the MP's along with the local police make sure the streets are clear."

About that time Keith heard someone calling out, "Hey Joe, throw me coins." He looked over the side of the bridge and there were two kids in what looked like a small canoe with an outrigger. "Yeah you. Joe, throw me coins," they repeated. Keith reached into his pocket and threw them each a fifty Centavo piece. They caught them with ease and beamed brightly. "Throw me more coins Joe." Keith knew where this was headed so he picked up his bags and continued across the bridge toward the base. The Marine sentry checked Keith's I.D. card and checked through his bags before allowing him on base. He joined Rotor at the taxi stand. They caught a cab to HC-7 Cubi Point. The driver dropped them off at the side of the road.

Keith could see all the helos from the vantage point of the road, and could tell that this was indeed a repair facility from the state of disrepair that the units were in. Everything was painted combat gray. Rotor and Keith got out of the taxi, grabbed their bags, and paid the driver. They took their bags down the long flight of wooden steps to check in at the duty office. They were told they could spend the night in HC-7's barracks and that they would catch the next VCR-50 COD to Da Nang. The duty officer instructed the duty driver to give Rotor and Keith a ride up the hill to the barracks. Rotor stopped at this point to talk to an old friend and Keith wandered out to the flight line to inspect some of the helicopters that were parked there. It was obvious that some of them had seen some rough missions. Keith stopped at an H-3 that looked like it had been damaged from gunfire, feeling a twinge of concern rising. A helicopter, points of light. Where had he seen that before? Keith realized that the driver and Rotor were yelling at him so he ran over and jumped in the truck. The driver ran them up the hill to Cubi Point barracks.

The road was paved, steep and meandered sharply back and forth through a thick jungle. The foliage was lush and green, covering the road like an awning, blocking out the sunlight, and giving an impression of a safe and serene hide-away. As they drove through the area, the screeching of birds erupted, disturbing the illusion of peacefulness. Keith started to feel a little braver again, "I'd like to walk this stretch sometime. Kind of restful, you know what I mean?" The driver glanced back over his shoulder, raising his eyebrows at the young man, "Not if you value your life." Keith looked at the driver, "Why?" He looked around trying to see what possible danger could be in this unpopulated area. The driver calmly replied, "Monkeys." Keith looked quickly around, "Monkeys?" The driver repeated his response, "Yeah, monkeys." Keith was dumbfounded. "What do monkeys have to do with anything?" The driver continued in the same steady voice, "They'll attack you, gang up on you, and rip you apart a piece at a time." The driver had a toothpick which he slowly cleaned his teeth with as he enunciated the words, "Can't outrun them either." He looked at Keith seeing if his words were having the proper effect. Keith looked closely into the tangled mess of the jungle, trying to spy the killer monkeys. "I don't see any monkeys," Keith replied, a little nervous, "Come on. Monkeys attacking men?" The driver smiled for the first time, "They're there fella. Believe it."

Keith remembered the monkeys he had seen at the San Diego Zoo and was sure that he was being fed a line. He looked at Rotor and Rotor nodded his head as if every word were gospel. Man-eating monkeys? They had to be pulling his leg. That would be just like Rotor. You just never knew in the military.

He remembered the time they sent him to fetch five gallons of rotor wash. He was sent from place to place, everyone telling him that they had moved the location of the rotor wash or that they had just run out of it the day before. When he had exhausted every location on the base, and it was starting to get dark out, it started to sink in. How was he to know that rotor wash was the air that the rotors blew down when they were turning? He'd have to be careful. Trust no one. Not even monkeys.

Keith and Rotor grabbed their bags and headed into HC-7 barracks. Keith wondered how he'd ever sleep in this place without air conditioning. They found two empty lockers and stowed their gear. Rotor suggested they head over to the NCO club and make plans for the rest of the day. "Is it air conditioned?" asked Keith. "Yup," said Rotor. "Does it have monkeys?" "Nope." Keith nodded his head, "Then it's a date."

Sitting over a cold beer at the NCO club Keith marveled at the view of the bay. Cubi Point sat atop a very large hill. It was surrounded by jungle on two sides and by water on the other two. There was a narrow road that led to the other side of the military installation, Subic Bay Naval Base. Three aviation squadrons were stationed on the Cubi Point side. Squadron VRC-50 transported personnel to and from the war. They had a daily flight to Da Nang and the carriers. Squadron VC-5 trained the A-4 jet pilots how to hit a target and HC-7 rescued those pilots when they were not so lucky. There were always those "other duties as assigned" of course, but this was the basic mission. "I've got it," said Rotor, "Lets go to Subic City." Keith hated being in the dark, but one had to learn somehow. "What's Subic City?" Rotor has assumed the fatherly role which Keith did not mind so much. At least he told the truth during these periods. "It's a town about eight miles outside of Olongapo." Keith was curious, "So what's Subic City have that Olongapo doesn't?" Rotor smiled from ear to ear, "Have you ever had a girl…" he paused for effect, "give you a bath…outside…" He had Keith leaning forward in his chair and he loved every minute of it…"under a hand pump?" Keith took another sip of beer, "Well, no, I guess I never have." Keith hoped he wasn't drooling. Rotor went on, "And all for about a dollar and a quarter." Keith set his drink on the table, "You're kidding." Rotor leaned back in his chair, "Wouldn't joke about a thing like that. How about it?" Keith finished off his beer, "Why not? I mean you've really been looking out for me so far. I mean we've only had to use our flare guns once, but then we've been in this country almost twenty-four hours already. I sure wouldn't want it to get boring." His attempt at sarcasm was having no effect whatsoever on Rotor, who knew that they'd be out of the club in less than five minutes. "Lets go, Rotor." Rotor got out of his chair, "Did anyone ever say you talk too much?" Rotor looked at Keith who pretended to zip his lip and smile. "First," said Rotor, "We've got to lock everything in our lockers except what we really need. And what we really need is about fifty pesos, I.D. cards, and our flare guns. Got it?" Keith just continued to smile and follow orders, giving Rotor a mock salute.

Thirty minutes later the two sailors were at the front gate of the U.S. Naval installation. They retraced their steps once again back over Shit River, and threw a peso at the kids still sitting in the bonka boat. There were two boats down there now and the activity in Olongapo had also picked up. Girls were waiting on the other side of the bridge for any able-bodied man with ten pesos in his pocket to cross over. "Hey Sailor, buy me drink." One gal called out as Keith and Rotor passed by. "Hey Sailor, I'm plenty good fuck." When Keith hesitated, Rotor steered him through the crowd and motioned for a waiting jeepney. "Patience, my young apprentice, patience." He smiled at his anxious little friend. They climbed in the jeepney and the driver looked back over the seat at them, "Where you go, Joe?" Rotor replied in Tagalog and afterwards told Keith he had made a deal with the driver to take them directly to Subic City. This cost extra, of course, but Rotor figured that they could spare the dollar and a half. It sure would beat making all the connections. They drove down the street of Olongapo and everywhere they could see the little brown girls with sailors. Many of the girls yelled at them as they passed by. "Hey Joe, take me with you…Where you headed…Joe, stay with me, Joe."

Keith felt that it would not take too long for him to begin to hate the name Joe. Keith noticed what he thought were Philippino soldiers sporting M-16 or M-1 rifles. In fact, wherever Keith looked he saw locals carrying guns. He commented on this to Rotor, who looked around him, "You bet, and they're all loaded. This place can get very wild at times, just like cowboys and Indians. Stay close, Boot Camp."

They soon found themselves on a potholed highway that curved and wound its way around Subic Bay. Rotor explained that the first set of curves were called the zig-zags by the Americans. The countryside outside of Olongapo was mostly jungle, like on the base. The vegetation was dense, with palm trees growing everywhere, and, of course, it was hot and humid. Keith felt that the climate was going to get old really fast. "You'll get used to the heat," remarked Rotor as if reading Keith's mind. "Once the rainy season hits, you'll be whining that you wished it were hot and humid again." "I doubt it," Keith felt a water pump would feel pretty good right now no matter who was doing the work.

There were a few white cement houses randomly spaced along the road. It didn't look like a great deal of planning had gone into their layout. Keith also spotted some bamboo huts with stilts under them located farther up on the hills. Rotor explained that this was more of the style house that most Philippinos lived in. "Why are they up on stilts?" asked Keith. "When it rains here it really rains, buddy. Flooding and all that shit. As long as the house is on stilts you can still screw on a dry floor. Got to have your priorities."

Keith had come to realize that everything Rotor explained was somehow equated to women, booze, or money. That should have made things easier to understand, but for some reason it didn't.

They arrived in Subic City, which was a much smaller version of Olongapo. The pair got out of the jeepney, paid the driver and headed toward a place called the Midway Club. There was an open courtyard with tables in front of the club and an armed guard at the entrance. Rotor and Keith walked past the guard and into the club. Rotor ordered the usual San Miguels and two glasses of ice. The hostesses were soon begging for their usual drinks. Rotor said something to them in Tagalog about benny boys and they left. Keith watched the exchange with interest. "So, what did you say to get them to leave?" Rotor took a long drink from his iced down San Miguel beer, "Oh, just told them that we were both queer and were not in need of their services." Keith was not smiling, "Well thanks a lot! I suppose before long you will tell them we want a room so you can give me a blow job?"

Rotor shook with laughter, "No, I'm not that desperate." Keith decided to move on to new things, "So what about all the talk about the bath...out-side...under the pump, oh wise peanut brain." Rotor continued to drink his beer, "Next bar, buddy. Be patient. Can't let just anyone man your pump. Ha! Get it?" Keith looked the other way, trying to ignore Rotor, but it wasn't easy.

There were only four other people in the bar at this early hour and as Keith drank his beer, two of them got up and left. He assumed the hostesses lived in the back of the club, because there were always more girls coming from the back and all were in a different state of undress. After about three beers, Keith was starting to feel relaxed.

He noticed two more Americans who had just gotten out of a taxi heading into the club. They must have been drinking heavily before they arrived, as they staggered and slurred their words. They were extremely loud and one of them grabbed a hostess as soon as he got into the club, threw some pesos on the bar and headed out back with her. The other one ordered a beer and when it arrived he paid the hostess and asked where the head was. She pointed him in the general direction and he got up leaving his wallet on the table. Keith was about to yell at him when he caught a glance of the young boy running into the club past the guard, and quick as a flash he had the wallet and was darting back out the door. Some sixth sense must have warned the guy who was heading toward the bathroom because he turned just in time to see the kid take off. "Stop thief!" No one responded. The American ran, half stumbling toward the front of the club stopping beside the armed guard and grabbed his arm and yelled again. "What the hell, aren't you going to do anything? That kid just stole my wallet." He pointed in the direction of the racing boy.

The armed guard looked at the American and very calmly pulled out what looked like a .45 caliber pistol, aimed at the small boy, and squeezed the trigger. The boy went down without a sound.

Everything slowed down for Keith; something acid-like rose in his throat. Sweat ran down the side of his face. The guard walked slowly over to the boy, picked up the American's wallet, and casually walked back. He handed the wallet back to the American. His mouth turned up slightly at the edges, but it didn't seem quite like a smile. "You happy now Joe?" The American just stared numbly at the limp body, his face pale, eyes wide. He ran over to the boy and felt for a pulse at his wrist, at his neck, and tried again at his wrist. The shot had gone through the back of the boy's head killing him instantly; a pool of blood spread out slowly from his small frail body. The American looked terrified at his red fingers, brushing smeary streaks against his white shirt, "For God's sake, call an ambulance or something!" Panic filled the American's voice and showed in his face.

Keith stood at the door with his mouth open. He didn't remember getting up from his chair or moving to the entrance. The whole thing had lasted less than two minutes and a small boy lay dead in the street. Rotor spoke in his ear, "Let's get out of here now." Rotor put strong emphasis on the word now as he grabbed Keith by the arm. Keith was still staring unbelievingly at the lifeless boy as Rotor drug him away from the scene. He finally found his voice, "Shouldn't we do something?" Rotor answered quickly, "We should get the hell out of here." Keith remembered thinking how strange Rotor's voice sounded so far away.

Rotor held his grip on Keith's arm, half dragging, half pushing him to the taxi across the street. He pushed Keith into the vehicle, said something in Tagalog to the driver, and they shot down the street taking a quick corner. Keith didn't know which direction they went. He only knew that he felt awful, and worse yet, he was afraid he might cry. He was aware of leaving the taxi and of Rotor saying something to him, but it did not register. He looked up at Rotor who looked like he was speaking, but Keith just didn't understand what he was saying. All he could think of was the small boy and a very large pool of sticky red blood. He didn't know how long he sat there, reliving the scene, trying to think of how he could have stopped it, changed it, prevented it.

The red fog finally faded; Keith saw that they were at a beach of some sort and that there were bamboo tables with bamboo roofs over them. He and Rotor were seated at one of these tables and there was the usual beer and glasses with ice. Keith looked directly at Rotor. He was surprised at how strong his voice sounded, "Why didn't we do something?" Rotor put his hand over Keith's shoulder, "Shit, Keith, it happened so fast. How could we?" Rotor ran his fingers through his hair, making it look worse than it already did, "Did you have any idea he was going to shoot that kid?"

"Hell no," replied Keith. Keith rested his head in his hands. Rotor looked Keith squarely in the eye, "Look, Boot Camp kid, you may and probably will see a lot worse than that so you'd better get used to it. This is where we separate the men from the boys. These folks don't put the same regard on human life that we do. This type of thing happens almost daily over here and no one seems to care much. Your main concern is that it doesn't happen to you. Got it?" Keith just looked dumbly back at Rotor as he spoke. He felt it so odd that they were sitting there drinking a beer while a little boy lay rotting in the street.

"I know it was a shitty thing to see and you aren't feeling so good about it, but get a grip on your feelings," continued Rotor. "We got some heavy-duty shit in front of us and you've got to get it together. Seems to me like that's all I'm telling you lately. Is any of this registering?"

Keith nodded and took a healthy swig of beer, hoping the anesthetic effect would take hold soon. And yet the pain was being replaced by something else-anger. What kind of country was this? "Is Nam this bad?" Rotor shrugged, "Yeah, mostly it's worse though. They got a war going on there, you know." Rotor was recovering more quickly from the episode than Keith, but then he'd seen it all before.

Keith's previous doubts about why he was here began to creep back into his mind. He tried to shake it off knowing that he had to maintain or he would lose it. Rotor deserved better from a partner. They stayed at the beach, each lost in his own thoughts. Rotor ordered another round of beers. Keith felt a need to talk about something else. "So tell me about why you're such a legend." Rotor smiled to himself and looked thoughtfully at the water. "All right," he finally responded. "I can tell you. After all, we're partners now." Rotor laid down in the sand beside the table and looked up at the stars.

"It all started out as a routine flight." Keith pulled one knee up under his chin and listened as if to a fairy tale. In fact, he was pretty sure that's what it was going to be. "We were just taking the bird up for a test flight after having replaced the tail rotor gearbox. The pilot suggested we do a little target practice, and I was mounting the gun in the port side door. Somehow," Rotor scratched his chin, "And I still don't know 'til this day how, but a round went through the M-60 and it fired straight up at the rotor blades. Well, then the helo began to spin out of control and I hung on for dear life. We no more'n hit the water and the bird capsized." Rotor sat back up in the sand as the story got more intense. No, not a fairy tale exactly, more like an action-packed adventure. "I didn't even have time to think about getting out, and when the helo turned over, the aft starboard door armor plating came down on top of me, and there I was - pinned. I tried to get out but couldn't move. I knew we were sinking fast because I could see the light receding as the helo went down. Shit, I was sure I was a goner."

A shiver ran through Keith; goose bumps rose on his arms, despite the heat. Rotor had described his dream. He hadn't told Rotor anything about it, yet there it was. He contemplated it further, the difference was the helicopter, Rotor shot down his own H-2 and Keith's dream took place in the H-3. No, in time maybe he would tell Rotor, but not now.

Rotor's face took on a strange glow as he proceeded with the story. Keith wondered if he was feeling the effects of his beer. "It was almost pitch black down there and I was holding my breath. Then suddenly," said Rotor, "From out of nowhere…" Rotor hesitated, but only for a few seconds and then continued rapidly with the story, "A man in a white suit with a white shirt, a white tie and white shoes came into the helo. He smiled at me and lifted the armor plating off of me and motioned for me to swim out. I wanted to thank him," said Rotor, matter of factly, "But he had no sooner arrived than he had gone. The next thing I knew I was on the surface."

Rotor looked at Keith like he was challenging him to question his story. Keith stared, blinking his eyes with his hand over his heart. Definitely categorize this as a fantasy. "The pilots had tried to go after me but the helo sank too fast. We had a raft and it took about thirty minutes for another helo to come and get us. That basically is it, partner. Want another beer?" Rotor turned away and motioned for the hostess. Keith looked at Rotor wondering if his leg was being pulled once again, but was afraid to ask. Then again, from the look on Rotor's face Keith knew that even if he didn't believe this story, Rotor thought it was true. "Tell me again the part about the man in the white suit," Keith's curiosity won over his common sense. "I know it's a hard one to believe," Rotor replied, "but I swear it happened just as I said." Keith sat waiting for the punch line. "By the way Keith…you're only the second person I have told this to; if it gets out I'm going to look pretty silly." Keith had never seen Rotor looking even slightly humbled. It was a nice change of pace. "So who was the other lucky guy?" Rotor didn't even flinch, "My mother." Keith caught this mid-swallow and beer went spitting out on the sand.

"I swear, Keith," said Rotor, "I'll kill you if you tell a soul." Rotor looked like his feelings had been hurt. "Scout's honor," said Keith, "Not a soul." God, who'd believe him? Keith contemplated the story, wondering if it made Rotor more human, or supported a growing suspicion that Rotor was not on the same level as the rest of the human race. And he's all mine, thought Keith, finishing off his beer and reaching for another.

Neither Keith nor Rotor said much after that and neither of them felt like leaving. They spent the night on the beach looking at the stars. Keith's thoughts wandered from home, to the war protesters, to the little boy, to Rotor's story, to his dream, to Cyndi. She probably had the right idea on this whole thing that he was the idiot. Well, he thought as he dozed off, only time will tell.

CHAPTER 15

▼

The sun was high in the sky when Keith felt Rotor tugging at his sleeve, "Come on buddy or we'll miss our flight." Rotor pulled Keith to his feet. It was past 0900 and their flight was due to leave at 0430. Keith quickly followed Rotor out to the highway where they caught a jeepney back to the base. They ran across the bridge into the base and caught the first available cab to Cubi Point. Rotor jerked open his locker, clearing everything out as fast as he could in order to catch their flight. Keith followed suit, packed, and caught a taxi to the terminal. They arrived at the terminal just ten minutes prior to departure of the C-2 aircraft.

The twin engine C-2 had a blunt nose that resembled the face of a bulldog, and looked like a bus with wings. There was only one small window on each side of the fuselage. When Keith had checked in for the flight he noticed that they were loading cargo and personnel through the rear cargo door. Rotor caught up with Keith and they entered the rear door to find about twelve passenger seats all facing aft, with the cargo storage area directly behind the cockpit. Keith grabbed a seat as close to the window as he could get and Rotor grabbed the one beside him.

The crewman gave directions on buckling up, and in the event of an emergency pointed out the one escape hatch on the top of the fuselage and also said that the two small windows could be jettisoned. Ninety percent of the light was shut out as the rear cargo door closed. This darkness gave the sensation of driving a vehicle through a tunnel. The two powerful T-56 turbo prop engines wound up and the aircraft began to taxi toward the runway. The din inside the aircraft made it almost impossible to carry on a conversation. Rotor leaned over and yelled at

Keith, "No wonder they call this thing the Flying Coffin." Keith yelled back, "Yeah, no shit."

The aircraft was soon airborne and all Keith could see out of the tiny window were clouds. There was nothing else to do but settle back to try and catch some sleep. Keith felt he was doing that a lot. It was the old "hurry up and wait" routine.

The C-2 landed on the base at Da Nang about five hours later and all the personnel aboard deplaned. The C-2 immediately loaded new cargo and new personnel and turned to head back to Cubi Point.

Keith and Rotor checked in at the personnel desk and were told they could catch a ride on a Big Mother as soon as it came in. They were told not to wander off as the helo could come at any time or be as late as four or more hours.

Viet Nam. Keith settled in for a wait. The base was about all he was to see on his first visit and it wasn't much. The climate seemed just like the Philippines, hot and humid. The surrounding countryside was hidden from view, but off in the distance rose some small mountains, looking more like foothills, but with nothing rising beyond. The base looked like a slum, with little ramshackle buildings packed closely together in scattered rows. A layer of dust hung over the base making everything look hazy, dreary.

He noticed that all the Vietnamese girls he saw seemed to be pregnant. He couldn't decide if that meant anything or not. He thought about asking Rotor, but knowing Rotor, he would probably claim responsibility. There were the usual frame buildings for offices, barracks, galleys, dispensaries, and armories found on any military installation, but the present picture didn't correlate with what Keith had seen on the six o'clock news. No rice paddies, no hovering helicopters, no back and forth gun fire, no children carrying arms.

The afternoon was peaceful and unless you knew there was a war going on, you wouldn't have suspected anything except for the fortified bunkers, the barbed wire on top of the fences and the six guard towers located at strategic points around the perimeter of the base.

It was around 1700 hours when the dull gray Big Mother landed. Keith and Rotor helped load the mail and assisted the other passengers aboard. It looked like more than a full load to Keith. There were eight passengers and seven sacks of mail all headed for the U.S.S. Kitty Hawk. Keith was just about to hop on board when the numbers behind the tail wheel caught his eye. The numbers "77" stared back at him, black, bold and foreboding. Reluctantly Keith climbed aboard and the Big Mother lifted off as they started out towards the carrier.

Keith could see the Kitty Hawk out of the starboard cargo door. He had purposely sat in back so he would be afforded a good view. It did not look like much at first but as they drew closer he could tell that the ship was a monster. She headed majestically in a northerly course and her escorts followed closely behind, leaving three white wakes in their passing. As the Big Mother came in closer view, the flight deck of the carrier grew to enormous size. She was as long as a football field. F-4 Phantoms, A-7 Corsairs, A-6 Intruders, E-2 Hawkeye's, and different versions of these planes sat on the flight deck along with tractors for moving them and a fire truck in case of disasters. When the helo landed, two men in brown shirts, denoting the status of plane captains, put chocks under the wheels and put tie down chains on the helicopter. The pilot shut the helo down and the passengers deplaned. As Keith stepped on the deck of the aircraft carrier he felt a movement under his feet and he staggered slightly. Rotor, who was right behind him teased, "You'll get your sea legs soon enough. Either that or you're going to be spending a lot of time on your face."

A man in a green shirt, which designated he was one of the maintenance men, told Keith and Rotor that he would be their guide and showed them the berthing compartment where they would spend the night. He led them toward the island that stood in the center of the flight deck on the starboard side of the ship. They stepped through a hatch and Keith bumped his knees on the lower part of the hatch. Rotor kidded him again, "You'll learn to watch out for the knee knockers soon enough, too, buddy."

Everywhere around them men were running here and there in organized confusion. The ship was a moving living city with every soul having a function and a purpose. They went down a steep ladder-like stairway. It was difficult enough just going down yourself, but carrying his bags, Keith found it a real challenge.

They finally made their way to a compartment with racks stacked four deep throughout the room. Space was constricted and men were everywhere. There was a small area with chairs and a sofa where some of the off-duty sailors were watching television. Keith soon learned that the ship had its own television station. Their guide, Wolden, told them where to bunk for the night and gave them directions on how to get to the chow hall. He said there were three chow halls on board where you could eat anytime you wanted. He also said they would probably be leaving for north SAR sometime in the morning.

After Rotor and Keith had feasted on overdone hamburgers and greasy french fries they hit the sack. Tomorrow promised to be another long day.

CHAPTER 16

▼

They were awake by 0600 and had their bags packed when Wolden came to collect them. He took them back up to the flight deck where a Big Mother already had her rotor blades spinning. Keith and Rotor climbed aboard and the Big Mother lifted off, dipped her nose and began forward flight. The helicopter headed toward north SAR.

They flew an uneventful flight and four hours later they landed aboard the U.S.S. Truxton. This was the first time Keith had landed on board such a small ship and he marveled at how the second crewman talked the pilot down on board the ship. The second crewman was leaning out the starboard side cargo door. He held this position until the helo was on deck. The crewman of HC-7 Det 104 also directed the pilot from outside of the helicopter and as soon as the orleos on the main landing gear compressed, the crew put chocks under the wheels and put tie down chains on the Big Mother helicopter.

Keith knew that they had set down but there was still a lot of movement. What he had felt on the carrier was magnified tenfold as the waves pushed this little ship around. Keith got off the helo and was immediately pulled into a bear hug by the crewman he was relieving.

"So glad to see ya pardner. The name is John. Everybody calls me Little John. You can just call me Little cause I'm so short you can't even see me no more." Little John laughed with his mouth so wide open, you could see the fillings in his back molars. He was hysterical. Keith thought someone should slap him.

"Come on over here and let me get you all your gear so that you are ready to take over and I'm ready to go and get the hell back ashore and drink some San Miguels, get me a little brown body and go to heaven for two weeks. Well, what do ya say?" There was no time to say anything as John drug Keith inside the hanger.

Keith was issued a Navy issue .45 caliber hand gun, one M-16 semi-automatic rifle, one survival knife, and one flare gun with reloads. Keith wondered what he would do with three flare guns. And last, but not least, he was instructed on how to load the M-60 into the cargo door. This seemed to be a shortcoming of Rotor's, so Keith paid really close attention.

Keith had brought his wet suit with him, along with snorkels and fins. He had also brought all the rest of his survival gear, which included among other things a compass, a mirror, shark repellant, a fish-hook and string, and emergency rations to eat and drink. Keith and Rotor were briefed and were then ready to assume their duties.

Little John introduced Keith and Rotor to Lt. John R. Rutledge. The pilot was cordial and very interested in Keith's training and background. He was about six feet tall and fairly stocky. Keith noticed that the Lieutenant had a picture of a helo stenciled on his helmet with the word Bossman underneath it. Keith also noticed that the lieutenant appeared to be ignoring Rotor. That should have been the first warning sign to Keith of things to come.

"Petty Officer Klein," Lt. Rutledge said, "I hope that you haven't taken old Rotor there too seriously. He tends to let his guard down a bit. I'm personally depending upon you to see that our flights are carried on in the most professional Naval manner possible. I don't expect any horseplay or gags from you two. We are here to do some serious business and we don't need that type of activity. Do I make myself clear, sailor?" Keith stood at attention, "Yes sir, very clear sir." Rotor sat off on one of the sponsons, which were mounted on the side of the deck. He smirked and winked at Keith. Lt. Rutledge continued, "Very well, we will be fly-ing this afternoon. I hope we will hit it off nicely."

Little John got aboard the H-3 helicopter, along with his partner, waving vig-orously and blowing kisses. Rotor waved in response, then turned his back on the helo and dropped his pants. Keith looked quickly around for the lieutenant who, thankfully, had already gone below. Keith wondered if he'd act like Little John at the end of his stint. At least he was alive. Crazy maybe, but alive. No, he thought, glancing back at Rotor, who was refastening his trousers, more likely he'd be court marshaled and sent home. He shook his head weakly at Rotor, then smiled. What a guy.

The helo lifted off and headed back to the carrier. Well, thought Keith, here we are…this is it. Little John had given him his old rack and locker, and Rotor had been given the one belonging to the other crewman.

After Keith had stowed his gear, he began making his rack and noticed two straps that looked like seat belts attached to the side of the rack. "Hey, Rotor, what are these for?" Rotor did not turn around as he stuffed his flight suit into the storage compartment under his rack, "Well, child, some things you just have to figure out for yourself…a little common sense and all that. Think about it." Rotor chuckled and finished making his own rack, letting Keith puzzle over his new dilemma.

The ship was not nearly as full of hustle and bustle as the carrier had been. It was like comparing a small town to a big city. This ship had only one galley and there was a set time for chow. There was a crew of five hundred forty-three plus fifty-three officers, not counting the Clementine crew. There was just enough room for one helicopter on deck at a time. The hangar was small and could hold only one helo, but the blades and the tail section both had to be folded in. This is where Clementine had been when the Big Mother landed. Keith and Rotor went down to the galley to grab some chow before their afternoon flight. They sat with the Petty Officer First Class O'Malley, Senior NCO, of the HC-7 crew. O'Malley had red bristly hair and a slight paunch. His face turned red when he laughed or, in any other way, over-exerted himself.

O'Malley explained to Keith that there were only five other than the three of them at this table. The eight of them would have to work as a team in order to get the helo out of the barn, get the blades and tail unfolded, and get the bird fired up and ready for lift off in case of a S.A.R. or other emergency. He assured them it could be done in under two minutes as long as the two new guys pulled their weight. Keith had known that the blades and tail rotor could be folded, but had never actually done it. "We're within spitting distance of Hanoi," explained O'Malley. "And so the top brass sometimes like to keep old Clem in the barn. Kind of an ace in the hole so to speak." He went back and filled another glass of bug juice, which was sailor slang for Kool-Aid. O'Malley took a long drink. He then sat down and continued, "As long as the gooks don't know she's there, they won't rush in so fast to get the pilots that are shot down close to North Vietnamese held territory. This definitely gives our pilots an edge but unfortunately it has some drawbacks. Life can get pretty boring out here with Clem locked inside the barn. No practice flights, no test flights, no nothing. And you can only perform just so much maintenance, and then you're just repeating yourself. Can't fix something that ain't broke."

O'Malley also explained that while in this blackout condition, they would push Clem out on deck at night and spread the blades just for practice, and didn't that sound like fun. Keith thought of the tiny flight deck and of the choppy seas and wondered if this wasn't a good exercise for going over the side. "Lucky for us," O'Malley concluded, "We're not in blackout at present, and hopefully it'll stay that way."

After chow, Keith and Rotor went up to the flight deck to meet the rest of the helo crew. O'Malley, of course, was the lead dog of the enlisted men. Then there was ADJ-2 Toman who was the lead mechanic, AT-2 Kimball who was the avionics technician, and AE-2 Smith who was the lead and only electrician. Next was AM-3 Duvall who was in charge of airframes and rotors, and last but not least was ATAN Clark, the plane captain, who was also new on the Det. Keith would be assisting Toman, as required, for mechanical problems. Keith noted that Toman was kind of the silent type but seemed friendly enough. Rotor would be assisting Duvall on airframes. Duvall talked even more than Rotor did, if that were possible, and Keith silently hoped that they'd drive each other nuts.

If something major was to happen on the helo, all the crafts worked together to fix the problem. These eight people along with the two pilots were a team. Keith was shown what he was to do when the helo was pushed out and the blades were to be spread. He was amazed at how well it went the first time it was tried. He knew he was working with professionals, and that gave him a sense of pride as well as a feeling of security, at least for the moment. He wouldn't let them down.

CHAPTER 17

▼

The pilots came back from their staterooms. Lt. Rutledge introduced Keith and Rotor to the co-pilot, Lt.jg Harry Babbot. He was a small wiry man with a toothy grin and a firm handshake. They chatted for a few minutes before the crew started up the helo. Keith and Rotor went to the back of Clementine and checked out their gear.

ATAN Clark gave the pilot directions through hand signals. He held up one finger on his left hand and made a circular motion with his right hand, which meant to start number one engine. With this accomplished, Clark held up two fingers on his left hand and made the same circular motion with his right hand, which meant start number two engine. When both engines were running, Clark pointed to the top of the helo and again started the circular motion with his right hand, which meant the pilot was to engage the main rotor. The big blades began to spin slowly at first and then faster and faster until they were at full speed. The helo sat on deck with the rotor and engines turning. Lt. Rutledge did his final checks before lift off. Keith and Rotor had completed their pre-flight inspections and were waiting. The plane captain gave the signal to remove tie downs and chocks, which was accomplished by the crew, and the liftoff signal was given. Clementine lifted off and started flight.

Keith watched as the ship faded quickly in the rolling waves. He was still amazed at how small it was in comparison to the aircraft carrier. The pilot radioed to Keith to check out his gear, especially the hoist cable, which was their main rescue tool over water. Lt. Rutledge said his call sign aboard Clem was to be "Bossman" to go with his present position. Lt.jg Babbot radioed his call sign aboard was "Humper" to go along with what he did best. Rotor snorted, "Maybe we'll have to have a contest, heh bud?" Keith rolled his eyes. Rotor got on and said he was sticking with his past sign, "Rotor." Keith didn't say anything.

"Well," Bossman radioed back. "What about you, Petty Officer Klein? What is your call sign to be aboard my helicopter?" Rotor hopped in. "We've been calling him, Roller, Sir, but that won't fit with me being called Rotor and all. Could be confusing. Sir, I think that for now since we have not had enough experience with the lad, why don't we just call him number four." This brought forth a series of chuckles from Bossman and Humper. Bossman finally composed himself enough to speak, "Yeah, it will be number four for now."

Keith gave Rotor a dirty look but it did no good. Rotor just ignored him, still chuckling. The pilot ordered number four to mount the M-60 in the port door and load it up. He was looking for something to do a little target practicing on.

The sky was a brilliant blue when they lifted off and visibility was clear to the horizon. Everywhere you looked in every direction there was only sky and ocean. Keith noticed that there were some clouds moving in but did not think much of it.

As they flew, Keith also noticed an occasional Vietnamese fishing boat. The farther away they got from the ship, the more of these fishing boats he saw. Bossman got on the radio again and said that some of these innocent boats were in fact spy boats picking up radio transmissions from the ship. Whenever a U.S. ship or plane would fly by, they would take down their antennas and act like they were out fishing. Bossman also explained that it was almost impossible to catch the suckers as they would immediately head into a group of other boats. They all looked alike.

They soon found themselves alone again and Bossman told Rotor to look in the back of the helo for an empty red can. Rotor reached in back and retrieved the can. "Throw it overboard," ordered Bossman. "Let's see what number four can do with that M-60." Keith opened up on the can after it hit the water and was able to sink it in under a minute, and was even feeling a little proud of himself. Bossman just grunted.

"Not too bad number four, but you could do better, the first few seconds you were off target." Keith glanced over just in time to see Rotor giving Bossman the finger. Humper broke in on the conversation, "With our present fuel state, we should think about heading back." Bossman redirected a course towards the Truxton and started flying at a speed of one hundred knots. They were about five minutes into this speed when it appeared. Humper was the first to speak, "Do you see that shit in front of us?" Bossman sounded more concerned, "Yeah, where the hell did that come from? This doesn't look real good." He increased speed to one hundred twenty knots. The cloud cover had moved in and visibility was decreasing rapidly. The clouds joined together like different army's merging for battle, their forward progression steady and ominous. Within minutes visibility was almost non-existent. Bossman lifted Clem higher hoping to fly over the top of the cloud cover but the muck was too thick, so he dropped altitude in hopes of getting below it. They were low and Keith could clearly see white caps on the water. Visibility improved only slightly. Bossman was flying by radar alone now, which would get them close to the ship. The air outside was like soup, thick, wet, and warm and if it was possible the visibility seemed to be getting even worse. Keith wondered how they would find the ship.

Humper jumped in, "According to my calculations we are about ten minutes out," They dropped altitude again and decreased speed to twenty-five knots. Keith kept his head out the side door looking for a sign of something, anything. All he could see was a thick dense fog. They should have been in the general proximity of the ship by now but they could see nothing. Bossman again radioed the ship. From the transmission they knew they were close but the ship could not hear them to talk them in. Everyone was quiet as they stared into the soup looking for a sign. Seconds turned into minutes. Suddenly Keith thought he saw something. He squinted, peering closely, as a form took shape within the cloud, and let out a sigh. He'd been holding his breath.

"There it is. I see the ship." Keith felt relieved. He had been having visions of ditching the helo at sea when she ran out of fuel. It had not been a pretty sight. "I see her at nine o'clock, Sir." Bossman pulled back on the cyclic and moved it to the left. They dropped altitude some more and this time they both saw it, the dim outline of a ship. They could barely make it out but it was there. "Okay," said Bossman, "You're going to have to talk me down onto that ship, number four. We need to find out what kind of stuff you are made of, anyway."

They moved closer to the ship, but visibility was still poor. Keith directed the pilot down. "Go to port, Sir. Down. Easy as you go." They got closer, and Keith started to see some of the details of the ship. He was concentrating so hard on talking the pilot down, that he did not immediately see the men removing a cover from a machine gun in the back of the ship. Now his eyes opened wide as he realized something wasn't right. He jerked back, yelling, falling on his butt in the helo. "Wave off, wave off!" The pilot immediately applied collective and the helo quickly lifted. "What the hell is going on, number four?" demanded Bossman. "That's not our ship, Sir. There's some fuckheads down there with a gun." Keith was back hanging out the door, trying to get a look at the ship. His breath was coming in short gasps.

"They're uncovering a gun on the aft end. The ship's not even the right color, Sir." Keith's heart pounded heavily in his chest. Scared seemed to be his normal state lately. Bossman radioed Truxton. "Bearcat this is Sea Devil four five. Did we just try to land on your fantail?" The Truxton was quick to reply, "Sea Devil four five, this is Bearcat. That is a negative. I repeat, we did not see you or hear you."

"Bearcat this is Sea Devil four five. We have an unfriendly in the area. Nationality unknown. Approximate size same as Bearcat. Will investigate further." Bossman radioed back to his crew, "We're going in for a closer look, number four, see if you can pick up any markings or any signs. Rotor, keep a sharp eye and see if you can see anything."

"Wonderful," Keith muttered under his breath. Keith pulled out the binoculars and the pilot dropped altitude once again. When they dropped through the cloud cover Keith saw that the aft gun was fully manned and that there was a forward gun that was manned as well. Both guns were pointed at Keith's helo. "Sir, respectfully request that you get us the fuck out of here. Two gun bores are trained on us at the moment." Keith was trying to find some identification that they could use. He tried to distinguish nationality of the crew. Something appeared curious about one of the aft gunners. Rotor responded before he had figured it out. "Tits. Tits on the aft gun. The guy's got tits." Keith studied one of the aft gunners, "Sir, it looks like there's a woman on the aft gun." Bossman keyed his mike, "Are you sure about that?" Keith responded quickly, "Can't be absolutely positive, Sir, but I've never seen a man with that big of a chest. I'd wager a couple days pay on it." Keith focused closer, "Yup, gotta be a woman."

Bossman radioed back to Bearcat. "Suspect origin to be Russian. Repeat. Expect origin to be Russian." The pilot immediately pulled up on the collective and pushed forward on the cyclic. He pulled into a hover a few minutes later, which put them in about a half mile radius of the Russian trawler. As visibility was zero, Keith felt safe at the moment. Bossman radioed the Truxton again requesting instructions.

"Approximately thirty minutes of fuel remaining. Request landing instructions." Truxton responded, "Direct Sea Devil four five to fly circular pattern from present position. Will try to pick you up on radar." They had completed two circles when they got called from the Truxton. "We hear you, Sea Devil four five. Proceed on a westerly course."

They flew west and Keith listened as O'Malley onboard the Truxton directed them left, then right, then left again. They were flying at about ten knots forward airspeed. The pilot was ready to draw back at a second's notice. The thick fog created a claustrophobic room, and nerves hung tense within its boundaries as the crewmen sweated, watched and waited.

The pilots saw the Truxton at about the same time, and Keith felt the nose go down before he heard the radio. Bossman directed Keith to talk him down. Keith leaned out the side of the helo and began the ritual of port, no starboard, too far forward, port again. Keith directed the pilot to line up the tail wheel with the corner of the flight deck.

If the helo landed wrong or the tail wheel jumped over the side he would have yelled "wave off." The plane captain had the same option. If he felt they were not coming in correctly he would have given the signal for wave off. It was not too difficult to land the helo on deck in calm seas, but it was very hard when the ship was lifting out of the water six feet at a time. Fortunately today, the seas were cresting at a mere foot, an elementary landing for an old salt like Bossman.

Keith gave the all clear to Bossman to land and the H-2 sat down hard on the deck. The chocks and tiedowns were immediately put into place. Clementine was shut down and the crew went forward for debriefing.

The skipper of the ship, Commander Ladbury, asked Keith to describe in detail the ship they had seen. They had already gotten its location from the direction the helo had flown and now they had picked the ship up on radar. Keith described the two encounters to the best of his recollection.

"There were no distinguishing marks on the other ship that I can remember, Sir, other than the fact that it was painted red," said Keith. He thought a little more. "Also, it was really in rough shape, Sir. Lots of rust. Nothing else, really."

"No matter, we are already on a course to intercept," replied the Skipper. "The U.S.S. Stanley is coming from the south to assist, as will the U.S.S. Jewett if required. I see no problem in intercepting this Ruskie if that is indeed what he is." The debriefing ended and Keith and Rotor went back to stow their gear. The helo was left on deck in case it would be needed. It was about two hours later when one of the lookouts spotted the trawler. The fog had lifted a little and visibility was improving. The small ship was flying the red banner with the bar and sickle on it. Truxton had one of its two MK141 launchers loaded with a harpoon anti-ship missile lined up on the Russian who in turn had its guns trained on the Truxton.

It took another ten minutes and the U.S.S. Stanley appeared on the other side of the trawler. The Stanley was also ready for action, if it came to that. Nobody wanted an international incident and the trawler finally decided to back down. The Stanley radioed the trawler and invited them to stay between the two ships as they escorted it out of the area. Failure to comply might result in severe retribution. The Russians chose to be escorted out of the area. They also unmanned their guns. Keith could clearly see the women on board the Russian ship now. When they were outside the normal U.S. patrol area, the two warships let their guest proceed on its way. The Stanley and the Truxton assumed normal stations once again.

Clementine was put back in the hanger and Rotor and Keith went below for some chow and then some shuteye. It had been a long and tiring day.

CHAPTER 18

▼

Keith saw the helo flying about one hundred feet above the water. He wondered vaguely why it was a Clementine rather than a Big Mother. He knew somehow he was supposed to be aboard, and when he turned around he was standing inside looking towards the back of the helo. He knew they would be there. The holes. Bullets. Keith didn't need to count, knowing there would be six, but wondering how he knew. He looked to his right and there was another crewman manning an M-60. He was confused, because that was his position. He tried to make out the face but couldn't, as it was hidden by a sun visor. He tried to call on the radio, but no one responded.

He inspected the bullet holes once more. They were from a large caliber rifle, probably an M-1 or something bigger. Looking down, there were two lifeless forms covered by a blanket. A voice screamed out, "Man your guns!" and Keith watched as the second crewman showered the area with his M-60. He knew that the helicopter would take off soon, leaving men on the ground. He should stop the pilot from taking off. But first he had to know for sure. Who was it that lay lifeless on the floor of the helo? Keith reached forward and picked up the corner of the blanket to reveal the face of the first man. The face was grey, the eyes closed and sunken. His hair was matted from being wet like he had just been pulled from the water. Across his forehead someone had written the numbers "seven-six". The corners of the mouth turned up in a smirk, almost like he'd told a joke he didn't expect Keith to get. Keith stopped breathing as he recognized the man and dropped the blanket.

＊   ＊   ＊   ＊

Keith woke up in a cold sweat, his mouth still formed in a scream. Everything around him was quiet, like no one had heard. He looked at his watch and saw that it was 0600 hours. Keith went over to where Rotor was sleeping and stood for a long time watching the slow rise and fall of his chest. Keith thought to himself, what the hell does this mean?

He went back to his rack and laid down. He felt nervous, tense, and found it hard to remain still. He went to the head, splashed water on his cheeks, and stared at a scared, pale face in the mirror. He stayed in the head, pacing back and forth. He had never had anything like that happen to him before. He began to study every detail of the dream. Six bullet holes. What the hell did that stand for? The numbers seven six and seven seven kept reoccurring.

Fuck this shit, Keith thought. It's just a dream, If I keep worrying, I'll drive myself nuts. He looked at his watch again. It was 0715 and he could hear activity in the berthing compartment. He and Rotor didn't have any flights today that he knew of but decided to try to maintain a routine. He went over and woke up Rotor who was really appreciative of this gesture. "You fucking shithead," Rotor responded to Keith's prodding. "We finally get a chance to sleep in and you wake me up. Are you fucking insane, you stupid asshole?"

Keith cowered just a bit from the string of obscenities but decided Rotor needed to get up anyway. Pulling Rotor's blankets off of his rack, Keith just smiled. "Call me number four will you? I think you're the asshole and if you ever stick me with a name like that again I'll personally see to it that you never sleep in another day in your entire fucking life, got it?"

Keith walked away, surprised at himself. Where had that come from? Out of the corner of his eye he saw Rotor look at him in a whole new way. Keith thought he saw…could it be…a little respect? Rotor got out of his rack and came over to Keith. "Let's go get some chow and we'll clean our weapons if the pricks in charge don't have something else in mind for us. By the way, if you ever talk to me that way again, I'll show you another use for a cleaning rod." He smirked as he walked back towards his rack, "What do you know, old Boot Camp's growing up."

Keith was running the cleaning rod through his M-16 when Bossman and Humper appeared. Bossman opened up the greetings. "Good morning number four, try landing on any Ruskie ships lately?" He laughed heartily, nudging Humper who joined in. Keith just smiled his most friendly smile and kept on cleaning his M-16, "No, Sir, I sure haven't, Sir." Bossman smiled inwardly at what was about to come, "That's good, because we took a vote and just to make sure you do not forget the incident we have opted to change your call name on board from number four to…Ruskie. What do you think of that?"

"That will be just fine, Sir, but to tell you the truth," said Keith as he smiled and looked steadily into the eyes of Bossman. "I was just beginning to like number four. It has kind of a charm…a certain ring to it, if you will." Bossman looked at Keith slightly worried. "Son, I think you may have already spent too much time with Rotor. I'm getting more than a little concerned about your sanity, especially if you like to be called number four." He stared back at Keith with a worried expression on his face, then continued, "No, it's Ruskie from now on, got it?"

Keith replied "Yes, Sir, I got it, Ruskie it is, Sir. From now on I'm the Ruskie from the boonies." Keith got up, untied his shoes, and with his shoelaces dangling did the Russian goose step across the flight deck. Rotor and the rest of the crew laughed hysterically. Keith couldn't believe he was doing this. Where in the hell was it coming from? Maybe he was going insane, but it sure felt good. After they had cleaned the weapons, Rotor and Keith went to chow and then decided to take in the afternoon movie. They were showing a James Bond flick, "Gold finger." Keith had not seen it so he thought what the hell.

CHAPTER 19

▼

They were halfway through the movie, when the ships one M.C. came to life. "SAR, SAR, SAR! Helo crew to the helo deck! This is not a drill!" Before the speaker got the word "helo" out for the first time, Keith and Rotor were already out the hatch and running back toward the flight deck. In less than two minutes Clementine 45 was lifting off the flight deck. She received her distances and vectors while en route from the Truxton. "Ruskie," said Bossman, "I want you to mount the M-60 in the port door and Rotor I want you to check out the hoist and cable in the starboard door. The pilot has punched out, we assume, over land but he may have been over water according to the vectors we received. We just don't know the exact coordinates. We will have to do a little search when we get there. Keep a sharp eye out for flares."

Keith had the M-60 mounted and had a round fed into the clip. All he had to do was pull the trigger that would lay out a salvo of lead. "Humper, let's start the search at sea and work our pattern inland," said Bossman. "That's affirmative, Sir." Humper drew a line on the map of the pilot's most likely course. Rotor suddenly yelled out, "Flare in the water at two o'clock." They were about a mile from shore when Bossman yelled. "Ruskie, get your wet suit on. You're going in to get those guys."

Keith did as instructed and was suited up in less than five minutes. Bossman had the helo hovering at about fifteen feet and was off to the side of the pilot and co-pilot in order to avoid spraying them with the rotor wash. Keith jumped out of the helo and swam toward the two downed pilots. One was in a raft and the other was holding on to the side of the raft. Because of the three-foot swells, Keith temporarily lost sight of the pilots, looking frantically around, but as the water lifted him again he caught sight of them directly in front of him. Keith approached the one in the water from behind. When he was about six feet away he yelled. "Are you okay, Sir?" Keith knew through his training that to approach a panicked person from the front was suicidal. He was trying to determine the man's state of mind. The pilot turned his head slightly towards Keith, "Fine, I'm fine." He appeared calm, but concerned for the man in the raft. "We should take care of my co-pilot first. He's unconscious and I think he may have some broken bones."

Keith swam over to the raft. He reached for the wrist of the co-pilot and after several seconds, he finally found a weak pulse. Keith signaled for Rotor to send down the stretcher and watched as Rotor lowered it with the cable. Keith grabbed the stretcher and just as he had been taught he maneuvered the co-pilot into it. Keith fastened the buckles and them motioned Rotor to take him up. Rotor pulled the co-pilot to the helo and then pulled him into the starboard door and sent the cable back down with the horse collar on it. When the cable was back in the water, Keith grabbed the horse collar and put it around the pilot. The round end went around the pilot's back and up under his arms to the hook. Held in this position, even if the pilot passed out he could not fall, as the collar would hold him. Rotor helped the pilot into the helo and sent the cable down for the last time to Keith who immediately crawled into it and was lifted up to the helo.

The rotor wash sprayed a fine mist under the helo so it made sight almost impossible. This was just as well as Keith didn't think there was anything to look at anyway. Keith felt really good about this rescue. Not only had it gone off like a textbook rescue, but he was sure there had to have been some kind of record set in the time it took. He had to have been in the water less than five minutes.

He made it back in the helo and proceeded to get out of his wet suit and back into his flight suit. When he put his helmet back on he heard Bossman on the radio requesting instructions. The carrier was out of range for Clementine, so the carrier instructed them to take the pilots to south SAR where a Big Mother could pick them up later. The co-pilot could receive medical attention onboard the U.S.S. Jewett, which was on south SAR station. Flight time to the Jewett was about forty five minutes. Rotor was giving the co-pilot the benefit of his years of experience. He had made him as comfortable as possible and was assuring him he was going to be okay.

"You die asshole, and it's going on my record, so you'd just best think twice." Keith thought it a blessing that the co-pilot was still unconscious.

The flight deck of the U.S.S. Jewett was clear when they approached and Keith assumed his position by the door in order to talk the pilot down. When

Clem was on deck, the corpsmen were in the helo before it was even tied down. The co-pilot was lifted out and the pilot took the blanket that Keith had given him and proceeded toward sick bay. They refueled Clem aboard the Jewett and then headed back home to the Truxton. It would be another hour back and Keith commenced cleaning up the back of the helo. Rotor was helping him when Boss-man came on the radio.

"Nice work men. Ruskie, I don't know if you knew it or not, but the gooks wanted these guys too. They were still about five minutes away in their boats. If you had made one slip up or if one thing had gone wrong, we could have been in serious trouble. This was a textbook rescue that this crew handled it like real pros." Rotor looked over at Keith while they listened and gave him the thumbs up sign. Bossman continued his speech, "I'm proud of all of you and I'm sure we will get some kind of a commendation for this one, but before our heads get too big we had better get home and put Clem here to bed."

Keith was just starting to let the words sink in. If they were five minutes out, they could have started shooting in less time than that. If he had messed around in the water only four more minutes, they could have been in serious trouble. Bossman landed the helo, disengaged the main rotor, then shut the engines down. The helicopter crew was cheering them as they got out of the helo. O'Malley came over and shook Keith's hand, "Good job you son of a gun. This will put us on the map."

They put Clementine away in the garage, as O'Malley liked to call it, and went down below for chow. Bossman and Humper went to officers' country. After chow and the evening movie, Keith decided to go up on deck to get some air. The ship was now in a blackout condition, which meant that it emitted no light to the outside. When he went out an outside hatch, he had to pass through a series of partitions, which kept any light from going outside. When Keith got through the outside hatch, he was amazed to find that he couldn't see a thing. He held his hand directly in front of his face, but could not make out his fingers. No problem, he thought. I will just wait a few minutes until I get my night vision. He stood outside the hatch for five minutes but still couldn't see a thing. It was like someone had taken all the light out of the world. He felt his way along the handrail until he came to a sponson. He sat down and listened. The only sound that he could hear was the ship sliding through the water. An occasional whitecap hit the side of the ship sending spray into the air. The cool night sea air felt good in Keith's lungs. He thought about the activities of the last two days and decided that Cyndi must be wrong about the war. What he was doing here was good and necessary. He had helped save someone's life today. Everyone out here had a right to feel good about themselves because they were doing a job that needed to be done. And yet what about all those protesters back in the States? They surely couldn't all be brain dead, could they? Well, maybe they could be, a lot of them were on drugs.

Keith decided that there were no easy answers. He shouldn't make any judgments yet. He had taken an oath to serve and to protect against all enemies both foreign and domestic. There was still a lot of time for him to serve, and a lot of things he needed to do. He felt his way back to the hatch along his original route, and went back into the ship. He proceeded to his berthing compartment and found Rotor lying on his rack, curled up with a Louis L'Amour Western, Matagorda. Keith's mouth fell open, "Rotor! You can read?" Rotor turned over and looked at Keith, "Yeah, I can read. The code of the fucking west and all that. Why ain't you never read a book? Don't tell me you're some kind of illiterate bastard or something." Keith squirmed under Rotor's scrutinizing gaze. As usual, his attempt at getting the best of Rotor was backfiring. "I read a lot. I've just never read any westerns." Rotor shot back, "You ain't read a book till you've read a western, Son". Rotor was sounding just a bit like John Wayne. "Here, have one of mine." Rotor pulled out a dog-eared paperback written by Louis L'Amour entitled *Silver Canyon*. Keith sheepishly grabbed the book and went to his rack. He was not very tired so he opened the cover and began to read. Keith read the first page, then put the book down. Keith looked over to see if Rotor was watching him and then tucked the book under his pillow, "Get real," he muttered as he rolled over and went to sleep.

CHAPTER 20

▼

The next day was not what one would call exciting. In fact the next week was just a routine of eating, sleeping, and watching movies. They cleaned their weapons, went through their gear and checked and rechecked Clementine. Everything was ship-shape and they could only do helo maintenance so much before it started feeling like punishment. At the end of this first week Keith went to Rotor, "Hey Pard, I'm about to go nuts here. What can we do for excitement?" Rotor smirked, "What? Did you finish reading your book already?" Keith stared at Rotor with a bored expression. Rotor tried to poke fun at Keith, but to no avail. Finally he gave in, "Okay, okay, I suppose it's about time. We need to introduce you to the fine art of poker playing. I'll see if we can't set up a game in the garage tonight. How about that?"

Keith sounded intrigued, "So, what are the stakes?" Rotor rubbed the stubble on his chin, "Nothing you can't handle, but there ain't no way we're playing for toothpicks." Keith nodded and smiled, "Well, okay, I'll give it a shot." Rotor sighed deeply, "Great. Now go away and leave me alone."

*   *   *   *

That evening after chow Keith and Rotor made their way back to the hangar. It was dark and they had to feel their way along the deck. When they reached the hangar, they went inside to find there were three others already waiting. O'Malley was there shuffling the cards with a shit-eating grin on his face. Kimball and Duvall were also present, seated around a make-shift table. Duvall immediately greeted them in his familiar non-stop chatter. Kimball had a fat little baby face that made him look like a young boy as he listened quietly to the conversation and counted out quarters from his pocket. "Did anybody bring any food?" he asked. O'Malley pulled out a can of Planter's peanuts and threw them at him.

"Come on, fifty cents for the fund. Fork it over." Kimball carefully counted out fifty cents from his cache and pushed it across the table. They had moved one of the cruise boxes out and had thrown a blanket over it. For chairs they used some five-gallon cans and a couple boxes they'd found laying around.

"Ladies," said O'Malley, doing a little fancy shuffling, "What we are playing here tonight is dealer's choice. Bets are as follows. Quarter is the limit and there will be a maximum of three raises. Are there any questions?"

"Nope, sounds good," said Rotor. Rotor nodded towards Keith, "Think this will break you, Grandma?" There were no other comments, so O'Malley started dealing.

"First jack deals." Rotor got the first Jack so he picked up the cards.

"Ante is a quarter for this here game, gents. You want to play, you got to pay." Keith threw in a quarter.

"The name of the game is High Chicago." Rotor dealt everyone two cards face down and one card face up. Keith had played some poker before, but this game was Greek to him. "How exactly does High Chicago go?" he asked sheepishly. Rotor didn't blink.

"High hand and high spade in the hole split the pot. Your bet, Kimby, or you scared of that little old eight?" Kimball checked as he stuffed in another mouthful of peanuts. The bet passed to O'Malley who had an ace of hearts showing. O'Malley bet a quarter.

"Quarter to see your next card gents, what'll it be?" said Rotor. Everyone threw in a quarter and Rotor dealt everyone another card. This time Kimball paired up his eights. He bet another quarter. Keith had a pair of fours, but he had the Queen of Spades in the hole. If the King and Ace should be dealt out he was sure to have at least half of the pot. He had to stay, and he got lucky as the Ace was dealt out the next round and the King was left in the deck. "Yes!" Keith took half of the first pot with O'Malley taking the other half with three Aces.

Kimball dealt next and he played Low Ball followed by O'Malley who played No Peek with deuces wild. When it was Keith's turn he played straight poker, five card draw, nothing wild. Rotor won that hand. They were about two hours into the game, Rotor was dealing again, when the ship's one MC came to life.

"General Quarters, General Quarters! All hands man your battle stations! This is not a drill!" Keith and the rest of the crew scrambled to get rid of the cards and any evidence of their game. Keith looked over at Rotor, "What is our general quarters station anyway?" O'Malley was the one to answer, "Your in it son, just hang tight. We don't do nothin' 'till we hear from Bossman or Humper." The rest of the helo crew stumbled in about a minute later.

"What the hell is going on?" Smith asked. Even though everyone else looked a little ragged after the long day, Smith, as usual, looked like he was ready for a date, every hair perfectly slicked back and not a wrinkle in his clothes. "Don't know," said O'Malley. They waited a few more minutes without receiving word.

"This is really creepy," said Duvall. "Sure wish the pilots would get their asses back here and let us know what the fuck is going on." The crew all stood by Clementine watching for someone to enter through the hatch on the side of the barn. Another minute passed and the outside hanger hatch opened and Humper came in. "Rotor, better get that M-60 mounted. Ruskie, you'd better get the rest of the small arms loaded aboard."

"Small arms already aboard, Sir," said Keith. Humper responded, sounding slightly confused, "Oh! Yeah right." He paused and paced back and forth in front of the helo, then stopped and looked at Keith, "Well, maybe we should unload them, then." Keith and Rotor exchanged glances. A few eyebrows raised among the crew members. O'Malley was the first to respond. "Lieutenant, Sir, what is it that might be going on? Maybe we could help you get a handle on this thing." Humper looked directly at O'Malley, "Has everyone been assigned a life boat station?" O'Malley looked at Humper in disbelief.

"Sir, with all due respect, you'd best be telling us what the fuck is going on here." Humper paced the floor and looked like he was going to have a nervous breakdown, finally he responded, "Actually, I'm not positive, but I heard one of the ship's crew say something about a fleet of Russian ships headed in our direction." O'Malley, who had been in the Navy for close to twenty years; decided he had better take some control here since Humper was a young officer with very little experience, "Has there been any confirmation of this?"

Humper had his hands behind his back and was pacing again, "I have no confirmation. They won't let us on the bridge or into Combat Information Center. Until we get word, we will just have to stay here and remain calm." Humper looked nervously at Clementine, "Rotor, better unload the M-60. Ruskie, better load up the small arms." Rotor shrugged his shoulders and motioned Keith to do as he was ordered. The young junior officer continued, "Bossman is standing by outside of CIC awaiting orders for the crew." Humper shuffled back and forth, "I was instructed to come back to keep everyone from panicking."

"Well, that's a relief, Sir," O'Malley smiled. "I sure feel a hell of a lot better having you here." Humper ran his hand through his hair, knocking off his hat, sweat beaded visibly on his forehead. He reached down, picked up his cover and put it back on his head, then looked over at Clementine, "Rotor," said Humper, "Load up the M-60, and Ruskie, take the small arms out of the helo." Rotor was starting to get a little fed up with the countermanding orders, "Sir, are you absolutely sure this is what you want?"

Humper stopped pacing and glared at Rotor, "Are you questioning my authority, sailor?"

"No Sir, I'd never question your authority, Sir. Getting right on it, Sir. Consider it done, Sir. It's in its mount even as we speak, Sir." Rotor backed away saluting and bowing to the officer's shoes, "On my way, Sir." As soon as Humper turned his back, Rotor flipped him off and went on his way.

The helo crew waited impatiently in the hanger for some word of what was going on. There was a squawk box in the back of the hanger, but they did not want to use it for fear of raising the anger of someone on the bridge. After about a forty-five minute wait, the word came over the ship's one MC again. "Secure from general quarters." About the same time Bossman appeared. "Any word yet, Boss?" asked Humper.

"Well gents," replied Bossman, looking like he had been made privy to a private joke. "It seems we had this unidentified radar contact bearing down upon us. It would not identify itself. It was coming straight toward this here ship, and, well I'll tell you boys, the skipper wasn't sure what the hell it was. The X.O. had his finger on the button ready to blow whatever the hell it was clean to kingdom come when someone finally figured out what the fuck was going on." Bossman paused for effect, smiling at the crew.

"Turns out it was a civilian airliner on a different radio frequency." Chuckles broke out and the crew sighed in relief. Bossman continued, "He couldn't hear us and we couldn't hear him. It was pretty hairy there for awhile. Can you imagine what the press would say if something like this ever got out? The skipper handled her right. I wonder how I would have handled it. If you guys want to go below, you sure can." Bossman looked at the port cargo door on Clementine. "Why the hell did you mount the M-60?" Everyone turned in unison in Humper's direction. Humper gave his final order for the evening, "Rotor, please unload the M-60." Rotor smiled inwardly, then clicked his heels together and saluted, "Yes sir, I am on it for the fifth time tonight." Humper ducked his head and made a speedy exit.

The helo crew headed down to the berthing spaces except for Rotor and Keith who put the M-60 away and put the small arms back in the helo. Completing that, they headed down too.

CHAPTER 21

▼

Mail came about twice a week via the Big Mother helos. Sometimes the helo would stay for awhile but mostly she would land, drop off mail sacks, pick up mail sacks, and be on her way.

By the end of his second week at sea, Keith had grown his sea legs and could walk level on a heaving deck. This came as second nature after awhile and he didn't think much about it. They had not flown Clementine but twice the whole week and each time was for only a half-hour or so just to stay proficient. Bossman tried to convince the skipper that they needed to keep their skills sharp and honed in, but the suggestion didn't meet with a lot of success.

It was Wednesday of the third week at sea when the Big Mother brought the mail over. Keith went up to greet her as she landed. He ran to the aft cargo door and the second crewman flipped up his sun visor, "Woody!" Keith was ecstatic to see his old friend, but there was no time to talk as the Big Mother had to get back to the carrier. Woody reached inside his flight suit, pulled out a letter and gave it to Keith. He yelled into Keith's ear, "Special delivery. Gonna cost you." He laughed and the next thing Keith knew Big Mother was lifting off again. Keith went into the hangar, sat on one of the cruise boxes and pulled out the letter.

Oct. Seven, 1969

Dear Keith,

Every time I smile, my head hurts, and I think of you, and then I smile. It's kind of a vicious circle.

At the time of this writing my uncle is still based at Atsugi but will be moving to a place called Baguio in the Philippines around the 15th of December. And I, being a prisoner of war, will be transferred as well.

Ron has kept me updated on your location and I thought it sort of an interesting coincidence that we may be able to see each other in the Philippines. My uncle has forbidden that I ever be in the presence of another enlisted man, and I see that as reason enough for you to look me up if you should ever be in the general area.

Thanks for visiting me in the hospital. Then again, wasn't it your fault that I was there in the first place?

Hoping this hits you at a good time, and you're not dead or anything. I would hate to think this was a wasted effort. If it's any comfort, if you should be killed in the service of your country, I promise to protest your useless life and senseless death.

Take care,

Cyndi

Keith folded the letter carefully and stuck it in his pocket. Whistling an indistinguishable tune, he walked out of the hanger and to the fantail. As he passed by Rotor, he punched him in the shoulder, "She loves me." Rotor turned on his heel, "What?" Keith continued his trek across the helicopter deck smiling and whistling with Rotor watching him with a strange look on his face. Keith headed down to his berthing compartment, thinking now was as good a time as any to write a letter to his babe. Rotor stood on the flight deck staring at the space his partner had just occupied, "Crazy fucker must have got a letter from his favorite sheep back home." Rotor shook his head, wondering if there was any hope for someone so naive.

CHAPTER 22

▼

On Tuesday of the fourth week on detachment, Keith and Rotor were sitting down for lunch when the call came over the ship's MC, "SAR, SAR, SAR! Helicopter crew report to the helo deck, this is not a drill!"

It took them less than a minute to get to Clementine. By the time two minutes had elapsed, they had pushed Clementine out of the hanger, had spread her main rotor blades and unfolded the tail section. Both engines were running and the rotor blades were engaged. It took another thirty seconds with Bossman on the radio to base, and then liftoff.

Humper kept an eye on the clock, frowning as the minutes ticked by. Bossman instructed Keith to load the M-60 as they might be going inland. Keith did as instructed and commenced loading the rounds from the ammunition box. Bossman got on the radio, "Okay listen up, we will use the same search pattern as last time," said Bossman. "The last contact vectors with the plane was over land, but they could have made it out to sea. We will plot their course and fly toward land from the seaward side of the plot."

After searching for about ten minutes, Rotor spotted what looked like bits and pieces of a plane. "I think we've got her Bossman. There is lots of debris at one o'clock." Bossman took Clementine down for a closer look. The four studied the area intently but could see no flares or any other signs of life. "The plane was an A-2 Tanker, with three aboard." Bossman pulled the H-2 into a hover and looked out the door down at the wreckage. He got on the radio, "Ruskie, put on your wet suit and go down and check out the area. There may be someone down there who could be unconscious or hurt and can't see us."

Keith suited up and jumped out from about fifteen feet. He was careful to jump where there was no debris floating in the water, and swam over to the most concentrated area of debris. He saw bits of twisted aluminum, lots of oil floating on the surface, pieces of hose, some plexiglass from one of the windows, and chunks of rubber, probably pieces of a tire. There were pieces of cloth like that of a parachute, and one complete parachute floating in the water.

Finally, up ahead of him about twenty feet he saw the helmet. He felt exhilarated to have located one of the crew and swam toward him hoping to grab him from the rear. He reached for the top of the helmet, to pull the wearer over on his back. The helmet gave way too easily in his hand, and Keith felt instant surprise. But this turned quickly to horror as the helmet flipped over and inside Keith saw what was left of the wearer's head. The only recognizable part was a small hunk of his forehead and one eye, which stared up at him as Keith screamed and threw the helmet across the water.

The motion pushed Keith down, dunking his head under the water. He gasped as he regained the surface, panic building, as he fought to maintain control, his arms splashing like a drowning victim. He saw the helmet still bobbing in front of him, and felt the bile rising in his throat. He vomited forcefully into the water, and continued throwing up, until he was finally able to signal Rotor to send down the cable. He climbed into the horse collar and allowed Rotor to lift him up to the helo. Rotor pulled him in. Keith was taking in air in quick gasping breaths and couldn't speak. Bossman knew something was wrong but would not leave until he knew what it was. He did not expect to see any survivors from the look of the wreckage.

"God, his head!" Keith moaned between gasps. "Just part of it!" Keith sat on the floor clutching his stomach. Beads of sweat and vomit dripped from his wet suit. Rotor looked ahead to Bossman shaking his head, "No." Bossman looked back at Keith who was still retching but had nothing left to throw up. He slowly turned Clementine and they headed for Truxton. Bossman radioed ahead. "Be advised there were no survivors. Repeat. No survivors."

Forty-five minutes later they landed aboard Truxton. Keith went through the motions of assisting in shutting Clementine down and pushing her back into the garage. He was unusually quiet, but the guys knew better than to push him once they got the sign from Rotor to leave him alone. After all the gear was stowed, Keith headed down toward the sleeping quarters. He sat down in a vacant corner of the berthing compartment and rested his head in his hands. He sat there long after the rest of the crew had come, cleaned up and had gone to chow. As Rotor passed him he stopped briefly and put a hand on his shoulder, "Hang in there guy, it sure as hell won't get any better." Keith smiled weakly, "Gee, that makes me feel better." Rotor was not about to let up, "Good, then get off your ass, and let's get something to eat. The last thing Keith felt like doing right now was eating, "I don't think I could eat just yet," said Keith. Rotor shrugged as if he didn't care, "Good, then I'll eat yours too. Just don't come in later and puke in my plate."

Keith nodded, "You go ahead. I'll be all right. I just need a minute." Rotor stopped suddenly, "Oh, sure, now I get it. You just want to see Rosie Palmer and her five sisters."

Keith looked at him questioningly, until it dawned on him what he was talking about. Rotor went through the motions with his hand, pumping it up and down, "You know...." Keith stood up suddenly, "Get out of here, you asshole." Rotor took off again, heading up the ladder to the next level, "Just wanted to see if you were going to be okay. Later, buddy."

Keith got out of his flight suit and slowly and methodically put away his suit, washed up, and crawled into his rack. He lay staring at the overhead long after Rotor had returned, crawled into bed, and his soft snores filled the room.

✳   ✳   ✳   ✳

Keith sat on the floor of the helicopter, clutching his stomach, his vomit covered the entire surface area. As the helo dipped in the air, he slid towards the door. No, this wasn't really happening, just a strange twist to an old nightmare. He would refuse to play the game this time.

"Man the guns!" He looked towards the mini-gun, but it was already manned as a crewman sprayed a ground cover. The foliage was thick, but he could see two of their own men running towards the door of the helo. They looked familiar. Despite his oath not to get involved, Keith reached out to help them in just as the helicopter went into forward flight. He was knocked off his feet and slid forward. The blanket that covered one of the men slipped to one side. There was no mistaking Rotor's face, blueish grey, his eyes closed, the head wound, a trickle of blood running down his forehead. But the other body remained covered, but Keith already knew who that was. Keith reached to take a second look, but jerked back his hand as if the blanket were hot. No, why torture yourself, get to the cockpit so you can save them, he had to warn the pilots, "Stop! There are men on the ground! Go back!"

The pilot didn't turn around, but sat motionless in his seat, the helo heading out towards sea. Keith grabbed the pilot's helmet to get his attention, knowing the instant that he touched it that he would be sorry. The helmet came away in his hand. Keith closed his eyes, but turned his face toward the helmet, knowing that there would only be a partial head, one eye. He held his breath and opened his eyes. Keith stared at the empty helmet as the unmanned helicopter took a sudden dive and plunged beneath the waves. The last thing he saw were the numbers on the seats, "seven-six and seven-seven."

CHAPTER 23

$$\blacktriangledown$$

The normal tour in the Tonkin Gulf for the ships was thirty days and Truxton was due to head out. Keith had grown to like the sleek nuclear-powered frigate, but the Truxton was scheduled to be relieved by the U.S.S. King. The King was much smaller than the Truxton and didn't have one of O'Malley's garages. Unlike the ships themselves, the helicopter crews stayed out ninety days, so whenever a new ship came on line, the helo crew would pack up all of their equipment and belongings and cross deck to the new ship.

On Thursday morning the King made her appearance and the cross deck began. On the first trip over they loaded Clem up with four cruise boxes, Toman, and Duvall. They landed on the much smaller flight deck of the King, and Toman requested permission for the helo crew to come aboard. Permission was granted and the cruise boxes were unloaded. Toman and Duvall stayed aboard the King, and Clem went back for another load. Five trips were made until all personnel and equipment were across. When Clem had landed for the final time on board the King, Keith inspected the clearance between the rotor blades and the superstructure. The tail wheel was as far back as possible and still there was only about a twenty- inch clearance. This gave the pilot less than a two-foot degree of error when landing. It wasn't much. Bossman shut down Clem, and the skipper of the King came back personally to welcome the helo crew aboard.

Commander Price was what the Navy called a Maverick. He had come up through the ranks and expected excellence from everyone around him. Bossman saluted the commander. Price returned the salute and shook the Bossman's hand.

"Expect we'll be getting along just fine, Lieutenant. I'm sure you won't mind flying a few flights for me and my men. We have a lot to accomplish in only thirty days so I expect we should get settled in here this morning and by this afternoon we should be able to check out the area a bit. Do you have a problem with that, Lieutenant?"

"That will be just fine, Sir," replied Bossman. Commander Price smiled as he turned to walk away, "I don't expect this crew will become bored on my ship as I plan on giving you your freedom to fly at will, but don't mess me up, understood?" The helo crew replied in unison, "Yes Sir."

One of the ship's crew showed the enlisted men where they would bunk. The accommodations were not as good as the Truxton, quarters were close and tight, but the ship was clean. That afternoon they gave the Executive Officer, or the X.O. as he was referred to, a ride aboard Clementine. They flew to the coast careful to avoid the known anti-aircraft batteries of North Vietnam. The X.O. seemed very interested in something ashore. The binoculars never left his eyes, but Keith was sure what held the executive officer's interest would be shared with Commander Price and only Commander Price. Keith knew enough about the Navy by now to know that even though they were all in the same service, each ship or unit commander had his own ideas or agenda on how things should be done. This was okay as long as they carried out their primary directive.

When they got back from the ride, the X.O. suggested to Bossman that it would be good for his crews' morale if they could all have a helo ride. He stated that there were only two hundred and ninety crew members, but he was sure some of the chiefs would not want to go. The X.O. went on to say, "You don't have to do this, but it might be a way to break up some of the monotony. It can really get boring out here." Bossman looked from the X.O. to his crewmen who were exchanging doubtful glances. Bossman nodded, "Well, let's give it a shot and see how it works out."

The ship's operations officer came back later that day with a schedule for the flights. Clem was to haul four of the crew at a time for at least a half hour. Bossman calculated that if they flew for two hours a day, it would take them around seventeen to eighteen days to complete the schedule. The rest of their days could be spent on flying missions for the captain or SAR missions.

There were some concerns about the joy rides from the helo crew, but since it was good to be flying again, no one protested too loudly. It sure beat the boredom of the Truxton. Keith felt relieved too. The busy schedule would keep his mind occupied, and lately he felt it was better if he didn't have too much time to think. The nightmares had become more frequent; the adventures more varied. The only stable feature of his dream was that there were two men down in the helo, two men down on the ground, the numbers seven-six and seven-seven and the helo diving into the ocean. He knew he should talk to someone about it, but the time wasn't right; the crew was just beginning to trust him. He didn't want them to think he was losing it, or worse yet, that he was afraid.

They began the next morning around 0400 hours with their first group of four. Bossman tried to make it as interesting as possible and flew them past some of the Vietnamese fishing boats. Some of the crew swore they saw radar antenna on these fishing boats, but as soon as Clem flew back over them it would disappear.

The ship's crew was very excited about flying and their enthusiasm carried over to the helo crew. The first day they exceeded their schedule by eight people. The ship's cook made box lunches for the helo crew and promised many more if his people could have a second ride. The ship's CIC people promised a tour of CIC if they could have a second ride. Everyone offered something and the helo crew was instantly popular. Someone was always willing to take them somewhere or show them something. True to his word, the cook brought up bug juice and more food than they could ever eat or drink. Time passed quickly on board the King.

Keith noticed that the Skipper kept the ship close to the coast of North Vietnam. They were always within sight of land. Just off the coast, about one mile, was a small island, about a mile long and two hundred yards wide at its widest point. It had steep cliffs and was easily defendable. Keith knew from the flight over with the X.O. that there were gun placements, but no anti aircraft batteries on the island. Subsequent flights also indicated activity on the island, but so far no fire had been drawn from it. After they had shut down for the day Commander Price would stand on the helicopter deck and stare at the island like he had something in mind. One night he happened to mention to Keith that if they were attacked while pursuing normal duties, they would be obligated to return fire in self defense. Keith didn't think much of this until later when he noticed that they kept getting closer and closer to shore with each passing day.

One day as he stood observing the Skipper watching the island, he pulled Rotor aside to express his concerns, "What the hell's going on here, guy?" He pointed to the Skipper obsessed with watching the shore. Rotor shrugged his shoulders, "We're in the middle of a war, buddy. That's what's going on." Keith glared at Rotor, "Being in the middle of a war is one thing, but looks like this guy is trying to start his own war." Rotor rubbed the stubble on his chin, "He's just trying to expedite things a little bit, nothing wrong with that." Keith was adamant, "But this is bullshit. He's purposely trying to draw fire on this ship, just so he can get into the fight. We both know that's not his mission." Rotor looked thoughtfully at the captain, "I see where you're coming from, but do we really know what his mission is? Have you got the inside scoop? Even if you did know, what the fuck are you going to do about it? This is war and when you fight, you fight to win, second place just doesn't get it." These guys know a hell of a lot more about strategy and winning than you and I ever will, so let's let them give the orders and we will stick to what we do best." Keith contemplated Rotor's little speech, "Yeah, guess you're right, still it makes you wonder sometimes, you know, what with all the war protestors and all."

"Okay, Mr. Righteous, you tell me just why we're here, and we'll go explain it to the Skipper. Get things back on track. Quit playing with all these nasty little guns and ships and helos. Make the world right again. Make Keith feel like a safer little boy. Sound good to you?" Keith spun on his heel, "Get fucked." Rotor smiled, "Thank you. I'll work on it."

The flights continued on a daily basis with more and more time being devoted to checking out Vietnamese junks. On day twenty-one aboard the King, a message was received that there was a massive storm building up in the Sea of Japan. Commander Price stared at the Teletype message, "*Storm brewing Sea of Japan. Wind intensity 120 knots. Classify storm as typhoon class, name Typhoon Bruce. Typhoon headed south southwest. Advise all ship captains Tonkin Gulf, storm on present course, will hit within twenty-four hours. Advise all captains to take immediate evasive action to avoid Typhoon Bruce.*"

The commander elected to stay on station as long as possible. Skippers like him were not called mavericks for nothing. He fought and clawed his way up the ranks and was now in charge of his own ship. This did not happen often. Keith decided it might be a good idea to trust the commander, anyway, what choice did he have. The U.S.S. King was the only U.S. war ship on station in the Tonkin Gulf that night. Even the carriers left station to avoid the storm. Commander Price decided it was now or never. He took the U.S.S. King in closer to shore, under the guise that the storm had blown him in. He apparently got too close for the liking of the North Vietnamese as they opened fire from their shore placements.

Commander Price ordered General Quarters to be sounded which immediately placed the ship in a battle-ready condition and all men at battle stations. Keith and Rotor reported to the helicopter deck awaiting further orders. Keith leaned against Clementine, "I just knew it, get through all this shit and end up drowning at sea because our ship will be sunk." Rotor laughed, "Ah come on, Ruskie, this is probably the most fun you're going to see during this war. Except for maybe when we almost landed on a Russian trawler. Now that was kind of fun too, don't you think?" Keith stood up straight and put his hands in his pocket, "Yeah, I can hardly stop laughing." Keith looked nervously around him as the men manning the six-inch guns swiveled their turret. Keith watched as the drama unfolded, "This is fucking nuts." Keith was feeling helpless and suddenly out of control of his life. As the ship turned, he could see the waves starting to break over the bow; and reminded him that there was more than one storm brewing.

Commander Price opened fire on the shore placements with the ship's six-inch guns, and at the same time ordered the following message to be sent to the Commander of the Western Pacific Forces.

"*U.S.S. King under fire. U.S.S. King returning fire. Requesting air strike, following coordinates.*"

About five minutes later, message was received on the King from Commander Westpac.

"*Cease all hostile action. Take immediate evasive action to avoid Typhoon Bruce.*"

Commander Price read the message, rolled it up in a ball and threw it on the floor. He turned to the bridge crew, "Cease fire. Secure from General Quarters. Set course for Subic Bay, Philippine Islands. Get Lt. Rutlidge on the horn. Advise all hands to prepare for riding out heavy seas." The commander sat down heavily in his chair, grabbed his coffee and took a long drink, muttering to himself, "Damn, typhoon." The Petty Officer of the watch handed the Skipper the phone, "Lt. Rutlidge, Sir." Commander Price grabbed the phone and talked to his chief pilot, "Secure that helicopter immediately, we're going to be seeing some pretty rough weather."

CHAPTER 24

▼

O'Malley supervised the tying down of Clementine. She was positioned directly fore and aft along the centerline of the ship. Her blades were folded and tied down. All tie down points were secured to the deck and additional tie downs were added as precautionary measures. Keith felt relief at the change in orders and found new energy in readying the helo for the storm. He counted twenty-eight separate lines leaving Clementine.

The U.S.S. King was fighting twenty-foot swells by the time the ship's weather decks were fully secured. All personnel were restricted from all outside decks. All unnecessary ship activity was also secured as the ship was already doing twenty-degree rolls. The helo crew was the last crew to go below, and they headed down to get into some dry clothes.

Keith and Rotor sat down in a corner of the berthing compartment. "Ruskie, I think we should get out into the barrio this time when we go into the Philippines." Keith shrugged his shoulders, "What's the difference? Besides, we still have another thirty days to go at sea before we are due for rotation."

Rotor smiled knowingly, "I don't think we'll be going anywhere with this helo any more. She's fucked. She's already taken on a lot of salt water and before we get through this thing she'll have drank gallons of it. Clem's gonna be a bucket of shit in a couple of weeks and there ain't crap we can do to stop it." Rotor rubbed the stubble on his chin in a gesture that had become very familiar to Keith.

"No, my guess is that we'll get to the Philippines and we'll be getting a little R&R. I can just feel my little brown baby now, yeah!"

Keith thought this as good a time as any to ask. "Rotor, do you know where Baguio is?" Rotor answered instantly, "Yeah, I know where it is, but why in the hell would you want to know?" Keith shrugged, trying to appear nonchalant, "Just curious." Rotor studied Keith, trying to read his thoughts, "Yeah! My ass you're just curious. What in the fuck could you have going on in Baguio?" Keith got up to walk toward his rack, "If you don't want to tell me where Baguio is, no problem. Don't tell me. I don't have to know where Baguio is. Just thought I'd ask, just curious. So don't tell me. See if I care. Don't bother me a bit. I knew a guy once that it would bother. But it wouldn't bother me. No, Sir. Maybe O'Malley would know. I suppose I can ask him." Rotor shook his head in disbelief, "Screw it, you'll tell me why you want to know where Baguio is when you're ready, I aint going to worry about it. I am going to worry a little about getting through this fucking typhoon in one piece and if that happens, we'll have her made, Ruskie." Keith had thought he'd gotten the better of Rotor for maybe the first time, but then realized he still didn't know where Baguio was.

Rotor's mention of the word "typhoon" brought back the reality of the situation. The ship was doing some serious rolling now. She would roll over to one side and just hang there for about thirty seconds, which seemed more like minutes, and then ever so slowly she would start the return roll, race through the center, and roll back in the other direction. She would roll to around twenty-eight degrees, hang there for another thirty seconds, and then finally come back again.

"Should we try and get some chow before it gets too late?" asked Keith. Rotor was having trouble just standing up, "No, problem, but we ain't going to Baguio to get it. In fact, I'm not even sure we'll make it to the galley."

They started the normal two-minute trip to the galley, crawling up the ladder and entering the passage way. From here they had to maneuver one hundred feet to get to the galley. At first they just hung on to the bulkhead railings and waited for the ship to level, then they would cover as much distance as they could before the ship rolled back again. At this rate, Keith figured they'd get to the galley in time to watch them put the food away. Following Rotor's lead, they tried another approach. They would put one foot on the bulkhead and one foot on the deck then run as far as they could. When the ship rolled the other way, they would shift to the other side, put one foot on the other bulkhead and one foot on the deck and go as far as they could that way.

Fifteen minutes later they finally made it to the galley where soup and sandwiches were being served. Some of the napkin holders and some of the salt and pepper, shakers were sliding across the deck in motion with the ship.

Keith and Rotor hopped from the bulkhead to the first supporting stanchion and on to the next stanchion, and finally grabbed trays in the serving line always holding onto something for support. The cook only filled their soup bowls about a third of the way with good reason. They each grabbed a sandwich and headed for a table when the ship was at center.

Keith looked back at the kitchen just in time to see a baker close the oven door after checking a batch of pies. He watched the baker attempt to flip the latch just as the ship rolled. The baker ducked as the door flew open and the pies flew across the galley. One slid under the table where Rotor and Keith were sitting, and Rotor scooped it up, "Thanks!" he hollered back to the kitchen, then looking at Keith he yelled, "How's that for service, 'eh buddy?"

Keith wrapped his leg around the table leg and held onto his tray with one hand to keep it from sliding off the table. He held his soup with his other hand to keep it from slipping off the tray or from spilling. This left no hand to eat with. He had no spoon nor did he have anything to drink. Well, he thought, they do it in Japan so why not here? He slurped some of his soup directly from the bowl. Rotor followed suit, and after their bowls were empty, Keith combined the trays while Rotor rescued the pie that was wedged between his feet and then went back to get some forks and something to drink.

There were now fifty to sixty cherry and blueberry pies sliding back and forth with the roll of the ship, along with the baker who was trying without much success to retrieve them. This had created a very slippery, slimy walking surface, and had also formed a type of obstacle course.

Rotor had almost made it back to the table, when the baker slid towards him with one pie in hand, was reaching down to pick up another, not knowing that the sailor was standing in his path and gracefully gave Rotor the first taste of the pie directly in his face. Keith watching the drama unfold, started laughing, lost his foothold on the table leg, and soon joined Rotor as they slid across the galley on the river of pie slime. They were joined by several other sailors who finally decided to give up the fight, and they huddled in one corner eating pie with their fingers directly from the tins as they floated by.

This was the opportune moment that Commander Price decided to check on the condition of his crew and stood braced in the forward hatch, looking astonished at the sight before him. Someone yelled, "Attention on deck!"

The sailors immediately attempted to stand at attention without much success. They supported each other, leaning against the stanchions, but lost their footing and slid across the galley ending up in a slime-covered pile of bodies. Without speaking, the Commander shook his head, and retraced his steps. The galley broke out in uproarious laughter.

After wrestling with the rest of his lunch and sliding by a port hole on his way out of the galley, Keith looked out to see what must have been seventy-foot waves coming down on top of the ship. He had to look up to see the tops of the waves. Rotor was right, the helicopter would be absolute shit with all this salt water on it. Keith and Rotor headed back to the berthing compartment using the bulkhead, deck, bulkhead, deck technique.

They attempted to play cards when they got back, but the ship would not cooperate. There was just too much movement to do much of anything except to get seasick; lots of men were starting to do just that. This in turn got more sailors sick as they vomited at the smell of the initial vomit. Keith was surprised that all the motion didn't bother him much; he hoped that meant his stomach was getting tougher. Keith grabbed a swab and cleaned the deck as best as he could under the circumstances. There were lots of sailors who were not faring so well. Keith decided the best thing to do was to hit the sack.

It was around 0200 hours. The ship was moving forward, coming off of a swell and going down into the trough, bringing the back end out of the water, when another wave hit the side of the ship. Keith went flying through the air and found himself in the rack of the fellow who slept directly across from him. The wave must have hit with such force that it sent him sailing across the passageway without even hitting the deck. He did not get hurt as the body of his shipmate broke his flight. The fellow woke with a start, "Just what in the hell do you think you are doing here, fella?" Keith tried to explain, but the other fellow cut him off, "See them damned straps buddy? They are here for a reason." Keith got out of the other fellow's rack and back into his own and carefully strapped himself in. He could hear Rotor chuckling in bed three racks down, "Fuck you, Rotor." Rotor blurted, "Well, that's one way to figure out things for yourself."

The storm started to subside about noon the next day and by 1500 hours sailors were again allowed on deck. O'Malley was the first to get some fresh water onto Clementine. She was all in one piece but needed to be washed badly. The salt water was already beginning to show its effects. Bossman got permission from the Skipper to run a garden hose back to wash her off. This would help but it was not the total answer. It looked like the ship would probably head into Cubi Point to offload the helo. Confirmation came via message traffic the next day.

Rotor began to make plans for the Philippines. Keith was just a little concerned. Some of Rotor's plans made him more nervous than the war itself. He was talking about going out into the barrio. Keith didn't really care where they went; he figured he could get drunk anywhere and that is just what he planned on doing. Cyndi would be in the Philippines soon. He could go with Rotor until she got there and then he would have to find her. Keith wondered where Baguio was in relation to Cubi Point. No matter, he was sure he would find it and he would see if he could get some time off to go there, wherever the hell it was.

CHAPTER 25

▼

The U.S.S. King was still sixty miles from the Philippines when Bossman, Humper, Keith and Rotor lifted off with Clementine. They would fly her in but they would not take a lot of chances with her. The corrosion caused by the salt water bath was spreading rapidly. The four men had brought their baggage along with them as they did not plan on returning to the King. The rest of the crew would offload when the King reached Subic Bay.

Bossman radioed Cubi Tower and received permission to land at HC-7's helo pad. After landing and taxiing to her parking spot, Clementine was shut down. Bossman took this opportunity to line up the crew and thank the men for their performance at sea, "Well, men, I appreciate your efforts. We've had some rough times. We've had some good times..." Keith yawned and Rotor scratched his crotch. Bossman was not concerned, "Ruskie, you really did a good job on that first rescue. I'm sorry you had to experience the second. But I think it's all part of being a crewman. You can fly with me anytime." Bossman offered his hand to Keith, who took it in a firm grasp.

Rotor looked over at Bossman, "Well, seems to me, I was part of this crew too, probably the best part." Bossman stood firm, "I was getting to you. Rotor, I really appreciate you not shooting us down or anything. Thanks for not making our lives as miserable as you did the last time." He reached and shook Rotor's hand as well. Keith muffled a laugh.

"It was tough, but I towed the straight and narrow for you. Wanted to set a good example for Boot Camp, here. Can't promise I'll do the same in the future." Bossman smiled, "Thanks for the warning."

Bossman and Humper secured Rotor and Keith and told them to hit the beach. They were to report in at the duty office by 0700 the next morning.

Not waiting to be told twice, Rotor and Keith made their way to the duty office to get a rack and locker. They caught a ride to the barracks, showered up, and changed into civies. They were in the N.C.O. club drinking beer less than an hour after shutting Clementine down.

Feeling a little guilty about the rest of the crew, Keith decided it would be a good idea to get some beer and ice it down to take to the guys when they pulled in. They got two six-packs of Budweiser and caught a cab to Subic Bay where the ship was to tie up. When the King was tied up and the helo crew was allowed ashore, they had cold beer waiting for them. The two six-packs were gone within minutes and plans were made to further the cause of a drunken night on the town. The HC-7 duty truck was there to pick up the cruise boxes and the rest of the gear. O'Malley asked the driver if he would just offload the boxes in a secure area and the crew would take care of them in the morning.

The crew all headed back to Cubi Point to get ready to hit the beach except for Keith and Rotor who said they would meet them at the Roofadora, a club in Olongapo.

Keith flagged down a taxi and he and Rotor headed for the main gate. Keith had never been to the Roofadora, but Rotor knew the location. They had walked down Magsaysay Drive for about five minutes when Rotor turned to his left down a street. This street forked into two more streets and at the corner of this vee, sat a club with a sign above the door proclaiming it to be the Roofadora.

Rotor went through the front door, with Keith following close behind. The club was air conditioned and cool. Rotor ordered two beers. Keith was surprised to learn they were cold and they did not have to order any ice.

"This is the only place in Olongapo that has cold beer," said Rotor. "…and this is the only club in Olongapo that does not have a lot of hostesses. Also, this is the only club in Olongapo that caters exclusively to HC-7 personnel. The only Philippinos you will see in this club are the owner, his wife and the staff and of course the HC-7 guests."

He pointed to a sign above the door that said, "HC-7 welcome here." Keith inhaled his first beer and ordered another for each of them. They were on their third beer when the others finally showed up. Duvall threw himself into a chair, making sure everyone in the club knew he was present, "Give me a beer. I need one bad." Kimball also sat down, "Do they have any food here?" Toman and Clark just smiled as they sat down across from Smith who was already talking to a hostess.

Keith ordered a round for everyone and the beer began to flow. They stayed at the Roofadora until about 2000 hours, when Rotor started to get restless, "This is getting boring, guys. Let's try someplace else." Duvall was feeling the effects of all the beer he had consumed, "Sounds good. I can get drunk anywhere. Got any ideas?"

"How about someplace with food?" asked Kimball. The sudden chorus of jeers quickly quieted him. Smith reluctantly left his hostess as they staggered out the front door.

From the Roofadora they moved on to the Bright Star Club. It was around 2300 hours when O'Malley's face turned a bright red, and his head fell forward hitting the table with an audible thud. They stuck him in a jeepney that was headed for the front gate. Toman volunteered to go with him in order to keep him from being mugged. The plan was to meet up with Toman at the Sierra Club in twenty minutes.

Toman got back just in time to see Kimball pull an O'Malley. He passed out on the table just as Toman walked in. Toman looked at Kimball, "I got the last live one." Keith was looking at Kimball as well, "Maybe we should have fed him something." Rotor grinned broadly, "talk about stating the obvious!"

Duvall and Clark volunteered to take Kimball back if the rest agreed to wait for them. They all ordered another round as Duvall and Clark drug Kimball out to a jeepney. It took two of them, because Kimball was quite a bit bigger than O'Malley.

Twenty minutes later they were back. For about five minutes, they just sat looking at each other, waiting to see who would be the next to drop. Since everyone else seemed to still be functioning, at least at a rudimentary level, the group headed out bar hopping once again.

They found themselves around the first curve of Magsaysay Drive in the Orbit Club drinking mojo. After about ten minutes, the hostesses seated at their table told them they would have to drink up and go back to base or pay the girls' way and stay overnight. The bar was about ready to close. Keith found himself just building steam, "Buddies, we been through some shit here and there's no way we can quit drinking tonight. I feel the need to party hearty." Rotor, who seemed to be the most sober of the bunch spoke up, "Well, we can always head down the road a piece to Subic City if you're up to it, Ruskie. We can drink there 'til they close up for curfew. If we get lucky, they may stay open all night." Smith was the most enthusiastic, "Yeah, and if they kick us out there, we can always head out to Paradise Beach. Hell, I can find a woman anywhere."

This brought a round of cheers from the group and they headed outside to catch a jeepney. Rotor did the negotiating with the driver and soon they all piled in. Rotor sat in front with Toman in the middle. Smith, Duvall, Clark, and Keith all climbed in the rear. They loaded up with two beers each for the trip.

Keith got quiet for a moment thinking of the last time he had gone out to Subic City and what had happened with the little boy. He thought of the odds of something like that happening again, but brushed it off. They all deserved this little party. After all, they had just spent over sixty days at sea. Keith forced himself to relax. He guzzled his beer and opened another, wondering vaguely how many he had drunk so far this night.

CHAPTER 26

▼

The driver was starting up the last little hill before Subic City when a car pulled up within two feet of the jeepney's rear bumper. The driver of the car started flipping its lights from bright to dim to bright again and laying on the horn. The poor jeepney driver was going as fast as that old jeep could go. Keith looked back at the car but could not see past the headlights, "What an asshole! What's his problem?"

In response to Keith's question, Smith, who was sitting next to him and smoking a cigarette, took the butt and flipped it out the rear of the Jeepney so that it landed on the hood of the car. The car had no markings of any kind to denote that it was part of a military or secret service organization, but it did have three different types of sirens, along with multiple emergency vehicle lights, all of which went on only seconds after the butt struck the hood.

The Mercedes Benz pulled along side of the jeepney and forced it off to the side of the road. Five Philippinos with M-1's got out and quickly surrounded the jeepney. One of the Philippinos held his gun to the Jeepney driver's head and another went on the other side and held his gun to Rotor's head. The other three went to the back of the Jeepney. Two of them reached in and grabbed Smith. They pulled him out of the Jeepney and one hit him in the stomach and the other hit him in the face with the butt of the gun. The three remaining passengers sitting in the back of the Jeepney-Keith, Clark, and Duvall-were told, "Fick a sfot on the ploor and glue your eyeballs to it."

Keith had just enough to drink that he wasn't as afraid as he probably should have been, and watched the beating out of the corner of his eye. He suddenly found himself being dragged from the jeepney, and soon felt a gun butt to his gut and a knee to his forehead.

Suddenly the beatings stopped, and two of the Philippinos walked across to the other side of the road. Keith was for the most part unharmed, but Smith was holding his stomach and was bleeding from a cut over his eye. Blood ran from his left ear down his neck, staining the collar of his shirt. Keith placed an arm around his friend's shoulders as Smith's legs threatened to buckled beneath him. The third Philippino looked directly at the two sailors. "Are you ready to die?" As if it had been a command, the two Philippinos across the road raised their weapons and pointed them directly at Smith and Keith. Keith saw a gun aimed directly at him and could almost feel the bullet entering his gut. Amazingly, he felt no fear, but only wondered if he would be found the next day lying here in the ditch and if Cyndi would ever know how he died.

This was it then; this was where it would all end. He felt some relief knowing he would not drown. The thought almost made him laugh and a hint of a smile turned up the corners of his mouth. He thought he might be close to losing it, yet he stared steadily at his executor. The seconds ticked by. Still they did not shoot. There was no movement in the car. Everyone waited for the next sequence of events. The quiet was unsettling. Keith felt like screaming at them, "Go ahead, get it over with!" but knew better than to open his mouth at this point.

Finally the Philippino who stood at the rear of the jeepney spoke to his two comrades across the road, "Ready...aim......."

Keith held his breath and waited for the bullet to rip through his body. From the angle of the gun, he knew it would hit directly below his heart. He wondered how long it would take to die. He had heard that being gut shot was the worst way to go. Finally after what seemed an eternity the Philippino closest to Keith said, "Did you two pucking Americans learn your lesson?" Keith hadn't realized he'd closed his eyes. He opened them in surprise, suddenly realizing that he'd been given a reprieve. Both Smith and Keith bolted upright and responded in unison, "Yes Sir! You bet!"

The Philippino said, "All right. You turn this pucking jeepney around and you get back to Olongapo. If I ever see any of your pucking paces around again, you will all be dead." Keith quickly helped Smith into the jeepney and crawled in himself. If the situation hadn't been so desperate he may have found some humor in the vernacular problem of the P's and F's.

The driver tried to turn the jeepney around, adrenalin pumping, but in his panic pulled the shifting lever right out of the floor. The Jeepney was now stuck in second gear. This enraged the Philippino from the Mercedes even further. His face turned red and he began shouting, "Out! Out! Everyone get out of this pucking jeepney and fush. Everyone!" Keith didn't know whether to laugh or cry.

All the sailors, except Smith, who was nursing his wounds, got out and began pushing the Jeepney backwards and forwards and backwards again, desperately trying to get the vehicle moving before the Philippinos changed their minds. The group finally managed to get the jeepney turned around, and pushed it down the hill until it started and took off. They all jumped back in and watched out the rear of the jeepney as the Philippinos got into the Mercedes and headed off in the opposite direction. Everyone must have been holding their breath. They all sighed heavily exchanging nervous looks. The driver held up the shifting lever, looking very distraught, "Where am I going to get a reflacement fart por this?" Rotor was the first to laugh, "What a rush! Ruskie, you should have seen your face when they were aiming at your balls. God, I thought I'd cut up then and there." The others joined in the laughter, but only halfheartedly as they continued to glance behind them for signs of the Mercedes.

Keith looked at the cut over Smith's eye, which was puffing up and turning an angry looking purple, "Gee, this looks pretty bad. We should get someone to take a look at it." He looked so serious, Smith started to get concerned, "Do you think it will leave a scar?" As if in answer, Duvall leaned over and poured his beer over the cut, "Nah, not as long as we disinfect it." Keith laughed, "What you need is a woman. You'll be fine. You can have her kiss all your sore parts." Smith relaxed and tried to save a little face, "Hell, those guys hit like old women. If it wasn't for their rifles, I wouldn't even have a scratch." Smith laughed weakly, suddenly feeling braver as they were heading down the road in the opposite direction as the Mercedes.

Keith felt pretty much the same way, but the incident did have the effect of sobering up the group. He thought it was just as well that they were heading back to Olongapo. They had to report to the duty office by 0700 hours and it was past midnight now.

The Jeepney was pulling up its first big hill, and since the driver could not grab a lower gear, the vehicle sputtered and died. The group sat in silence for a minute, looking at each other, wondering what to do. They spotted some headlights coming from the opposite direction and Rotor jumped out and waved the vehicle down. It was a taxi and Rotor came back to life, "Subic City here we come," he yelled.

Keith was about to protest, but suddenly the other guys started to pick up as well. "Women, here I come!" shouted Smith, who was suddenly feeling a lot better. Duvall, who had been unusually quiet all evening suddenly joined in the chorus, "God, I need a drink bad!" Smith nodded in agreement, "Yeah, I could use some pain killers in addition to the women."

Duvall seemed to be getting wound up, "We can't let no Philippinos push us around." Rotor laughed loudly, "Yeah! we'll smash their pucking faces in this time." Keith was the only reserved one, "Right, I didn't see you guys talking so strong just a short while ago." Smith just shook his head as he climbed into the taxi. Clark looked sick, but didn't say a word. Keith knew how Clark felt, but there wasn't a whole lot a person could do except hope to live to see tomorrow.

Keith shrugged his shoulders, threw some pesos at the Jeepney driver and climbed into the cab with everyone else. Rotor instructed the cab driver to approach Subic City very slowly, which the driver did. Everyone looked around for a Mercedes but none was spotted. They all climbed out of the cab, paid the driver, and headed for the nearest club.

Keith headed into the Number Nine Club and asked for a room. Since all the rooms came equipped with little brown women he let himself get pulled to the back. He sat on the bed while the events of the past hour sank in. He began to shake as he thought about how close to death they had come. It was beginning to seem to Keith that Vietnam was safer than the Philippines. It seemed that everyone here still had the old wild-west mentality, but it did make for some exciting times.

He asked the girl who was with him if she would wake him up at five. "No froblem Keet. You be my number one boyfriend?" Keith just smiled as he rolled over thinking he would get some sleep.

As the warm hands roamed slowly over his tense and tired body, the events of the evening slowly moved far away from his thoughts. Keith rolled to his back as the girl, who called herself Precosia, began to run her fingertips lightly up and down his body. Through half closed eyes he watched like a spectator as she expertly brought his sleepy member to attention and seated herself upon him, moving slowly and sensuously to a much needed release. Keith suddenly felt a lot better about the world and its state of affairs. He rolled over, pulling Precosia close, and went to sleep.

CHAPTER 27

▼

At 0500 hours everyone appeared on the street as if by some prearranged signal. The sorry looking group caught a jeepney and headed for Olongapo. Duvall and Toman looked like they'd slept in their clothes, which they probably had. Clark was complaining that someone had stolen his underwear and was walking slightly funny. Smith had somehow gotten some Band-Aids for his cuts and looked pretty much as if he would live, despite the God-awful hangover he kept whining about. Only Rotor and Keith had smiles on their faces, Rotor grunted in the standard HC-7 mating call, "Aauurraaahhh!" Keith, who was feeling pretty proud of himself, responded with a loud, "Ditto."

The group made their way to the base, past the Marine guards, and up to Cubi Point. They changed at the barracks and still had five minutes to spare when they reported for duty at 0700.

O'Malley looked them over with a scowl. He commenced to speak on the evils of drink, but stated that as long as one took care of their leader, their leader might just go easy on them. O'Malley went on to explain, "A new crew is headed out to Det 104 with a new bird. It's our job to fix up the helo we just brought in."

The group was looking like they would all fall over at any minute. O'Malley kept talking but everyone seemed to be having a hard time paying attention. O'Malley finally felt sorry for them, "All right. Listen up. I know you all feel like shit and I know why you feel like shit. And since you all did a pretty fair job at sea this time out, we are going to give you the rest of the day off." Rotor nudged Keith and winked. O'Malley was not done, "You are all to report here Monday morning…bright eyed and bushy tailed." O'Malley put great emphasis on the final words.

Keith gave a sigh of relief. He was going to go directly to the barracks and go straight to sleep. The group caught a ride up to the barracks and Keith was headed toward his rack when Rotor caught up with him, "Come on partner. Get your civvies on. We got us a trip to make."

Keith didn't even bat and eye as he responded, "Go to hell. I'm going to get some sleep and no one is going to talk me out of that." Rotor looked at his friend with a look of amusement in his eye, "Could be we'll be getting very close to Baguio." Rotor pretended not to notice the change in Keith's expression at the mention of Baguio. Rotor was enjoying himself now, "But that's okay. If you're too tired, I won't push you. No problem. Never let it be said that old Rotor forces his friends to do something they don't want to do. If you're tired, I understand. You go on ahead and get some rest, you need the shuteye. Don't let me stand in your way. No sirree. Not me."

Keith froze for a moment, "How close?" Rotor acted as if he didn't have a clue, "How close to what?" Keith spun on his heel, "How close to Baguio, you idiot?" Rotor grinned again. "You just never know, and anyway you can sleep on the bus on the way. It's at least a five-hour ride." Keith sighed, gave up, and started getting dressed.

One hour later Keith and Rotor were at the front gate. They had each packed a small bag to take with them. They also carried their flare guns and flares. Keith didn't need any more convincing that this was just a part of the civilian apparel in the Philippines. The ever-fresh scent of Aroma River assailed their nostrils as they crossed the bridge to Olongapo. They caught a jeepney to the Victory Liner Bus Station, where all the buses were a bright red. Rotor purchased two tickets to Tarlac and Keith and Rotor boarded the bus.

Keith sat down next to the window. Across the aisle from him sat a Philippino woman with her two chickens. Rotor sat down next to Keith, "Time for a nap my friend." Keith smiled back and nodded at the chickens, "I sure hope the poultry don't mind if I snore a little."

The woman pulled her chickens closer, not knowing what the men were talking about, but certain it had something to do with her property. Rotor smiled and slouched down in his seat for a much needed rest. It didn't take long before Keith joined him in sleep. The big bus stopped numerous times on their route but Keith was able to sleep most of the way. They arrived in Tarlac about three hours later. Rotor said they needed to switch buses here. Rotor bought two more tickets to San Carlos. Fifteen minutes later they were on another bus, only this one had many more chickens and even a few pigs. Keith punched Rotor in the ribs as he sat down, "First class accommodations buddy." Rotor smiled slyly, "It gets better as we go."

Keith sat up straight, warning bells ringing, "Just where in the hell are we going anyway?" Rotor turned to his side, trying to get comfortable on the hard seat, "Just a small barrio outside of Tonton." He glanced over his shoulder to see the perplexed expression on Keith's face, "On the coast," he added.

Keith suddenly felt a bit bewildered by the change in surroundings and the lack of American faces, "What is so special about this barrio? There must be thousands of other barrios on this island. Why do we have to go all this way just to get to this barrio?"

Rotor turned back to Keith, smiling patiently as if talking to a small child, "Because, Dickweed, the other barrios are not having their fiesta like this one is. Also, I just happen to know the mayor of this little village, so we will be assured of having a good time." Keith felt somewhat reassured and muttered an audible, "Oh!"

They arrived in San Carlos about two hours later and got off of the Victory Liner. They walked to the end of a street where a jeepney was waiting. Rotor talked to the driver and then motioned for Keith to get inside. Rotor followed him and they sat toward the rear of the jeepney as there were other passengers already seated. The driver waited for a full load before he took off. It was not long before there were thirteen people inside the jeepney and the driver finally left. Keith glanced at Rotor who acted like he did this sort of thing every day. He was talking away in Tagalog to the Philippinos on board the jeepney. Keith knew he was the topic of conversation as everyone looked at him and laughed. He elbowed Rotor, "So, what the hell are you talking about at my expense?" Rotor sat back, crossed his arms and smiled contentedly, "Gee, maybe you should learn the language, then you'd know."

To Keith, the jeepney ride lasted forever. Rotor and Keith were the last two passengers to get off. When the road finally ended, so did their ride, and they got out. Keith looked at Rotor, "Well boss, what now?" Rotor walked down a path a short distance, "We wait here for the tricycle."

Keith looked at him incredulously, "A tricycle?" Rotor didn't respond and Keith knew it would be futile to push for an answer. Unfortunately he knew he'd find out soon enough.

Ten minutes later a small motorcycle with a side car came along and Rotor and Keith got in. The driver apparently knew where they were heading as Rotor did not say a word. This ride lasted for a half-hour and when the tricycle stopped, it was dark. There was nothing to see except some lanterns here and there. Rotor called out something in Tagalog and some folks appeared carrying lanterns and talking up a storm. Keith and Rotor were led to a small hut where they were told they would spend the night. It wasn't the Hilton but it had a floor and a roof. Keith was whipped and after drinking one warm beer, he and Rotor passed out on the floor of the hut.

Keith woke very early to the sound of a rooster crowing. He crawled out of the hut and was immediately surrounded by a dozen kids who were all holding out their hands and talking at the same time, "Hey Joe, give me peso."

Keith did his best to ignore the kids and looked at the sea, just outside the opening of their sleeping quarters. It was calm, with just very light waves lapping at the shore. It was calming and soothing and Keith walked closer and sat down. He soon had a dozen or so new friends who sat beside him, "Peso Joe, give me peso," they held out their hands palm up. Keith smiled at the young boys and soon many of them shrugged their shoulders and left. Keith then studied the village. The tiny hamlet was made up of a series of huts all on stilts, with one cement block building in the center of them. Not all of the huts were the same. Some of them were quite large that resembled houses and some were small with only one or two rooms. All of the buildings except for the center cement one were made of bamboo.

There was a lot of activity farther down on the beach and it looked to Keith as if they were roasting some pigs over hot coals. The pigs were on bamboo poles and were constantly being turned by hand. Rotor got up about this time, yawned, stretched, and looked over at Keith, "You just can't get a better night's sleep than you can get in the barrio." Keith chuckled, "I'm starved." Rotor looked around as he scratched himself, "Yeah, I'm damn hungry himself. Maybe we should head down the road a piece and get some chow, since the Barrio festivities will not start until later today."

They walked to the road where they were dropped off the evening before. A large group of people came out to talk to Rotor like he was their long lost friend. Just as soon as Keith saw Rotor handing over Salem cigarettes to the locals he knew part of the reason for Rotor's popularity. Rotor and Keith left the group shortly after, with Rotor explaining that they would be back before the festivities started.

They walked down the road for a few minutes until another tricycle came along and they caught a ride. They finally came to a small town with a building that looked like a store of some sort. Rotor assumed his fatherly role, "Keith, this here is your Philippino version of your local American convenience store. Nice huh?" Keith looked skeptical. Rotor saw the look of disbelief, "It's a Sari Sari store. They sell everything from a single cigarette to a case of beer. What more could a body want?"

There were two tables in the store and one was occupied by four Philippino men. Keith and Rotor sat down at the other one. Rotor looked like he was at a loss for a second, he fidgeted then finally spoke, "Well, Boot camp, there is someone in this town that I'd like to check out, on this personal matter, you see. Do you think you could stay out of trouble if I left you alone for awhile?" Keith shrugged his shoulders, not wanting to hold Rotor up, "Go for it. I'll be all right. You said they serve beer here, how about food?" Rotor nodded just as the store owner delivered what appeared to be beef stew to the other table. Keith wondered vaguely what Rotor was up to this time, and just hoped that it didn't involve him.

No sooner had Rotor left when one of the Philippinos at the other table turned to speak to Keith, "Hey Joe, you want something to eat?" Keith smiled brightly, "You bet, that's why I'm here. I'm hungry enough to eat a bear." The Philippino laughed, "We don't serve no bear. There no bear in the Philippines, but what we're eating here is good. Do you want some?" Keith smiled, "Sure, I said I was hungry."

This brought more laughs from the Philippinos. The owner of the Sari Sari store brought Keith a bowl of the same menu item the Philippinos were eating. Closer inspection revealed that it must indeed be beef stew. It had carrots, potatoes, and thick gravy. Keith dipped in a spoon full and couldn't believe how good it tasted. It didn't take him long to finish the bowl, "This was really good. How 'bout some more?"

This brought another round of laughter from the Philippinos. Keith could not figure out what was so funny but did not care. He was hungry. The second bowl of stew came out and Keith dove in again. He was about halfway through this bowl when one of the locals came over to the table, "Hey Joe, do you know what you're eating, Joe?" Keith stopped eating for a moment, looked at the contents of his bowl, then replied, "Looks like beef stew to me." Keith kept on eating. The Philippinos laughed again and the one who had elected himself spokesperson venture another comment, "It is not beep stew, Joe. It is stew but not the beep type." Again he laughed.

Keith had visions of snake or monkey dancing in his head, but did not want to let on that it bothered him in the least, so he tried to ignore him. The spokesperson peered closely in Keith's face, "You are eating aso adobo, Joe." Keith did not blink an eye as he wondered to himself, did he say asshole? He didn't have to think about it long as the Philippino enunciated the food slowly, "You eating dog stew, what do you think of that?" Keith kept on eating until he had finished the bowl and wiped his mouth on his napkin like he was eating in a fancy restaurant, "I think that's just fine, and I really could use another bowl, 'cause it's really tasty and I'm really hungry." The spokesperson howled with laughter, "If you eat more, I buy por you, Joe. One time only good deal, just 'cause I like you Joe. You want more beer?"

Keith sat in the little Sari Sari store for about two hours talking and drinking beer with the Philippinos, like they were old friends. Rotor finally showed up, apparently surprised that Keith had survived on his own. He commented on this to Keith as they left to go back to the village.

"Well, you sure seem to have hit it off okay without me. There might just be some hope for you yet." Keith smiled, "Well, you know the code of the West. Stare 'em down, show 'em who's boss, and don't pull the big gun, unless you absolutely need it." Rotor sneered, "Yeah right. Like you had a big gun to show them." Keith shrugged his shoulders, "Okay, so actually we found some common ground in our love for animals." Rotor looked at him strangely but didn't ask any more questions.

"So where'd you go?" asked Keith. Rotor was intent on something as he replied, "Have to keep all the women contented, you know. It's a tough job, but I can handle it." It sounded logical to Keith that Rotor would have a gal tucked away in every barrio, and yet a slight doubt hung there in the thick humidity.

CHAPTER 28

▼

They got back to the barrio about 1000 hours and were invited to the mayor's house for drinks. The mayor, as it turned out, lived in the block house in the middle of town and owned the town's only television, and had the only electric wire running to his house. They were given Philippino rum, which Keith did not particularly care for, but forced it down anyway. It was the closest thing to kerosene Keith had ever tasted. He watched as Rotor dumped his out the window when no one was watching. He suddenly wished he'd been a little more creative and wondered what the concoction was doing to his organs.

They were each offered another drink by the mayor but said they preferred beer. They left the mayor's house just as the festivities outside were getting under way. The celebration started out with a big meal. There were foods that Keith had never seen before including black rice and eggs, about half the size of a chicken egg, which they later told him were dove eggs. There were vegetables in different shades of blacks, purples, and greens—one that looked kind of like black puffed rice. There were many different kinds of noodle dishes, chicken, and mangos. Keith tried many of the dishes he felt he could identify or looked like they wouldn't do him any harm. The main course for the meal was the roast pig, or leechon, as they called it.

After everyone had eaten, they brought out some bamboo poles of equal length and placed a young man on each end of two poles. The men had a pole in each of their hands while they knelt on the ground facing each other, the length of the poles between them. They started to beat the poles together, then against the ground. They formed a sort of rhythm going twice together then twice down. As soon as they had a good beat going, a young girl jumped in between the poles and started to do a dance. It looked as if the poles were sure to catch her legs but she always moved her feet just in time. She jumped out and soon someone else jumped in. Keith found out the name of this dance was Tinikeling.

Despite his earlier fears, Keith found that he was enjoying himself and was glad Rotor had talked him into coming. This was really turning into a good time as Keith continued to pour down the beers. People kept coming and going all the time. There was laughter and frivolity everywhere. The children played games and the teenagers danced while the adults mostly talked or fussed over food and other activities. Around 1600 hours Rotor came up to Keith.

"I'm really sorry buddy, but I am going to have to head out again. I've talked to the mayor and he'll look out for you. I'll be back to get you before tomorrow, but just in case I don't show up, make sure you leave here by 2200 hours tomorrow evening in order to make it to the base by 0700 Monday morning."

Keith listened with a dazed expression on his face, his eyes glazed over. As mellow as he felt right now, Rotor could have told him he was going to attack Hanoi single-handedly and Keith would not have cared. He shrugged and turned his attention back to the dancing girls.

"No problem. Take care of business, buddy." Rotor grabbed Keith on the shoulder, "Thanks, I appreciate this," and he was gone. Keith continued to drink beer with the local constable who spoke fairly good English. The mayor directed a question at Keith. Keith did not even know he had been addressed until everyone got very quiet. The constable looked at Keith, "He wants to know ip you are married?"

Keith laughed, waiting patiently for the music to resume, "No, you can tell him that I'm thankfully not married and not even engaged." The constable translated that to the mayor and everyone laughed. The mayor then asked another question and everyone again waited to hear the answer, "Do you have any girlpriends?" asked the constable.

Keith was beginning to wonder where this was leading to, "Well, maybe one, but she doesn't know it yet." Keith laughed, but the constable didn't seem to see the humor in that. Keith could see he had not made any points, "Okay, I guess to be honest with you I would have to say no, no girlfriends at this time."

The mayor's next question really threw Keith for a loop, "Do you like girls?" asked the constable. When Keith answered he almost sounded angry, "Of course I like girls." Keith looked from one to next of the approximately thirty people surrounding him and hanging on every word that he spoke. He had this foreboding feeling that something was not quite kosher. He watched the mayor's lips move again, dreading the next question, "Have you ever considered marriage?" Even the constable was starting to appear nervous.

Keith considered his answer very carefully, "Well, if the right girl were to come along I might give it some thought," he responded slowly. This again brought a chuckle and everyone went back to the festivities and left Keith alone. Keith felt relieved, thinking this must have been some kind of an initiation process. Maybe they were just trying to get to know him a little better. The constable struck up a conversation about the American bases in the Philippines, which always seemed to be a hot topic amongst the Philippinos, and Keith continued to pour down the San Miguel's.

A short while later the mayor returned and motioned for Keith to come with him. There was a small army with the mayor and as Keith followed behind he noticed that the army was growing. Keith's stomach started to knot. It hadn't been that long since he had stood before a possible firing squad; the situation appeared similar. He looked around for possible avenues of escape, and briefly thought if he ever saw Rotor again, he was going to personally kill him.

The mayor stopped shortly and motioned for Keith to stand beside him. Keith came up beside the mayor, thinking the best action would be to play along with him. Standing in front of the mayor were five young ladies all lined up in a row and all smiling at Keith. The mayor made a gesture towards the young women with his left arm. Keith looked toward the constable for help.

The constable looked as surprised as Keith as he looked over the girls. The mayor spoke again and the constable translated, "He said the choice is yours. Take your fick, but take your time, one does not choose a wipe in haste." Keith's mouth fell open. He looked to the constable for help but all he found was a confused face looking back. The mayor put his arm around Keith's shoulders, "You choose, Joe."

Keith looked around astonished by this sudden change in events. He wondered what his next move should be. "Damn you Rotor," he thought. He started babbling to the mayor that he could not possibly pick a wife this way, but could tell he was not getting through to him as he kept pointing back at the girls and telling Keith he needed to pick one. "Choose, Joe, choose." The crowd was getting impatient. Keith was feeling panicky, and he could not think of a way to get out of his latest predicament. Boiling water. Yes, he'd boil Rotor in a tub of water. No, there had to be a worse death. He needed to give it more thought. The mayor smiled at him impatiently and spoke to the crowd. Keith pulled the constable aside.

"Can you tell these nice people that I can't possibly do this?" Sweat was beading on Keith's forehead; his teeth clenched as he spat out the words slowly but with emphasis as he enunciated his words carefully. The constable looked nervously around at the mayor and grabbed Keith by the arm, "Very insulting not to fick most beautipul woman in village." The constable wore a dejected look since the woman he loved was in that lineup. He looked dejectedly at his mistress standing there in her bright red dress, but he was helpless to do anything.

Keith thought once again that he should buy some time and play along. He walked around the girls as everyone kept an eye on him. Keith felt like he was picking a cut of beef at the meat market and unfortunately none of it was marked Grade A Choice.

The five young girls were of different sizes and shapes, and several had very distinguishing features. They were all smiling broadly at Keith except for one who smiled shyly with her mouth closed. The others had brownish teeth, some missing, some seriously crooked, one had big buck teeth, and one had a silver tooth. When he could get past the teeth, he noticed one was so ugly, words to describe her didn't form in his mind. Two were extremely heavy, the other three looked almost gaunt. The shy one that only smiled had on a bright red dress, and based on that alone, he felt she was the lesser of all evils. Keith had made up his mind and if forced to pick it would be the one in the red dress. "I'm going to kill you Rotor," he muttered again to himself. It was becoming a sort of avenging prayer, and he knew that if he survived this, Rotor would definitely pay.

Keith could tell the mayor was getting impatient. He stood with his arms crossed, defiance showed in his face, "Okay Joe, you pick now!" Keith saw no way out, "I choose this one," Keith choked slightly but managed to finish the sentence. The crowd cheered and Keith and the girl were whisked away by some of the older women in the barrio. Two hags grabbed Keith, and two grabbed the girl in the red dress and escorted them down a path that led away from the village. When they were about a half mile away, the two old women let go of Keith and motioned that he should walk beside the girl. Keith asked the girl her name. He was surprised when she seemed to understand, and thought that perhaps there was a God. "Rosita," she answered. And with that she smiled. It was not a completely toothless smile, but the two front ones were gone. Keith's smile, on the other hand, disappeared, and he thought that maybe he would become an atheist after all.

She explained in a broken English that they were on their courtship period and that was why they were being chaperoned by the old women. Keith desperately needed a beer and wondered how he was ever going to get out of this, get back to Rotor, and murder him.

They were finally escorted back to the village and separated. Keith was taken to the hut where he had spent his previous night. He found himself with constant companions, none of which spoke English. He was isolated in a sea of brown humanity, but at least he was given back his beer, and he asked to talk to the constable.

The constable arrived shortly thereafter, but was suddenly distant as if he no longer had even the slightest interest in Keith. Keith felt the change in temperature becoming slightly colder, but was hard pressed to understand why the constable suddenly appeared to be mad at him. He had thought for a moment back there that they'd almost become friends.

Keith finally realized that the entourage meant to spend the night. At least this meant that this would not be his wedding night. He slept only after many futile attempts to figure a way to slip out the door and run far, far away.

*   *   *   *

The six bullet holes littered the side of the helicopter. Keith could see the blankets with the lifeless forms beneath them. He knew he had been here before but he couldn't quite remember what he was supposed to do. He grabbed the M-16 and shot a clip out through the side door.

He knew one of the forms was Rotor, but that didn't fit, Rotor was firing the M-60 out the other side of the helo. That was all wrong too, because that was his job. He reached over to tap Rotor on the shoulder, but the man would not turn around. It had to be Rotor. But if it was, then who was this guy under the blanket that looked just like Rotor? The pilot's yelling brought him back.

"Gooks on the ground! Ruskie, shoot, damn you, shoot! They're going to fire at us if you don't keep them down!"

Keith opened up on the trees and fired clip after clip from the M-16 into the area. He felt the rifle getting hot, but still he kept firing. He wondered to himself why he was doing this, "Why are we just sitting here?" No one answered. He looked to the front of the helo and both pilots were gone. He looked at the other crewman and he was gone too. The two forms still lay under the blanket. Keith jumped into the pilot's seat, lifted the collective and pushed ahead on the cyclic. The helo lifted and they went out toward the sea.

"Stop! Go back! There are men on the ground!" A voice like his own, shouted from the back of the helo. My God, how could he have forgotton?

They had just crossed over the beach; Keith felt the helo shake uncontrollably. He felt the helo waver, then shudder as she started her downward spiral. The helo hit the water and Keith watched helplessly as the water rushed in. He was pinned behind the armor plating of the pilot's seat. The blanket in the back had rolled off Rotor, and Keith could now see the other man clearly. He turned again, faced forward and saw the numbers seven-six and seven-seven painted over the instruments, just then the helo hit the water and capsized, water rushed in…

∗   ∗   ∗   ∗

Keith knew for sure that he had screamed. He looked around the darkened hut, but was only greeted by silence. This dream was really having an effect on him. What the hell did it mean? He laid back down and ran the dream over in his mind, coming to no conclusions.

The events of the day came back to him and he realized he had more serious problems than the dream at the moment. He wondered how he was going to ever get out of his present situation in good enough shape to do bodily harm to Rotor before he was killed in the helo. At least Keith felt confident that he was not going to drown. Not in the next couple of days anyway.

CHAPTER 29

▼

The sound of the rooster crowing brought Keith out of a restless sleep. He stretched and looked around, saw his guards still sleeping and unfortunately recalled the sorry state of affairs he was in. He stepped outside to relieve himself, and surveyed the area, thinking that the only way he was going to get out of this was to physically run away from it. He started casually walking toward the road glancing over his shoulder as he went.

He was maybe twenty yards from the hut when he saw the first activity. His entourage exited the hut, surrounded him excitedly, and pulled him back inside.

"Shit," muttered Keith. "Just taking a pee…you know, piss. Nothing to get excited about. God, what the hell do you people know about anything?" Keith sat on the floor of the hut. "I'm doomed, dead, screwed, blued, tattooed. Fuck you Rotor. So are you."

His watchdogs sat on the mats staring at Keith. They constantly smiled, babbled, and nudged each other, pointing at Keith, "So what's happening, guys? Any of you assholes want to give me a blowjob? How about just ruining my life?" The group nodded and smiled, not having the vaguest clue what the sailor was talking about. Several minutes later, the mayor stopped by and invited Keith over for breakfast, "Joe, come eat. Yes?"

Keith followed, glancing around him for a possible means to get away. His entourage followed closely behind. They arrived at the mayor's house and the mayor's wife prepared a feast of fried eggs and dry bread. The mayor seemed particularly pleased with the eggs, gesturing towards them and excitedly chattering in Tagalog, "Joe like eggs, yes?"

Keith wanted to tell him what he could do with the eggs, but ate them, and smiled to show his appreciation. Keith's entourage shifted out one by one but there were always at least four there for him to look at. They were a very happy lot, unlike Keith who was quickly becoming a wreck. He wondered if today was the day he would have to bite the big one. A crowd was already gathering outside the mayor's house. If Keith could only talk to the constable, he felt he would be able to straighten this whole mess out.

Keith was brought a cold beer right after breakfast and he drank it, feeling somewhat hung over from yesterday's binge. He drank that one and soon another and another and before long he was at the point where he didn't much care if they made him get married or not. Lunch came with another large feast, but Keith didn't eat much. It was just after lunch that the constable came by, "How you doing, Joe?" He asked somewhat stiffly. Keith smiled, feeling the effects of the beer, "Oh, just wonderful, and you?"

The constable shuffled his foot, kicking at the dusty street, "I'm here to wish you long and haffy marriage." He shifted from one foot to the other, and Keith wondered why the constable seemed uncomfortable. He wasn't the one getting married. Keith decided he had to confide in the constable. He grabbed the constable by the arm and pulled him away from the crowd. "I can't possibly do this," Keith blurted, "I just can't get married." Keith thought for a moment that he was going to cry. He felt awful, and it wasn't just from too many beers.

The constable looked at him in awe, "Why? Very beautipul woman." Keith, ever the diplomat, knew it was now or never, "You just don't understand, in my country you just don't rush into these things. These things take time. I'm too young. I shouldn't have even been here, but this asshole of a friend, you know Rotor, brought me here and took off." Keith knew he was babbling but he was desperate, "You've got to help me here. I thought you were my friend. If I've done something to make you mad or something, it wasn't intentional. You've got to help me. I'll do anything. But I just can't get married. You've got to help me explain this to the mayor so he doesn't kill me."

The constable stared thoughtfully at Keith, as if an idea were forming. He rubbed his chin thoughtfully, "Can you keef secret?" Keith knew that something important was about to be said, "I can do just about anything, just give me a chance." The constable hesitated, took a deep breath, as if he were reluctant to disclose anything to Keith, "Rosita…my woman." He waited for Keith to respond, and suddenly Keith felt a glimmer of hope. The constable had taken a chance, "If this get out, we both be run out of village."

Keith was dumbfounded, "So how can you stand by while they marry her off to another man?" The constable explained slowly as if he were talking to a retarded child, "Por village…means big money to marry American G.I." Keith looked confused, knowing that he wasn't actually rolling in the dough. The constable continued, "You marry Rosita. Navy gives money to Rosita. Rosita gives money to farents. Farents fay mayor for arranging marriage. Everybody haffy except you and Rosita…and me." Keith was starting to feel like his old self again and he was starting to get an idea. Yeah, he thought, this could almost work, at least it will buy me some time, so I can get back and pour boiling oil all over Rotor.

Keith said, "If you back me up, your secret will be safe, but I need your help." The constable nodded slowly in agreement. Keith put his arm around the constable and started telling him his plan as they walked toward the mayor's house.

The mayor was just getting up to come and get Keith. He stepped outside his house and addressed the crowd that was gathering there.

"It is time por wedding. Soon dis American will be known as Keet. No more will we call heem Joe." It was at this point that the constable spoke up, "The American cannot be married today." A hush fell over the crowd and everyone looked from the constable back to Keith. Keith tried to look appropriately saddened by the change in events, but felt at this point, his life was back on track. He was wishing with all he had that he would make it through this so he could choke the shit out of Rotor himself. That son of a bitch was going to die just as sure as he stood here. So involved was Keith with his thoughts of revenge that he almost did not hear the constable speaking to him, "Please exflain again why you cannot be married today." Keith took a deep breath and explained, "The U.S. Navy requires all of its personnel to request and receive permission before they can be married." Keith stopped, waiting for the constable to translate. The constable poked him in the ribs, "Tell them the rest, the imfortant thing about the money."

Keith looked around to see if everyone was listening closely. All eyes stared at the American symbol of money and prosperity, "If I fail to get permission, my wife will not receive any money from the Navy." The constable again translated as Keith continued. This caused a major ruckus as everyone started talking at the same time. The mayor looked visibly upset, called some of his chiefs into his house, and closed the door.

Keith sighed. He felt he may have at least bought some time. The constable and Keith waited for news from the mayor's house. Keith wished he had not drunk quite so much beer. A messenger finally came out and motioned Keith and the constable to come into the mayor's house. When they were inside and seated, the mayor addressed Keith through the constable. He explained that Keith must apply for permission to marry as soon as he got back to the base tomorrow and that as soon as permission was granted, Keith was to report right back to the village to be married. The mayor also added that men from the village would be sent along with Keith to…insure his safe return. Keith felt it only fair to point out to the mayor that it could take up to three months to receive permission. This was translated to the mayor and the mayor's face turned bright red. The mayor responded back through the constable, "In that case, you will refort to Manila every weekend to Rosita until fermission is granted. You will be chaferoned and must be introduced to Rosita's farents, who could not be here for this pestival, but would be most haffy to see their daughter married to such a pine young American Sailor." The constable explained, "Rosita's pather is very resfected government emfloyee. He works at the defartment of labor and makes almost ten pesos a week. Rosita stays in her home barrio most times, but visit her farents on weekends, but not this weekend because of the pestival."

Keith smiled at the mayor and thought to himself, "Yeah, a pine American sailor with money. I wonder what your cut will be. Fucking Rotor, wait till I get my hands on that bastard. He will surely regret the day he was born."

Keith and the constable left the mayor's house and went out to the hut where Keith had spent the night. The constable was not so sure that all their problems were solved, "Ip you try to get out of this marriage, the mayor will see to it that you die a slow and miserable death. This is reason he is sending along men from village." He was wringing his hands, feeling that he had lost Rosita for sure, "They will hurt you ip you do not come back. Navy no helf you. They kill you. They haf way to get on base around guards. You die on base, not haf a chance." This was very reassuring to Keith who stared down at the beach thinking that a death by drowning may not be so bad after all. It was 2100 hours and still no Rotor so Keith got his things together and headed out of the hut. He was greeted by two young men and one older one. They each had a small bag and when Keith stepped out, they immediately grabbed his bag and headed down the path. Keith followed slowly behind, his shoulders crunched over, his feet dragging on the dusty road.

CHAPTER 30

▼

Keith thought to himself that at least he would not have to worry about finding his way back. He also noticed that one of the younger men carried a big bolo knife; he didn't doubt that the man knew how to use it. He tried not to think, but his thoughts involuntarily drifted to Cyndi. He'd had such high hopes of seeing her again, but now everything looked pretty bleak.

Keith did manage to get some sleep on the Victory Liners on the return trip and was not feeling just too awfully bad when he finally came to the front gate. His escorts stayed on the Olongapo side of Shit River and Keith made his way to the HC-7 barracks feeling grateful to be home, and also feeling a false sense of security. So what if he could never leave the base again?

When he got to the barracks he showered and got ready for work, still looking for that bastard, Rotor. He made his way down the hill to the duty office where they were to muster. Keith still did not see Rotor and was beginning to wonder if anything had happened to him. He would have felt cheated had someone or something gotten to him before he had the chance. It was 0658 when Rotor showed up just in time for muster. He did not look any worse for wear, in fact he looked well fed and happy. Good, thought Keith, right after muster I will murder him.

Keith and the crew were all present and accounted for and O'Malley started giving out instructions on what was to be accomplished in the upcoming weeks. Major priority was getting Clementine back into ship-shape condition. O'Malley also explained that there was to be a dress white inspection on the following Friday. All hands were to be present and accounted for. "So," explained O'Malley, "What this means, to all of you elementary school drop-outs who don't understand what I'm trying to say, is that you shit birds better get your uniforms ready."

"Great", thought Keith, "Just fucking great. That's all I need yet is a fucking inspection. When it rains, it pours." Then again, if he made it to inspection, it would mean he had lived another week. As if in answer to a prayer, it started raining—not just a drop or two, but a downpour, the kind that you could only see in the Philippines or in Viet Nam. The rain came down in heavy layers, so dense that Keith could see only about a foot in front of his face. Everyone was soaked within seconds. O'Malley immediately dismissed the crew.

Keith never hesitated as he sprinted over to Rotor and grabbed for his neck. Rotor did a quick duck and Keith ended up face down on the deck. He rose quickly and swung hard and fast with his right fist, slipping on the wet surface, and landing with a thug on his back. Rotor leaned over and looked down at Keith, "Easy there buddy. If I didn't know better, I'd think you were a little teed at me." Keith struggled to get up, "Teed?" asked Keith, his face turning red. "Teed? You fucking asshole! You rotten no good bastard!" Keith got to his feet and pointed his finger in Rotor's face as he advanced on him. The rain eased a little but continued steadily, doing nothing to improve Keith's already foul state of mind. The smirk on Rotor's face only made him more angry.

"You dirty son of a bitch. You damned near got me married off to some toothless wonder and you think I might be a little teed?" Rotor's eyes grew wide, and for a moment Keith thought he was going to laugh. Keith was not about to let up, "I'm not teed. I'm fucking pissed off, you fucking prick! I'll be back tomorrow you said. I'll be back to get you." Keith was almost screaming at this point. He had both hands clenched in fists ready to strike, "But did you show up? No fucking way. What was all that talk out at sea about sticking together and looking out for one another?"

Keith became aware that he was talking rather loudly and that many of the other sailors were looking on amusingly, but he didn't care. He did notice that Rotor was no longer smiling. Good. "Well asshole," said Keith, "Now that you got me married off to one of your local babes, I suppose you will go celebrate and tell your buddies this amusing little story. You're no friend; you're just a fucking asshole." With that Keith turned and stormed off toward the helo unaware that he was soaked to the skin. Rotor turned to O'Malley and smiled, "Little misunderstanding. I'll have it straightened out before lunch." O'Malley just shook his head, trying to stifle a small smile.

Keith did not talk to Rotor the rest of that day. On Tuesday Rotor approached Keith cautiously, carrying a white handkerchief he'd taped to a pencil, "We have to talk eventually, buddy. And if you want the help of a friend, you're going to have to tell me what happened."

Keith still felt that he would like nothing more than to wrap his fingers around Rotor's scrawny little neck and squeeze, "Don't 'Bud' me. If I want the kind of friendly help you'll give, I might as well pray to the devil." He again scowled at Rotor, turned, and walked away. It was hard for Keith to stay mad, however, as he and Rotor had to work so closely.

By Wednesday after work, Rotor again approached Keith. They were in the barracks, and Keith sat on his rack thinking about Friday, and how he was going to get out of his mess. Rotor came over and sat beside him, "I think you should tell me, buddy, maybe I can help."

Keith broke down and told him the whole story. Rotor listened in amazement. When Keith told him the part about the entourage watching him take a pee, Rotor actually laughed and Keith considered once again if he should just bash him in the face and get it over with. Rotor put his arm around Keith's shoulder, "Wow! No wonder you were pissed! I really feel like shit now for leaving you there." He almost seemed sincere for a moment, but Keith was leery. Rotor looked closely at his friend, "I had no idea anything like that would happen…honest. Let me think about this a little. Maybe I can come up with something." Rotor got up and left the barracks. Keith didn't know if he felt any better or not.

Keith had gotten his dress whites into the cleaners and was working on his dress shoes and his cover. He surely did not want to get any demerits or he would probably be in more trouble.

Thursday at noon Keith and Rotor were eating when Rotor jumped up and said, "I've got it!" Keith looked at him and replied, "You've got what?" Rotor chuckled and cocked his head, "I've got a way to get you out of your situation." Keith rolled his eyes back and shook his head, "I'm almost afraid…no I am afraid to ask. I'm sorry, dickweed, but I just can't get too fired up over your ideas anymore." Rotor smiled, "This one will work. You'll see, buddy."

Rotor put his arm around Keith's shoulder in his typical fatherly mode and explained his plan to him. When he had finished, Keith had a look of hope on his face once again. He smiled, thinking that it just might work. Either that or he was being fucked again. By the end of the day Keith had convinced himself that Rotor's plan would work, but only if Rotor came with. It would take the two of them to pull it off.

Later that day Keith and Rotor were sitting in the NCO club drinking a beer. It dawned on Keith that the bastard Rotor had not shown him where Baguio was even after using it to lure him out to bum-fuck Egypt. He was about to bring it up but decided to let it drop. *Just let me out of the mess I'm in now, and I will stay away from this clown and his hair-brained schemes for the rest of my life. I'll find my own way to Baguio.*

Friday after work Keith and Rotor again headed out the main gate, and there across Shit River awaited Keith's three escorts. They caught a jeepney to the Victory Liner Bus Station and were soon on their way to Manila. After about three hours they arrived in Manila, where the three escorts arranged transportation to Rosita's home. The last jeepney finally left them off and they walked for the last two blocks.

Manila was a large city with big city traffic. The only difference that Keith noticed here was that even though everything seemed to move at a faster pace, they still had their horse drawn carts in the city center. There was a great deal of Spanish influence, especially in the architecture on many of the buildings, mostly the churches.

They arrived at what looked like an apartment house. The oldest of the three escorts knocked on one of the doors and was soon admitted. He came out a few minutes later and motioned for Keith and Rotor to come in. When Keith and Rotor entered the house they saw an older man and woman seated on a sofa and Rosita was seated in a chair. The mayor and the constable were present also. The escort went outside and closed the door. Rotor immediately went into his rapping mode and soon had the older man and woman laughing and chattering pleasantly back to Rotor. The mayor finally interrupted, "Keet, you get fermission to marry Rosita?"

Keith promptly replied, "I have put the request in and hope that I have an answer by next week." Keith watched the expression on the constable's face turn from sad to miserable. Keith could not stop now, "I am looking forward to making the plans for the wedding now and maybe we could even get married this weekend." This set the mayor back a little and even the constable was sitting with his mouth open. Rotor put part two of the plan into effect by addressing the parents, "Will your daughter be giving a dowry? This is customary in the United States." Rotor continued, "I need to look out for my friend and his fiancés best interest. Of course there are some problems so they will need to dowry to live on." Keith threw in his follow thru, "Yeah, we will really need this money in order to set up a house in Olongapo." The constable translated all of this and the mayor wanted to know why Keith and Rosita could not use Keith's Navy pay for that purpose. Keith looked at the floor for a while, then, he looked up at Rotor who was also staring at the floor. The room was deathly quiet. Keith spoke softly,

"Well, I kind of got into some trouble not too far back…and my wages are going to be garnished for the next ten years." He watched the expression on the faces of the mayor and the parents as the constable translated. He noticed that the constable was starting to catch on and seemed to be enjoying the exchange now.

"It was either that or go to prison," continued Keith. "I figured I'd be better off just giving up wages. That won't be a problem will it?" Keith finished looking innocently at the mayor. The mayor looked at Rosita's parents, who looked like they'd just eaten spoiled fish. He spoke directly to them, and the constable translated back to Keith, "The mayor says that maybe we should wait a little while on this wedding. There is no hurry. And besides, maybe you would want to invite your pamily to the wedding?"

Keith replied, "I don't think it will be a good idea to wait. We should get married right now. And as far as my pamily, I mean, family, coming to the wedding, we don't have to worry about that. I'm sure they will not be able to make it. My dad won't be able to get out of prison for at least two more years and my mother has her business to run so she won't be able to take off."

Rosita's mother spoke up after the constable had translated and she wanted to know what kind of business Keith's mother was in. Rotor translated the question to Keith and he looked her right straight in the eye, "Why, she's a prostitute, has a nice little place just outside of Vegas."

When the constable translated this, Rosita's mother went hysterical, covering her face with her hands and wailing loudly as she rocked back and forth. Rosita's father started shouting and pointing his index finger, carefully including the mayor, his wife, and Rotor, as centers for his anger. Rosita and the constable exchanged knowing looks, their eyes peaceful. Rotor turned to Keith, his usual cocky self, "Show's over, buddy. This kind gentleman is asking us to get the puck out of his home." Keith and Rotor left quickly, prodded on by both the mayor and the constable.

When they were outside, Rosita's father politely asked Keith to please not come back here anymore. "You stay away, Joe. You stay par away or you be one sorry American."

Keith felt as if he had been given a second life. As much as he hated to admit it, he couldn't have pulled it off without Rotor. Then again, one still had to remember the fact that he wouldn't have had to go through all of this in the first place if it had not been for Rotor. He didn't know if he should hit Rotor or hug him. He smiled broadly. Life was good, at least for the moment.

CHAPTER 31

▼

Keith caught the next Victory Liner back to Olongapo. Rotor had wanted him to stay but Keith felt the need to be away from Rotor for awhile. As soon as Keith returned to Olongapo he caught a Jeepney to Subic City and went to the Number Nine Club to order a beer. Precosia came over immediately and sat down beside him. He hadn't exactly planned on seeing Precosia again, but there he was and there she was, and Baguio was still only a mystery spot on the map. He ordered a drink for the pretty young girl and another beer for himself. Precosia crawled up on his lap and played with the buttons on his shirt. Hell, he didn't even know if he'd ever see Cyndi again. Finally he sighed, paid his twenty pesos and went in back with Precosia.

They were just inside the door and Precosia turned towards Keith with a small seductive smile. She slowly worked her hands inside his shirt unbuttoning as she went. Keith suddenly felt impatient and helped her with the buttons, popping one button loose as he pulled off his shirt. She opened his trousers and pushed them down, letting him know that she was in charge. She gently pushed him onto a chair beside the bed, removed his shoes and socks and then pulled his pants off over his feet. As he sat there waiting for her next move, she simply pulled her dress over her head showing she was naked with the exception of her panties. She pulled Keith to his feet, pressing her body against him. Keith felt himself harden and he tried to direct her towards the bed but she only smiled and took his hand as she pulled him towards the door. He tried to protest, "What the...?" Precosia kept pulling, "Wash, Keet, wash."

They left the room in a state of undress, Precosia in her underwear and Keith with a hastily grabbed towel, which he held in place with one hand. Precosia led him to the back of the club where there was a small room with a hand pump inside, "Keet you pump for me?"

Keith readily complied with her wishes, watching her work up lather as she soaped and washed herself. Precosia had an excellently proportioned body. She must have weighed all of ninety pounds soaking wet. When she had finished she took the handle from Keith while he washed. The water was cold and made his member shrivel temporarily. Keith finished soaping and rinsing, then he and Precosia moved back to the room. The door had no more than closed and he had his hands on her breasts. They fell onto the bed and he moved his hand between her thighs, feeling her wetness. Her legs fell open for him and he positioned himself between them. She helped guide his penis into her, her eyes open and smiling, as she stared intently into his eyes. Precosia giggled and was soon wiggling anxiously to draw Keith deeper. They fell into a steady rhythm, which quickened as they reached orgasm. Keith moaned out his pleasure and, as he erupted inside of her, Precosia locked her legs around him preventing his escape. Keith lay on top of her, breathing heavy. He lay there for a few minutes and rolled off. Precosia immediately got up and began getting dressed, "Where are you going?" asked Keith. Precosia continued to dress, "I want Keet por number one boyfriend," replied Precosia, "but I must also fay my way out of club. I must get another customer to fay unless you stay."

Keith thought about this for a moment, "Well, how much would it cost to stay." Precosia smiled brightly, "Thirty pesos for all day, one time good deal, just for you, Keet." Keith considered. "Yeah, right." Keith was tempted, but felt restless and thought he should move on. He smiled at Precosia, "Next time maybe." Precosia's smile dropped only a little, "You bet, we puck very hard next time."

Keith got dressed, went outside, and caught a Jeepney that was headed in the direction of Olongapo. He had the driver stop at the entrance to White Rock Beach and walked from there to Paradise Beach, which was well hidden from view. This was HC-7's private beach, and Keith felt drawn there. He walked up to the bar and ordered a San Miguel. He took his beer and went down to the beach. He took his shoes and socks off and laid down in the sand, one arm under his head. Thoughts of Cyndi crept in and he wondered once again where Baguio was. Keith knew she was due in the next weekend. Thank God, he was able to get out of his marriage engagement. He smiled thinking back, surprised that he'd ever find that situation humorous. His thoughts were interrupted when he felt sand in his mouth and he looked up to see Duvall grinning down at him, "Hope we're not disturbing any wet dreams or anything." Clark stood next to him with an extra beer, which he was holding out to Keith. Keith grabbed the beer, "Hey, buddies, I'm just laying here enjoying the warmth, the sun, and the sand." Keith felt lazy and contented, "Pull up a piece of the beach and take a load off."

Pretty soon the three of them were all laid back in the sand, drinking beer, and feeling no pain. Duvall lit up a Marlboro, "This is the life, man this place is great, eh buddy?" Clark nodded in agreement, "Hurry up and drink your beers, and let's have another."

Keith and Duvall guzzled their San Miguel's. Duvall raised his hand and waved at the bartender for three more beers, and she brought them down. Keith asked her if they could get something to eat. She later brought down some kind of chicken concoction. They were afraid to ask exactly what was in it, but it didn't taste too bad and they were hungry so they forked it down.

Several beers passed and it finally became dark. The guys became deeply engrossed in a conversation on life, death, women, and work thinking they were experts on all three areas. They had not paid a great deal of notice to the large crowd of Philippinos who had gathered at the bar, but then they hadn't really been interested in what was going on. There was some shouting and name calling, but they continued their conversation, not wanting to get involved.

As the evening dragged on, they felt a little tired, but weren't quite ready to leave, so they finished their beers and waved at the bartender. Apparently she didn't see the three young men vigorously waving their arms, or else she was purposely ignoring them. Keith finally decided he'd walk up to the bar to get a round.

As he walked up the beach, he noticed the large crowd who was now blocking the area around the bar. They were standing in a circle surrounding two men who were at the center shouting back and forth at each other. Keith didn't really pay a whole lot of attention, neither was he in any shape to really analyze the situation, "Excuse me…excuse me," he said politely as he worked his way through them to the bar. When he got to the middle of the circle where the two men were shouting at each other, he again excused himself.

"Three beers, "Keith held up three fingers, just in case she didn't understand. The bartender looked momentarily stunned. Not too bright, thought Keith. She stared at him as he walked between the two arguing men and up to the bar. The whole circle became quiet as they watched Keith pay for the three beers. He turned around, feeling the crowd's eyes upon him and feeling like he was expected to do something. He raised the three beers in the air like a toast, "Long live Philippinos."

Mouths dropped open, some men exchanged glances, others continued to stare. Keith shrugged and walked back the way he had come. When he got back,

Duvall and Clark were on their feet, looking at Keith like he was totally insane. Duvall was the first to speak, "You must really be thirsty." Keith was taking a long drink from his beer and when he finished he wiped his mouth with his arm, "Why?" Keith asked the question as calmly as he felt. Clark took a sip from his beer as well, when he stopped he looked up at Keith, "Didn't you see the guns pointing at you?" Keith stared dumbly at his shipmates, then back up to the group of Philippinos. It was then that he saw the two men in the middle were both armed. They were arguing once again and the gun pointing and the shouting was getting louder. Clark muttered, "Damdest thing I ever saw, when you went up there they both quit arguing, stepped back a little to let you through, and then they both waited till you had your beer before they continued with their own fight. Seems to me like beer has a definite priority around here." Clark was shaking his head, "You must live under some kind of gold lined cloud as close as you have come to being shot on how many occasions." Keith did not want to admit that he had drunk so much he was oblivious to the guns and the argument, "I live a charmed life, so you gents have to remember to stick close to me."

"Right," laughed Duvall, "You might lead a charmed life but the rest of us don't and the bullets that may be intended for you just might end up getting embedded in us, because I do not lead a charmed life."

The three laid back down in the sand drinking their beers. Keith hoped they didn't notice that he suddenly felt a little sick. The color had drained from his face, and his stomach had resumed its normal churning state. He wondered if he was getting an ulcer. At least he couldn't blame this one on Rotor. Not yet, anyway.

When Keith woke up, the sun was shining in his eyes. He kicked sand in Duvall's face as he rose to his feet. He felt like the entire Russian army and all their horses had slept in his mouth. He ordered a beer to clear his taste buds. At first Duvall and Clark laughed at him, but pretty soon they had ordered one also. They finished their beer breakfast and headed down the road, deciding it was time to go back to the base.

As the three sailors passed the Roofadora club, Keith decided he would like another beer. He felt a sudden need to contemplate all the things he'd been through lately. Duvall and Clark chose to keep on course and they parted company. Keith walked into the "Roof" and ordered a beer. He picked a table over in the corner and sat down. The table was partially hidden by a support column, giving Keith the privacy that he felt he needed at the moment.

In a few minutes he heard voices coming from the other side of the support column and he unconsciously listened to the conversation. Keith could not see who was speaking but he heard one fellow say, "I'm sure of it, they blew the whole damn boat up. I'm not kidding. They blew the boat up and they killed everyone on board." The other fellow let out a long breath and asked, "Are you really sure they did that? How can you be positive unless you saw it?" Keith sat up straight in his chair and continued to listen.

The first fellow replied, "The second crewman told me. He made me promise not to tell anyone but, shit, this is really bad, and I don't know what to do. Somebody should report it." The second fellow whistled and said, "Bamboo told you that? But, when? He and Hero are still out on Det one-zero-seven." The first fellow replied, "Well, you know I just came in from Det one-ten. Two nights before I left we had flown the Big Mother over to the USS Chicago and spent the night there. Bamboo was pretty excited when he told me. He said that it had happened only two days before. He said they were on a test flight because they had just changed out a hydraulic pump and while they were flying they drew fire from one of the Vietnamese junks. Hero got excited and automatically returned fire. Hell that damn junk didn't have a chance and it sank quicker than an anchor. The pilots looked back and yelled cease-fire but it was too late. Bamboo said it only took about two minutes and the whole thing was over."

The second fellow was quiet for a minute and finally said, "Well, if the pilots know I'm sure they will report it." The first fellow again responded, "Yeah and I'll bet Hero gets his ass fried on this one, even though they fired first." The second fellow responded, "I'm not so sure, you never know, they did fire first after all and he has a witness to prove it."

The second fellow again let out a deep breath and said, "Yeah, well lets just hope that it goes that way, after all we all know there are three ways of doing things, the right way, the wrong way, and then there is the Navy way. There is no telling where this could go and I know I sure as hell would not want to be involved. Come on, let's get out of here."

Keith listened as the two men slid their chairs back and got up to leave. He did not see their faces and he did not feel like meeting another new shipmate now but the gravity of their voices and their concern they expressed in their story struck home. How would he react under a similar circumstance? He though about how he felt when they almost landed on that Russian trawler. He remembered the adrenaline rush and the pumped up feeling he had. It was almost enjoyable. This story however needed to be put aside. It was definitely none of Keith's concern. He had enough shit going on. He did not need to worry about this crap too. He had just made up his mind when he saw Toman and Smith come in. He motioned them over and ordered a round of beers.

CHAPTER 32

▼

At Monday morning muster, O'Malley informed Keith and Rotor that they were due to re-qualify for swims and that they also needed flight time to maintain their flight status. The decision had been made at higher levels, of course, to kill two birds with one stone. Keith, Rotor, and six other crewmen were to be flown out to sea five miles and would swim back. This would re-qualify them and they would get some flight time in as well. This was all to happen on Tuesday, so Keith and Rotor cooled it Monday evening, staying away from the clubs and resting for the big day.

Keith feared that this was going to be one of those weeks when everything happened. Dress white inspection on Friday, swims on Tuesday, maybe Wednesday and Thursday too, if they did not qualify. What else could possibly happen?

After muster on Tuesday, Keith, Rotor, and the other six crewmen suited up for the swims. The flight instructor informed them that they would jump from a flying helo, much the same as in an actual rescue. The helo would be flying at fifteen feet and at twenty knots. The instructor also explained that he would tap each of them on the shoulder when it was time to go. When the instructor gave them the order, they were to line up, with Rotor going first and Keith somewhere near the end. The instructor continued, saying that there would be check points along the way and someone would be keeping an eye on them in case they got into trouble.

After the instructions were given to everyone, they went outside to the flight line where a Big Mother was already turning up. The crewmen climbed aboard and the helo lifted off. The flight instructor put on one of the helmets in the helo that had a radio and talked to the flight crewman. Keith assumed he was giving him instructions on something or another and did not pay much attention. He did notice that the flight instructor was one of those people that talked with his hands, always gesturing in liberal and jerky movements.

When they were over the ocean, the flight instructor got Rotor up and positioned him in the door. Keith assumed they were close to the jump point. That was really fast, he thought. He had assumed the pilots would fly around a bit first and check the area out.

Rotor stood in the doorway and the flight instructor kept talking to the crewman. It looked like they were arguing about something as the flight instructor started getting pretty wild with his gestures. Keith was amused and watched the scene closely. The instructor got a little too carried away with one of his arms and it hit Rotor on the back. Rotor, assuming it was time to jump, crossed his arms, placing his hands on the opposite shoulders, and jumped out of the helo.

The flight instructor caught the movement out of the corner of his eye and looked to see that Rotor was gone. From the look on the flight instructor's face when he turned around, Keith knew they were not over the jump point. The flight instructor keyed his radio and the helo immediately came into a hover and lowered its altitude. The flight instructor and the crewman both looked out the door now looking for Rotor. He knew from the looks on the faces of the crewman and flight instructor that something had gone wrong and he was sure that Rotor had jumped before he was supposed to. He waited anxiously; it was hard to sit still, not knowing what was going on and wishing he could see for himself. What if? No. More than likely the old coot was fine, just another one of his stupid jokes.

The crewman must have spotted him, for the helo banked to the left and started forward flight. They flew in a circle and the flight instructor got ready to go in the water. The crewman got the stretcher ready and Keith knew now that Rotor was hurt, but how bad? The helo pulled into a hover and the flight instructor jumped out. A few minutes later the crewman hooked the stretcher to the hoist and lowered it out of the helo.

Keith unbuckled himself and went aft to where the crewman was lifting the stretcher. He helped the crewman pull the stretcher in and set it on the helo floor. The crewman then put the horse collar on the hoist and lowered it to the flight instructor. As soon as the flight instructor was in the helo he motioned for Keith to go and sit down. Rotor was unconscious and his legs were strangely twisted. Keith relaxed somewhat noting that Rotor's breathing was regular. It took the helo fifteen minutes to make the return trip. There was an ambulance and crew waiting when they landed.

Rotor was whisked away by the corpsmen and the helo lifted off once again. The swims were to continue, but off schedule, and with one less crewman. Keith had little time to worry about whether Rotor had broken his legs or whether he would be okay.

This time the flight instructor sat quietly on the aft bench and waited until they were over the drop zone before he had anyone stand in the doorway. Keith's turn came. He jumped and felt the water engulf him. He swam easily to the surface and began his long swim toward shore.

After two hours into his swim, Keith felt very tired but was still moving forward. It was at that time that he decided to give up cigarettes. Finally after some deliberation he also agreed to give up drinking beer. The water stretched on endlessly; the waves lapped gently, calmly. Often his thoughts would drift to Rotor and he forgave Rotor. He eventually forgave Rotor for all the rotten things he had done and hoped he would be okay. Finally, the shoreline was getting closer and Keith knew that his swim was almost over. All thoughts of giving up cigarettes and beer were gone—a guy had to have a few vices to keep him sane. Only Rotor remained in his thoughts.

Keith was greeted by most of the other crewmen, who made a point of noting that he was pretty much the last one in. He immediately sought out the flight instructor. "Rotor...how's Rotor?" His voice came out more anxious and concerned than he would have liked. The flight instructor hung his head slightly as if he were still taking responsibility for the accident. "Broke both of his legs." He shuffled his feet as Keith waited for further information. "...but they were clean breaks," he added, hoping that made the situation better. "Has a hairline fracture in one arm...and a couple cracked ribs." His voice got softer as he added to the list, "But other than that he is just fine." The instructor smiled weakly.

Keith asked," Will he be able to fly again?" The flight instructor shrugged his shoulders, "That ornery old cuss wouldn't die if his life depended upon it. He'll fly again."

That evening Keith went to see Rotor in the hospital. Rotor looked miserable lying there all bandaged up. Keith tried to cheer him up, "Guess it's a good thing it happened here. Blossom would probably compound your injuries if she gave you a hug now." Rotor showed just the tiniest hint of a smile. Keith decided it was up to him to keep the conversation going, "So, just how fast were we going when you jumped?"

Rotor replied somewhat unbelievingly, "We were going a one hundred and twenty knots and I jumped from one hundred feet." Keith whistled, "You are lucky to even be alive! Why the hell did you jump when you did? Couldn't you see how high we were? You must have noticed how fast we were going?" Rotor became a little irritated, "I don't want to talk about it now. I just had kind of a bad day, okay? Just about got killed here and you're asking me why I wasn't more careful? Could be I got some signals crossed or something, do you think? Can we just leave it at that?"

Keith recoiled from the defensive stance Rotor was taking; he had never seen this side of Rotor before, "Sure buddy, if that's what you want we'll leave it go, just trying to make conversation, that's all." Rotor's eyes looked dark, his hands refused to lay quietly in his lap as he played with his fingers, then his hair, and continually rubbed his nose, "Why the hell are you here anyway? Can't you tell I'm half dead? Can't you tell I probably need some recuperation time here?" Keith kind of got the feeling that Rotor wanted to be left alone, "Well I guess I'd better go. If you need anything just call." Rotor looked away as if preoccupied, "Yeah, I'll do that."

After leaving, Keith wondered if something more was bothering Rotor than the failed swims. He sure didn't seem to be himself. Keith shrugged and thought maybe if he were in the shape that Rotor was in, he probably wouldn't be himself either.

CHAPTER 33

▼

Keith got back to the barracks and laid down on his rack. The next thing he knew he looked at his watch and it was 0600. He hadn't realized how tired he was. He immediately got up and headed down for muster. After muster he checked his mail and found two letters from home and one from Cyndi. He opened the one from Cyndi first.

Dear Keith:

Got your letter. Hope this still finds you alive.

I will be in Manila, Saturday, November 18. I will be at the front gate of the U.S. Embassy at 8:00 a.m. If you would like to meet me fine, if not— drop dead.

All goes well here. The Uncle is still an asshole and watches me like a hawk. I'm working on organizing a peace rally, but am meeting heavy resistance from everyone - totally military you know. Not much job security in seeking peace.

Until Manila.

Peace and Love,

Cyndi

He could meet her in Manila alright. The front steps of the U.S. Embassy were an excellent spot. He would be there Saturday morning with bells on, but first he had better pass that damn inspection or he might just be screwed.

Friday morning came and Keith was as ready as anyone could be. He had his whites cleaned, pressed, and starched. He paid one of the houseboys to shine his shoes. Keith felt he could use the shoes as a mirror to shave with if he had to. He had purchased a brand new T-shirt and had his tie pressed and rolled. He pinned on his ribbons and put on his kerchief. The last thing he worked on was his cover, which he scrubbed with a toothbrush until it was spotless.

To avoid the possibility of getting dirty, he carried a sheet with him and put it on the seat of the bus. He carried his hat, to avoid rubbing it against something and getting it soiled. The bus stopped on the flight line, and it looked like everyone on the base was present. Keith had no idea there were so many sailors assigned to Cubi Point. He walked out to where the HC-7 personnel were mustering. He took short stiff steps to avoid putting creases in his shoes. As there were a lot of officers milling around he figured he had better put his cover on or he would get in trouble. He lifted his hat and began to form it with both hands.

High above, a sea gull circled the area, passing over the flight line. The feathered fowl surveyed all the clean white sailors below him and was having trouble deciding which one he should shit on. He swooped low, ever searching, until he saw one who was just putting his hat on. The sailor held the cover just perfectly and the bird from hell dove in for the bull's eye.

Keith stared dumbly at the bird droppings that had just fallen into the inside of his hat. If he could have, he would have opened up with his M-60 on all the sea gulls in the world. He felt like crying. All this work. All this time. Just to be foiled by some stupid fucking bird.

He thought of Cyndi's letter. If he didn't pass the inspection, there would be no liberty and no Cyndi. He shook his hat but the substance only slowly oozed to one side, there was no time to let gravity take care of the problem. He looked around for something to wipe it out, his mind racing, but nothing was available. If he didn't stand still, he would soon draw attention to himself. He cringed as he set his cover on top of his head, feeling the bird droppings spread as the hat settled. Keith looked straight ahead, his face emotionless, keeping one eye on the movement of the inspection.

It took forever for the inspecting officer to make his way around. Keith could feel the bird shit spreading down the side of his head. It was hot and he was perspiring, which did not help. He prayed that the hat would hold the goop in and not let it run down onto his ear, or worse, into his eye or something.

Out of the corner of his eye he saw the inspecting officer start down his row. He was moving along at a pretty good pace. Good, thought Keith just ten seconds more and this will be over.

The inspecting officer came up beside him. Then he was in front of him, looked at him quickly, and then he was on the other side of him. Keith thought for a moment he was in the clear; thought the inspecting officer was moving on to the next sailor. He almost grinned. But, then he was back. He got real close to Keith's face and peered closely at his head.

"What's that stuff running down the side of your face, sailor?"

"It's bird shit, Sir," Keith promptly replied.

The inspecting officer studied Keith for a minute then said to his yeoman, "Petty Officer Klein, shitty cover." The yeoman promptly wrote this down and the inspecting officer continued on. Keith swallowed hard; he physically shrunk in his place, as the disappointment set in. Good-bye Cyndi.

It took another twenty minutes for the inspection to finally be over. The inspecting officer walked up to the podium in front of the personnel, "Cubi point personnel dismissed. Report to your squadron commanders." At this point it was the usual tradition to secure all personnel for the day if the inspection went well.

Keith was walking dejectedly back to the bus when he heard someone hail, "Hey Ruskie." Keith turned to see Bossman bearing down on him. Keith, having removed his cover, quickly put it back on and saluted Bossman. Bossman asked why he was walking around with his cover off and Keith reluctantly showed him. Keith explained dejectedly what had happened while Bossman listened. "Damn Ruskie, you got a way of attracting shit, don't you?" He thought for a minute and then chuckled at his own joke and left. Keith muttered under his breath, "Fucking asshole."

The bus got back to HC-7's Duty office and the Commander of Det Cubi was outside. When everyone was again mustered, the Commander announced, "We will secure for the day except for the following personnel who will remain on base today and will be assigned special duty for the weekend. Anderson, Freesia, McKinley, Moos..."

Keith waited for his name to be called, swearing under his breath and wondering how in the hell he would get in touch with Cyndi to tell her he couldn't make it. The Det Commander finished up by saying, "Most of you made an outstanding effort to get ready for the inspection. For those of you who did not...well you're paying the price."

Keith was still listening for his name to be called. Finally the Det Commander said, "HC-7 dismissed." There were hoots and hollers as everyone around him took off. There were a few moans and groans too. Keith continued to stand there wondering what to do. They hadn't called his name. He went over to where Bossman was standing. "A second of your time, Sir?" Bossman turned and looked at Keith, "What can I do for you?" Keith spoke cautiously, "Sir, I told you about the bird shit and all, but they didn't call my name here at muster. I know the inspecting officer took my name down for a shitty hat. What should I do?" Bossman looked at Keith and put his hand on his shoulder in a fatherly fashion, "Son, let's just say the skipper saw you when the bird did his thing on you. He also noted how much work you had put into your uniform prior to the unfortunate incident. Let's just say he had a little disagreement with the inspecting officer and he won." Keith started to smile. Bossman took his hand off Keith's shoulder, "Go on now, get outta here and enjoy your weekend, you earned it."

Keith let out a whoop and headed up to the barracks and showered all of the bird shit off of himself. He proceeded to pack a bag for his trip to Manila. He was on cloud nine. He checked his bag over three times before he was satisfied that he had everything he needed. Keith was at the Victory Liner Station one hour later and purchased a ticket to Manila. He briefly thought of Rotor who had shown him the tricks of travel. He felt a twinge of guilt knowing his friend lay in the hospital. He probably should have gone to see him before he left. Oh well, too late now. Maybe Rotor needed the time alone anyway: he hadn't been too receptive to company the last time.

Keith tried to rest on the way to Manila, but was too excited. He would get to see Cyndi tomorrow morning.

Keith checked into a hotel directly across the street from the U.S. Embassy. As he went into his room he figured there was nothing that could keep him from making his date now. All he had to do was go across the street and there she would be waiting by the front gate of the Embassy.

CHAPTER 34

▼

The next morning Keith got up bright and early and had breakfast in the hotel dining room. He was at the Embassy gates a half-hour early. This street was known as Embassy Row. The embassies of the various countries lined the seaward side of the street.

Keith paced up and down the street waiting impatiently. He looked out into Manila Bay and saw what must have been a hundred ships of various colors and sizes, most of them at anchor but a lot of them were coming and going too. Keith looked at his watch for the tenth time. It was 0800 hours and he was standing at the U.S. Embassy front gate, with no Cyndi in sight. Keith started to panic. He looked up and down the street impatiently, but couldn't see her anywhere. He pulled her letter from his pocket wondering if he had misread it and was at the wrong place. He looked again at his watch; she was ten minutes late.

Keith decided to give her ten more minutes; then he would be history. Could she have stood him up? After all the work he had gone through with the inspection and all the agonizing after the bird from hell had violated him? Shit, he'd ring her neck. It would be just like her. She'd really get a big charge out of that. Keith paced up and down in front of the Embassy, getting angrier by the minute.

Thirty minutes later, Keith stormed across the street, nearly got run over by a cab, which brightened his countenance even further, slammed open the front door of the hotel, and headed for his room.

*   *   *   *

Cyndi maintained her position on the balcony by Keith's room where she had a perfect view of the sailor as he had paced and fumed in front of the embassy for the last forty-five minutes. She smiled to herself, but then got serious. It had seemed like such a cute joke to get Keith a little riled, but now as she got a glimpse of his face as he stomped across the street, she suddenly became concerned for her personal safety. She'd head him off. As the elevator door opened and Keith stepped out in a cloud of fury, Cyndi opened two buttons on the top of her blouse and struck a provocative pose, "New in town, sailor?"

Keith's mouth fell open at the sight of Cyndi standing at the door of his room, and it took him a few moments to get his bearing. He didn't know if he should rip off her head, or drag her bodily into his room to seduce her.

Keith stopped where he was and put his hands on his hips, "Where the hell have you been?" Cyndi smiled innocently, "I've been right here." Keith pulled the letter out of his pocket, opened and flashed it in from of her. "We were supposed to meet across the street."

Cyndi did not move, "Have you ever heard of being spontaneous? Living dangerously?" Keith moved closer to her and Cyndi wasn't sure if he had seen the humor of the joke or not. His eyes blazed, he looked menacing as he approached and Cyndi thought, probably not. Feeling a tinge of fear Cyndi was not so sure of her self. Keith advanced toward her, "So just how dangerously do you want to live?" Suddenly Keith felt like he was back in control of the situation, and Cyndi started taking a few backward steps, until she butted against Keith's door. He was standing directly in front of her now, glaring down at her. As she looked up to defend herself, it put him in direct line with her mouth, and he felt she had probably already said too much today, as he pressed his lips firmly against hers.

When Cyndi didn't protest, Keith moved closer, putting one arm around her waist and the other hand at the back of her neck, pulling her tight into his grasp. Her lips opened slightly, and Keith moved his tongue to touch hers, their mouths opening in a deep and intimate kiss. After a few moments, Cyndi finally pulled away breathless but smiling, "Do you think maybe we should go get some breakfast?" Keith was not about to let the moment slip away, "You want to eat at a time like this?" Keith looked from Cyndi's eyes back to her lips and moved to kiss her again. Cyndi kissed him quickly on the lips and then grabbed his hand pulling him back towards the elevator.

"Got to keep your strength up, you know. It's going to be a long day." She emphasized long, as if she had some hidden meaning, and they both laughed and entered the elevator. Keith and Cyndi entered the restaurant from the lobby of the hotel. They were escorted to a table and approached by a well-starched waiter. Keith considered asking how he got his creases in his pants so exact, but thought better of it. Keith reached into his pocket to pull out a pack of cigarettes and before he got one to his lips the waiter had a flame in front of the cigarette.

"Now this is what I call service," said Keith. Cyndi just smiled, and looked over her menu. Cyndi was hungry and ordered in the typical American fashion. She received large portions of scrambled eggs, hash browns, and sausage with buttered toast and steaming hot coffee. Keith just had coffee since he had already eaten. While Cyndi ate Keith asked, "Did you have anything special in mind for today or should we just take in the local attractions?"

"Make my day, Sailor," Cyndi smiled and Keith returned a lazy smile. Keith contemplated for a minute, "Maybe a museum, a park or two, a little shopping, and then a romantic candle-lit dinner followed by some drinks and dancing. What do you think?" Cyndi looked Keith in the eye, "What happens after the dancing part, Sailor?" Cyndi's eyes laughed at Keith as he returned a surprised look, like he didn't have a clue what she was suggesting. Keith was not about to be taken in by here friendly banter, "We'll play that part by ear, how's that? Maybe a movie?" Now it was Cyndi's turn to be surprised, "A movie?"

Keith asked the waiter to recommend a good park or museum. The waiter thought for only a minute, "You go to de San Augstin Church and Museum. You will have flenty good time there, Joe. Tell taxi driver to take you to intersection op Luna and Calle Real." Keith tipped the waiter and they left the hotel. Keith gave the taxi driver the directions he had received from the waiter and they stepped out in front of the church. Chinese lions carved of granite guarded the entrance to the church courtyard. It seemed odd that they would have non-Christian symbols guarding a Christian temple. The main door was carved of Philippine hardwood and was divided into four separate panels depicting the figures of St. Augustine and his mother, St. Monica.

Keith and Cyndi joined a tour in progress, and as they moved into the adjoining monastery-museum, the curator went into a lengthy rendition of Philippine artifacts and religious art. Keith had the feeling that this was not how he wanted to spend the rest of the hour. He looked over to Cyndi to see how she was reacting to this bit of culture and found her also looking at him for his reaction.

"What do you think, babe? Should we stay here or should we see if we can have some fun?" whispered Keith. Cyndi looked around a bit more, "Let's bust this joint." As the curator gave them looks of disgust, Keith reached for Cyndi's hand and they slowly backed out of the museum and out into the street. Once out on the street and into the bright sunlight, Cyndi looked at Keith, "Okay, so now that we're cultured, what should we do for the rest of the day?" Keith rubbed his chin slowly, "What do you think of the Chinese? We could go to Chinatown and eat Chinese for lunch. Maybe we could even do a little shopping."

Keith looked at Cyndi questioningly. Her approving smile and nod sent Keith scurrying after a taxi. After Cyndi and Keith were in the taxi, Keith requested the driver take them to Chinatown. Cyndi looked up at the driver, "Where is Divisoria?" Cyndi explained to Keith that she had heard this was a shopper's delight, "There is supposed to be like a thousand little stores selling anything from lace to fruit to handy crafts. This should keep us busy and out of trouble for a least a half an hour, but I hear it's a good idea to keep an eye on your wallet." Keith's forehead wrinkled in over exaggerated concern, "So what do I need to worry about the most, you or the pick pockets?" Cyndi laughed, "Both." Keith leaned back against the seat, "If I didn't know better, I'd think you had this planned all along."

"Me?" asked Cyndi innocently. "Didn't I tell you shopping was my middle name. Keith again rubbed his chin in deep thought, "I thought it was peace activist." Keith ducked the incoming blow aimed at his teeth.

Keith and Cyndi spent the next two hours roaming the shops in the area. Cyndi picked up several items she could not possibly go on living without, including an ashtray shaped like a frog with his tongue held out to receive ashes and a scarf done in every gaudy color Keith could imagine. Keith thought of a man dressed in yellow and purple, striped pants with a pink shirt containing green and orange polka dots and some earth tone strips, he shuddered. Cyndi was not unaware of Keith's disdain in her selection of the scarf. She folded it neatly and stuck it in her bag, "It's for an aunt back in the states." Keith was pretty sure that not even an eccentric aunt would be caught dead in an ugly thing like that. He decided it best to keep his opinion to himself. The day still held promises.

They ate a beef-like meat on a stick, which tasted like barbecued steak. They later heard that the Americans called it monkey meat, which took some of the pleasure away from the memory. As Keith licked his fingers, an idea came to him, "Are there any more priceless treasures you need to buy or should we hit the beach?" Keith asked cynically. Cyndi was still picking away at her snack, "I suppose I should probably save a few things for someone else." Keith couldn't resist, "If we did stay and you bought more scarves, you might be doing them a favor."

Cyndi chose to ignore his comment. She threw the remainder of her beef stick in the garbage, stood up and looked at Keith, "Let's go swimming."

Keith again hailed down a taxi and directed the driver to take them back to their hotel where they could pick up their suits. On the way he asked the driver how much he would charge to take them to Tagaytay, which was supposed to have some pretty neat beaches. When they had negotiated a price that was satisfactory to both parties, Keith and Cyndi ran up and got their suits and grabbed some towels.

The driver dropped them off at the Batangas beaches two hours later. It was a pleasant drive as Keith enjoyed the friendly banter he had with Cyndi on the way, mostly peace versus the war, but amazingly they kept the conversation light. He was really beginning to like Cyndi and he thought maybe the feeling was mutual.

They spent the next three hours laying in the sand and soaking up the sun. At one time during the afternoon, Cyndi handed a bottle of suntan lotion to Keith and he rubbed down all her visible parts with lotion, making a concerted effort to keep his lustful thoughts at bay. His mother would have been proud. At about 1700 hours, Keith waved down another taxi and they were back at their hotel by 1900 hours. They made a date to meet in the lobby and have dinner after cleaning up a bit. Keith sucked in his breath as Cyndi appeared wearing a tight red mini dress. She smiled teasingly and pivoted for him to get the full effect. "Like?" She asked.

Keith was not looking into her eyes when he replied, "Very much. Do you want to get something to eat or should we just go back to my room?" Cyndi decided it was up to her to keep this Sailor in line, "Get your head out of your pants, Sailor, and let's get something to eat. A little dancing would be nice too." She laughed as Keith made a pouty face, "I seem to remember that was your suggestion." Keith walked toward Cyndi, "Yeah, but I didn't think you'd take me up on it." He took Cyndi's hand and they walked into the hotel restaurant.

They ate a leisurely dinner by candlelight. The day had been so relaxing that Keith didn't remember ever feeling so good. After dinner they moved into the lounge and sat side by side sipping wine, getting more relaxed and lazy as the band began playing a slow tune. Keith pulled a non-protesting Cyndi onto the dance floor and they moved slowly around the floor, which was beginning to fill with other couples, mostly the elite and well-dressed of Manila, probably mostly American and military or government affiliated.

They spoke little and Cyndi rested her head on Keith's shoulder brushing his neck lightly with a kiss. He looked down at her, "What was that for?" Cyndi replied almost in a whisper, "That was for a fantastic day, and for not being the animal I thought I would be having to fight off all day." Keith puller her closer, "Me? Never crossed my mind." He thought briefly of the episode with the suntan lotion and smiled, "Well almost never." Cyndi lifted her head, "Now at least you're being honest, I mean after all you are a sailor, right? The way I hear it all you guys ever think about is getting laid." Keith contemplated her statement, "I'm a sailor, but I also care for you a great deal. I knew you were special from the first time I laid eyes on you. I would like to think you're a very good friend and I wouldn't want to throw that away on a cheap pass." Cyndi looked Keith right in the eye, "Well, Keith Klein, you do say the sweetest things." Keith smiled brightly, "That's right, and don't forget it." Cyndi grabbed Keith's arm and drug him back to the table. She gulped down the rest of her drink and looked up at Keith. "So, your room or mine?" Cyndi looked up to Keith to get his reaction. Keith smiled down at Cyndi planting a kiss on the tip of her nose, "Well, you little hussy. Will you respect me in the morning?" Cyndi shrugged, "Probably not, but then you're probably going to get killed soon anyway, so I don't have to worry about it. In fact, if I find my phone number written on any wall anywhere, I'll kill you myself." Keith leaned down and whispered in her ear, "Not a chance, babe. I never share."

Keith and Cyndi walked arm and arm from their table to the elevator, which they took up to Cyndi's room. There was a bottle of champagne chilling on a stand next to the bed. Keith chuckled, his eyes sweeping the room, "I think I've been set up. You thought I'd be that easy?" Cyndi smiled as she walked toward the bathroom, "No, I knew you'd be that easy." Cyndi was in the bathroom for only a minute and when she returned, Keith smiled at her. "Seems like you've thought of everything." She smiled, "Hope so."

Keith leaned toward Cyndi and held her face gently in both hands as he kissed her lightly on the lips. He pressed harder, wrapping his arms around her and pulling her close to him. One hand moved slowly up and down her back unzipping her dress from the neck to the waist in one motion. He began working on the clasp of her bra, but the damn thing was stuck and he couldn't seem to get it undone.

Keith opened his mouth and reached his tongue deep into the warmth of her mouth. He finally felt the clasp on the bra give way and his hand immediately went to Cyndi's breast. He caressed her breast lightly with his thumb as a weak moan escaped her lips. Their kiss broke and Cyndi stepped back letting her dress fall to the floor.

Cyndi unbuttoned Keith's shirt slowly, and zipped down his trousers. He sat on the edge of the bed and rapidly pulled off his shoes and socks, throwing them across the room. This brought a giggle from Cyndi who was left standing only in her panties at the side of the bed. Keith pulled Cyndi down on the bed next to him and kissed her fully on the lips again, moving down to her neck where he sucked and nibbled at the tender skin. His hands roamed freely over the soft curves of her breast, stomach, and thighs. As he nibbled the edges of her lips and tongue with his own, his hand explored her inner thigh.

Cyndi's breath came in quick, shallow breaths as she responded to Keith's touch. Her hands moved in response to her needs and Keith felt himself harden in her hand.

Keith rolled over on top of Cyndi and placed a nipple gently in his mouth, but Cyndi pulled his mouth back up to cover hers, showing a sudden urgency, and Keith moved between her legs, with a hand from Cyndi to guide him, slowly entering her.

They moved in slow blissful unison, their eyes locked, as Keith reached a height that he could not maintain for long. Cyndi increased her movement beneath him, dragging her nails across his back as they burst together in a long shuttering release. They lay in each others' arms, bodies glistening from the effort. Keith kissed Cyndi's nose, her cheeks, her eyes, and finally the tiny smile of contentment that remained on her lips.

*   *   *   *

They woke up the next morning in this same position, but with the sun high in the sky. Keith noticed the untouched and now warm bottle of champagne still propped beside the bed. He thought perhaps there would still be an opportunity to take care of that later today. He felt Cyndi stir in his arms and kissed her softly on the forehead which started the whole lovemaking process over again.

This time they joked about having worked up an appetite, but neither wanted to leave so Keith ordered breakfast from room service. He also ordered another bucket of ice. After breakfast, Cyndi went to the bathroom to take a shower and Keith followed her in. They soaped each others bodies and made love again in the warm stream of the shower.

Clean and relaxed, they sat on the bed while Keith attempted to comb through Cyndi's wet and snarled hair. Cyndi pulled away, "Is this supposed to be romantic? I think you're ripping out half my hair!" Keith smiled lazily, "Never had this much trouble with my dog, Spot." said Keith. "Are you a purebred?" Cyndi grabbed the comb, "Give me that thing before I go bald." Cyndi laughed, grabbing the comb away from Keith and finishing the job herself. Keith leaned against the headboard of the bed watching her.

"What's it like out at sea? What do you actually do out there?" asked Cyndi. Keith got serious for a moment, "Do you really want to know, or is this research for the latest newspaper documentary of a war monger?" Cyndi turned and planted a kiss firmly on Keith's lips, "A little sensitive aren't we? Of course, I really want to know. It just might help me to understand this mess a little better, not to mention you."

Keith lay back on the bed with Cyndi curled up next to him. He started thinking back to all the things he'd gone through since he had arrived at Atsugi. He told her about the little boy being shot in the bar, about his rescue at sea and the helmet, and how repulsed he had felt afterwards.

He talked about the helos he flew in and the camaraderie of the pilots and crew. Cyndi listened attentively and asked questions about his day-to-day routine. She seemed sympathetic to what he had gone through and at that moment he felt extremely close to her. She didn't judge and she didn't criticize. He even told her about the Vietnamese junk which had fired on one of their birds and how under pressure the gunner had fired back, sinking the small craft. Cyndi continued to listen intently. She asked questions and she seemed to understand his feelings. Keith felt a great deal better having someone to confide in. He felt that Cyndi was someone who he could really trust. Cyndi tightened her hold on Keith and he felt the increased pressure. He looked down to see a tear running down her cheek. "I'm sorry babe, is it something I said?" Cyndi sobbed softly, "no, its nothing you did but I really like you and now I am scared that I might lose you too." Keith held her tightly and the two of them lay in silence for a long time, each absorbed in their own thoughts. Cyndi finally broke the silence.

"You're a good man, Keith Klein." Cyndi reached out to straighten a tight black curl on his forehead. The curl bounced back. Their eyes locked, smiling at first, then serious. Moments later they were again entangled in each others arms and legs. War was temporarily forgotten.

CHAPTER 35

▼

It was right after muster on Monday morning when O'Malley told Keith that he was to report to the personnel office. Keith wondered what could be on the drawing board now. Was he being sent back to sea? It seemed a little soon, but one never knew. He hoped that he wasn't, not when things were just starting to go good with Cyndi. He walked into the personnel office and was told by the Yeoman that he had been picked for burial detail and that he was to report to the Cubi Point Air Terminal at 0600 the following morning. He was to report to Lt. Summerset and was to be in his dress whites.

Keith left the personnel shaking his head, amazed at the twists and turns of his life. Burial detail. What next? Why do I always get picked for this shit anyway? Oh well, how bad could it be?

The next morning Keith arrived at the air terminal and reported to Lt. Summerset. There were eleven other sailors in dress whites as well as six Marines. Lt. Summerset issued white leather leggings to all the sailors; he then called the group together to explain the detail.

"Men, we will be traveling to a small village called Papaya, which is approximately eighty miles north of Manila. We will be airlifted to what used to be United States controlled Sangley Point Naval Station, but has since been turned over to the Philippine Navy. From there we will be going by bus to Papaya." The Lieutenant glanced nervously around, his face grim. He wasn't happy about this duty, but orders were orders.

"Men, we will need to follow a few rules here. First of which is, there will be no drinking on board the bus or at the funeral itself." He hesitated letting this sink in with the men. "It will be okay to have a beer or two later. As I understand it, the local custom is to have a few beers after the funeral, but, I stress…" He hesitated again for effect, hoping ineffectually that they would understand the seriousness of what he was saying, "We are here to set a good example, so stay in control at all times and drink moderately." He paused. The detail stood at ease around the Lieutenant, listening to his directions, yet not at all sure yet what they were in for. Drink moderately. You bet, thought Keith.

"Second, we will not wander off. We are to stay together at all times. This is crucial both for your safety and for your availability in completing this assignment." This got Keith's attention. Safety? Why would a funeral be a dangerous situation? Then again, he didn't have to remind himself that he was in the Philippines. At least Rotor wouldn't be along to raise the odds of something going wrong.

"Third, we are all men here, so no games please. We are all members of the United States military. We represent the very fiber of the United States of America, so please act accordingly." After letting the appropriate amount of time go by for his message to sink in, the Lieutenant continued.

"There will be six sailors assigned as body bearers and six sailors assigned as body guards. The Marines, of course, will provide the honor guard and the final salute. Marines, make sure that your rounds are blanks. We don't want to kill anyone." This brought a few chuckles, and the men relaxed a little.

"The deceased was an E-5 with fourteen years of service in the United States Navy and rates a four-gun salute. Are there any questions?" No one responded. "Okay, if there are no questions, we will go out and board the helos. We will be back by this evening, so don't get too upset over being picked for this detail. Think of it as a one-day flu virus. I will make the final assignments when we arrive at our destination." The sailors and marines headed out to the helos and climbed aboard for the forty-five minute flight to Sangley Point.

When Keith got off the helo, the first thing he noticed was the sad state of repair that the runway was in. It was just a small runway but had large cracks and weeds growing through the cracks. Keith looked around and saw that this was the state of the entire base. They went into the air terminal. Keith went to use the restroom but found the urinal laying on the floor. He decided he could wait for a while longer, although he wasn't sure when he'd get another chance.

The bus that was supposed to have been there waiting for them was nowhere in sight. Lt. Summerset got on the base's only radio and called back to Cubi Point requesting assistance in contacting the party that was supposed to be there to meet them. Keith was beginning to perspire. Even though it was early in the day, he had the feeling that it was going to be a long, hot one. The Lieutenant was waiting for a reply from Cubi Point when the bus pulled up along with a private automobile. The sailors and marines boarded the bus, while the Lieutenant was given the deluxe accommodations in the green 1963 Chevy wagon.

As soon as the sailors and the marines were onboard the bus, the driver brought out a case of San Miguel and motioned for the men to help themselves. "Drink uf, Joes." He looked kind of confused when the group hesitated. The driver, who was the brother-in-law to the deceased, felt obligated to be a good host to these men, who were going out of their way to give his family a military funeral. He had hoped that this would be an honorable gesture of good will. He looked a little dejected when they wouldn't take the beer, but opened himself one, pushed in the clutch, started the engine, and put the bus in gear.

The sailors all looked at each other, knowing that less than two hours ago they had been lectured about doing just this sort of thing. But then the Lieutenant was safely packed away in the other unit, leaving no senior man in command. He was having champagne for all they knew. Suddenly everyone went for the beer at the same time, passing some on to the next guy. The marines were only a few moments behind in accepting the beer, but soon followed. The driver grinned from ear to ear, "You have flinty good time Joe. We really affreciate you coming to bury my brother-in-law."

When the first case of beer was gone, the driver stopped at a Sari Sari Store along the way and got another case. This was an important stop as there were other necessary items of business to be taken care of, and Keith finally found a urinal that was functional. It took a long time to get the twelve sailors and six marines through the single head. The driver realized they had fallen behind and tried to make up the time on the road, his leg stretched to keep his foot to the floor as the bus squealed around a few corners. Keith figured that was the dangerous part that the Lieutenant had mentioned earlier. When he told his thoughts to the sailor next to him, the guy laughed. Soon the whole bus was exchanging jokes.

The beer mixed with the heat, mixed with the lack of breakfast, caused Keith to feel quite lightheaded in short order. Going around the corners at the pace they were driving didn't help matters either. The second case was almost gone when they finally arrived at their destination. Everyone immediately tried to compose themselves. Clothes were smoothed out; shoes touched up with hankies, hair combed, and covers set on straight. Keith was sure no one would notice their slight failing; it was only a few beers after all.

The group of eighteen was shown into the living room of the deceased. They filed in somberly, making a concerted effort to appear sober and in control. One sailor brushed against a statue sitting on a stand inside the door, but the sailor behind him steadied it and they continued into the room. Keith noticed that the driver of the bus was having an argument with someone who was holding one of the empty bottles of San Miguel and waving it in the driver's face. It looked like an elderly man; Keith thought it might even have been the father of the deceased.

A few minutes later, the Lieutenant, looking slightly disgruntled, came in. He addressed the squad. "Okay…" The lieutenant took his hat off and wiped his hand across his brow. He appeared tired and slightly resigned. "Just exactly how much have you had to drink?" One of the marines spoke up first, "Awe, it was only one beer, Sir." This may have gone over well, except he slurred over the word beer and hiccupped at the end. Keith figured he must not have had any breakfast either.

The Lieutenant wanted to believe that the situation could be salvaged.

"Well, I guess one beer isn't so bad, but let's make sure we don't drink any more until this is over with." He looked the men over, not at all confidant that they could pull off this detail. He wondered briefly if a fuck-up here could mess up his entire Navy career.

The funeral was supposed to have started when they arrived, but due to unwritten Philippino custom, everything was running late, and the Lieutenant told them that the funeral would be delayed for at least another hour. He took this opportunity to brief everyone on their assignments.

Keith was assigned to be a body bearer and so he had to practice folding the flag over the coffin. He used two chairs to simulate the coffin and went over the folding until he was sure he could do it in his sleep, let alone half drunk. The Lieutenant looked pleased with himself. He seemed satisfied that everyone would do well, complimented everyone on a good rehearsal, and went to check on the status of the funeral.

No sooner had he left the room when the bus driver came in with another case of beer and started to pass them around. This time no one hesitated, and everyone had at least two more beers when word came that the funeral was about to begin. It was 1230 hours. The funeral was supposed to start at 1300 hours. The Lieutenant announced that it was show-time, and directed them to where the coffin was. Keith found that he was having a slight problem walking. He willed his feet to go straight but they just didn't seem to want to listen. He tried to compensate by holding his body very erect, eyes front. He did manage to make it to the coffin without stumbling, which in his present state, he felt was a major accomplishment.

The six body bearers positioned themselves around the coffin, three on each side, and at the signal from the Lieutenant, lifted it and started a slow and dignified, if somewhat unsteady, march toward the front door.

As if on cue, a wailing rose from a group of mourners huddled in a corner of the room. It reminded Keith of a wounded dog that hadn't been fed for a week. The single wailer would start low and build to a screeching crescendo, than taper off, only to begin again. Some of the mourners had pained looks on their faces. Keith thought it was probably from the wailing rather than from the grieving. He gritted his teeth and leaned slightly into the coffin to steady himself.

They made it through the door okay, with some assistance from the funeral director. As the bulk of men and coffin were too wide to walk through the door, the director held the coffin on one end while the bearers worked their way around the coffin and grabbed it from the other end. The procession continued with Keith peering at the gate at the end of the walkway. From his vantage point, the gate seemed to be awfully narrow but then he figured that may just be the beer.

The mourners and the wailer were coming out of the house. There were other family members and friends in the yard, making a body of about two hundred people. They all began forming up behind the honor guard. The din from the wailer was distracting. Some family members tried to console her but to no avail. If anything she became more vocal the more they tried to quiet her down.

Keith and the rest of the body bearers swayed on towards the gate. Keith was almost positive now that the gate was too narrow. They got closer and closer and Keith knew there would be no way in hell that the coffin could go through the gate. He glanced to the side with eyes only, keeping his head straight, trying to see if there was another gate. There was none.

They were at the gate now and sure enough, the whole solemn procession stopped when the coffin would not fit through the gate. The funeral director ran up to the gate frantically looking for a solution to the problem. The walls were six-feet high with no other gate. They had brought the coffin in through the back and had not run into this problem. The director finally looked at the fence and directed the Lieutenant to tell the body bearers to take the coffin over the top.

The Lieutenant's mouth dropped open for just a second but he quickly recovered his composure and looked at the wall. He reluctantly ordered the body bearers to side step with the coffin to the lower area of the wall, where they would lift the coffin over the wall.

The six sailors sidestepped about ten steps to the left to avoid a tree. Keith felt that was a major feat in itself that they had managed to stay synchronized. He almost smiled. Then they proceeded to lift the coffin over their heads, maintaining a dignified composure. Yeah, good, we're doing great now, he thought. This was accomplished in a somewhat unsteady fashion with beads of sweat breaking out on every sailor's face. It was up and over, and Keith felt the coffin being grabbed by hands on the other side. He felt the coffin leave his grasp and he felt somewhat relieved, until he heard a hollow thud, the kind of sound a coffin would make if it hit the ground, followed by what only could be swearing from the other side of the wall.

The funeral director screamed, "Bo tung eenamo, pucking wall." This was followed by hysterical screaming from the wailer on Keith's side of the wall. The Lieutenant had to have heard the noise, and made a gallant effort to maintain his composure. He ordered the body bearers quickly through the gate to the other side of the wall. They found the body guards holding the coffin upright, like everything had gone according to plan, except all the men had suppressed grins on their faces. The funeral director was perspiring heavily and wiping his face with his handkerchief.

The body bearers took the coffin from the bodyguards and all assumed their places in the solemn procession to the hearse. Keith noticed that the cover of the coffin was slightly ajar, another sign that the pass over the wall had been anything but successful. When the serious, yet slightly unstable procession reached the hearse, the funeral director had a small cart waiting to set the coffin on. As the coffin was slid into the hearse, Keith watched the director re-attach the cover. He also watched him brush some of the dirt off the bottom corner of the coffin. Keith wondered if the deceased was finding some humor in his last ride. He knew that if the situation were reversed he would be happy if his cohorts could make light of an otherwise bad situation. The bodyguards assumed their positions beside the hearse while the body bearers took up the rear. The funeral director got into the hearse and started driving slowly, while the honor guard made an effort to march alongside and behind the vehicle.

CHAPTER 36

▼

The trip to the cemetery took about thirty minutes, but seemed like hours to Keith. It was hot and the sailors had to stay in step and in ranks beside the hearse. The beer definitely did not help but somehow they made it to the cemetery. The coffin was lifted out of the hearse and taken to the gravesite.

The six marines marched to a formation adjacent to the coffin. The priest said a final blessing for the deceased. The Lieutenant took it from there. "Present arms." A slight pause as all the Marines almost moved in unison, "Ready." Another slight pause, then, "Aim, Fire." This was repeated four times. With each report, the wailer set up a new round of hysterics competing well with the marines report. The body bearers grabbed the edges of the U.S. flag from the coffin and brought them to the center, folding the flag in half. They went through the procedure until the flag was folded in a perfect triangle. The end body bearer handed the flag to the Lieutenant who presented it to the widow, who was bawling furiously. Keith began to feel she was overdoing it just a tad. The body bearers back stepped two steps away from the coffin.

The brother of the deceased, moved by the moment, decided that the widow should have one last look at the deceased. Keith had never seen this custom before but got a good view as he was standing right beside the coffin. The coffin was designed in such a way that the first cover lifted and there was a second see-through plastic cover inside that was not supposed to be removable, unless of course the coffin were damaged in some way, like if it were dropped or something.

The brother lifted the outside cover and the widow, who intended to kiss the inside cover, leaned forward. When her lips did not meet the plastic cover, she became unbalanced, falling headfirst into the coffin with legs straight up in the air. To make matters worse, the plastic cover that had been dislodged when the coffin had fallen, now slid ahead, pinning the upper body of the widow inside with her deceased husband. She screamed hysterically, and Keith noted that all was not lost in that it was somewhat muffled. She was kicking her legs wildly into the air around her, trying to free herself, rocking the coffin back and forth precariously on its stand. Keith could tell she took her mourning seriously because every stitch of clothing she wore was black, including her underwear.

Her brother-in-law was trying to free her, but every time he got close, he was rewarded with a kick. After a couple of futile attempts, another man from the crowd who must have lost patience with the situation, rushed forward, grabbed the widow by her legs and pulled her out of the coffin. The poor woman had totally lost control, was screaming hysterically, and bolted from the coffin, not looking where she was going. She ran straight into the Lieutenant who was trying to maintain some dignity during this whole fiasco. She and the Lieutenant tumbled to the ground and she came to rest with her crotch nestled in the Lieutenant's neck, her skirts billowing around her, covering the Lieutenant's head.

The crowd just stared dumbly, pretending not to notice, as she again got up and ran away from the grave site. Several of her relatives chased after her. The Lieutenant got up like nothing had happened. The honor guard never moved, but stared straight ahead. If they had been drunk before, they were perfectly sober now.

"Honor guard, dismissed." The Lieutenant's face was slowly turning red. Keith thought he might choke if he couldn't laugh pretty soon. "You men will be given a ride back to the house by bus."

On the way back to the house of the deceased, they passed the widow who was still running and screaming hysterically. The widow was still being chased by the other mourners, but they were falling behind. The sailor beside him poked Keith in the ribs with his elbow, "They sure do have some wild funerals in this part of the world. Guess I never did see one like this before." Keith had to agree. They were drinking beer in the house when the captured widow was drug in and carried to the bedroom. She was still wailing. This made conversation somewhat difficult, however the Philippinos seemed unperturbed and just spoke a little louder.

There was a feast being spread out on tables in the back yard and soon everyone went outside. The Lieutenant kept looking nervously at his watch. Keith knew they were supposed to be picked up at Sangley in less than an hour as the drive to Sangley was at least two hours. This, however, was not his problem. He had not volunteered for this shit detail in the first place, so he was going to enjoy himself. Actually, it had turned out to be a very interesting day; the men were still chuckling and whispering about the crotch-to-face incident. He grabbed another beer as he went to sit down with a plate full of food. As he did so he noticed what must have been one of the town dignitaries corner the Lieutenant. Poor bastard, Keith thought to himself.

It was about 1600 hours when they finally got on board the bus to go back to Sangley where they were supposed to have been picked up at 1500 hours. The bus driver had stowed plenty of beer on board and it looked to be an enjoyable trip. It took them two and a half hours to get back to Sangley because of three necessary pit stops. When the green Chevy and the bus got to the air terminal, the Lieutenant jumped out immediately and ran inside to use the radio. The helos were nowhere in site. The air controller told the Lieutenant the helos had waited two hours. The Lieutenant called Cubi Point and was told that the helos would be called back to get them. They were to sit and wait patiently.

This was unfortunate because everyone was nearly half primed and ready for more action. The Lieutenant was starting to get a lot of verbal abuse so he decided to call again. This time he was told that the helos would not come due to an incoming storm. New orders stated that they were to catch a ride from the Philippine Navy. The traffic controller told the Lieutenant where the boats were anchored and how to get there. The Philippinos would deliver them to the United States Embassy, which was across the bay in Manila.

The now thoroughly drunk crew of sailors and marines stumbled toward the waiting gun boats. Keith noticed that although the base looked like shit, the boats were well cared for and looked combat ready. The crew seemed very competent and made the Lieutenant and his crew wear life preservers. They were split up among three boats and the boats took off.

It took about forty minutes until they reached the dock behind the embassy. This dock apparently had not been used in a good many years as it was in a very sad state of repair. A short inspection found it to be totally unsafe. The gun boats took the motley crew as close to shore as they could get. The sailors and marines jumped, stumbled, and fell, disembarking any way possible. They took off the life preservers and gave them back, then clambered up the bank.

Ahead of them was a very large wall with a gate that must have been at least fifteen feet high. Everyone looked at the Lieutenant questioningly as they listened to the gun boats speed off. The Lieutenant pushed a button on the wall but nothing happened. He tried this several more times to no avail. Finally he said, "Well, they know we are coming. Let's just climb over the gate." No more said than done. It was an easy gate to climb. Keith had just swung his leg over the top when the spot light hit him and he heard a voice, "Freeze where you are or you are dead." Keith did not move a muscle. Everyone must have obeyed as it got very quiet. Keith felt the hair on his neck stand on end as the seconds passed. Finally the authority voice boomed out again, "Who's in charge of this sorry excuse for a military squad?" The Lieutenant spoke up weakly, "Well, I rang your doorbell three times, but no one answered. We're the burial detail that you're expecting." The authority voice shouted back, "Nobody here died and we don't plan on having anyone die so who do plan on burying?" The Lieutenant was feeling the effects of a very long day, "You were supposed to be contacted by Cubi Point. We already completed the burial and they could not get us transportation home so they told us to come here to spend the evening."

They waited several long minutes. Finally the spot light was taken off and Keith could see the marines with their rifles all aimed at the men coming over the gate. They also had dogs. Keith smiled weakly hoping they would recognize him as just another friendly animal. The marines finally lowered their rifles. "All right," said the head Marine. "Get down from there, but don't do nothing stupid. I'm still not one hundred percent sure you idiots are Americans." He and the Lieutenant went inside to straighten everything out. The rest of the group just stood there dumbly, under the watchful eyes of the marines. The Lieutenant came out twenty minutes later and told the group that they were being put up for the evening at a hotel just across the street. This brought a cheer from the group as they headed for the front gates of the Embassy. The Lieutenant told the group as he passed out vouchers for the hotel rooms, that they still had to stay together and be back here tomorrow morning for the ride back to Cubi Point. As soon as the Lieutenant went back inside, the group dispersed in different directions.

Keith was amazed at his luck. Things were finally going his way. This was the same hotel where he and Cyndi had spent the weekend. She could still be here. He inquired at the desk to see if Cynthia Croft was still a guest. He was told that indeed she was and was still in room 324.

Keith waited until he had been given a room and instead of heading to his own room, he headed to room 324. He knocked lightly on the door and heard Cyndi respond, "Who is it?" Keith was feeling great, "Its Santy Clause, And he's got a little present for you." Cyndi opened the door and stared at Keith, "What on earth are you doing here?" Keith quickly explained about the burial detail and how he ended up back at the Embassy. Cyndi laughed, a little nervously, glancing back inside the room. As Keith babbled on he suddenly got the feeling that he might be intruding on something. His eyes followed hers and he tried to look around her. Cyndi blocked his view and stood in front of him, "I have a few friends here who are sympathetic to the anti-war movement. We are planning on doing some demonstrating, maybe here at the embassy or maybe at Clark or Subic." Cyndi didn't look like she was going to invite him inside. Keith suddenly felt a stab of anger or jealousy, he wasn't sure which, but decided he needed to know what was going on inside.

Keith stepped around Cyndi and entered the room to see four guys and three gals seated on the floor in a circle. How convenient, Keith thought to himself. A perfect one-to-one ratio. Keith looked at the spot where Cyndi had apparently been sitting and at the long haired fellow who would have been seated next to her. He had a peace symbol hanging from around his neck and wore a flowered shirt. His hair was tied back in a pony tail.

He looked at Keith and spoke to the group, "Hey, who let the baby burner in." The room grew silent. Keith looked at Cyndi, expecting her to say something but she didn't. Keith decided it might be best if he got away from the present situation before he got really pissed, "Maybe I had better go, this doesn't look like my kind of party."

Cyndi stared at him, opening her mouth to speak, but was interrupted by the guy with the peace symbol, "Are we a little scared of the truth? The truth will set you free man. Brave man can kill babies but not justify it. I would like to know what justification you have to burn babies." Cyndi stepped in front of Keith, "Hold it Pete," Pete could tell he had riled the sailor, "Why? If the dude's cause is so righteous he should be able to defend himself." Keith cringed and heard the door close behind him. He felt as if he had just been sealed into someone's private hell. Keith knew he had to make the best of it, "I didn't know that I had a cause, I do know I have a duty. I was taught to honor my flag. I was taught that there is nothing wrong with being patriotic…" A young lady with straight black hair interrupted, "This wouldn't be the brave young man you told us about who watched an eight year old boy being shot and did nothing to stop it?" Keith turned to look at Cyndi, but she wouldn't meet his glance. Cyndi finally spoke, "Hey guys…let's cool this, okay? He's got a right to his opinion." Keith turned to leave, "I've got to go. There's no way I'm going to take on eight of you who already have me convicted and hanged." The black haired girl laughed, "Well, maybe you should be hanged for not protesting the sinking of an innocent fishing boat?" Keith turned again to Cyndi. He spoke calmly as he stared into her eyes, "And you're version of the story is that it was an innocent fishing boat?" Cyndi was looking at Keith now, eyes pleading for him to understand, "I was just…"

Pete was enjoying this and was not about to let Cyndi explain a thing, "Our version is the truth man…what chance does a small fishing vessel stand against major firepower like yours. We are going to stop you war mongers from doing things like blowing Vietnamese fishing boats out of the water. Man you people are all the same-kill, maim, burn, you're nothing but a bunch of warmongers. Don't preach this God and country crap to us, we are not buying into the lie."

Keith's whole body felt hot, his fists clenched at his side. He turned and looked Cyndi in the eye, "Thanks for the swell time. I'm really glad I had some-one like you to share some bad times with."

"Please, Keith," Cyndi reached for him, but couldn't get anything else out as he stalked out slamming the door behind him. Pete laughed, "Let him go. You don't want anything to do with guys like him, come on over here and sit down. I got some really good mescaline that will blow your mind."

CHAPTER 37

▼

Keith didn't sleep that night. The word "betrayed" ran like a marquee around and around his head in never-ending cinema. When his 0700 wake-up call came he was ready to go. He skipped breakfast and went straight over to the Embassy. He figured he could wait there just as easily as the hotel. He spent the next two hours as he had spent the sleepless night. He kept going over the confrontation with Cyndi in his mind. He finally came to the conclusion that Cynthia Croft was a spoiled rich bitch who had nothing better to do than to go around questioning the establishment about things that she knew absolutely nothing about. Words like duty and honor held no meaning for people like her. You would think that she of all people, the niece of an admiral would understand. Well, piss on her, he was doing something important. He had already helped save lives. What was her fucking problem, anyway?

Keith watched as the helo that would be taking them back to Cubi Point came in for a landing. Cyndi didn't know shit. Keith vowed he wouldn't think anymore about it as he got onboard the helo. They arrived at the base at 1000 hours and Keith checked in. The Lieutenant told him to take the rest of the day off. Keith figured he would use this time to visit Rotor.

Keith got to the hospital at about 1400 hours and walked into Rotor's room. There was another American visiting Rotor. As Keith walked in, the man pushed something under the mattress. Rotor appeared to be a little flustered at seeing Keith. He fidgeted with a water glass and nervously ran his hand through his hair. He looked back and forth between the American and Keith. The other fellow excused himself and quickly left. Keith was curious, but didn't pursue it as he was anxious to tell Rotor the latest atrocity with Cyndi. He needed to tell someone who he knew would understand. He sat in the same chair the other fellow had just vacated. "Hear any news from Blossom? How's the family doing?" He thought he should cover a few formalities before he got down to the real important stuff, like himself.

Keith noticed right away that Rotor still wasn't himself. He kept glancing around. He looked at his watch. Keith waited for an answer, but it was like Rotor hadn't heard him speaking.

"Okay, buddy," asked Keith, waving a hand in front of Rotor's eyes. "What's going on?" Rotor glared at Keith, "Not a fucking thing, might have been nice if you had let me know that you were coming." Now Keith was feeling a little irritated, "No problem, next time I'll check in with your secretary and see how your schedule looks." Rotor didn't respond. Keith got up to leave, "Just thought I'd stop in to see how you were doing, you being my partner and all. No problem. I'll just leave. We'll see you sometime." Keith turned towards the door, hoping that Rotor would not catch his bluff. He looked over his shoulder to see if Rotor had softened.

Rotor turned in his rack to ask Keith to stay. As he turned a bag fell from the mattress. Keith saw it and Rotor saw it. It was a small plastic bag filled with a white powdery substance. Keith reached down, picked it up and looked at Rotor in disbelief. Rotor almost yelled at Keith, "What in the fuck did you think?" Rotor grabbed the bag out of Keith's hand. "Oh you're mister goody two shoes. Running along sweetly, following all of life's little rules. Well, some of us need a little help to make it through this shit. All you got to worry about is your sweet little ass. I got my ass and your ass, Blossom and the kid's ass, plus every other fucking Boot Camp that comes along." Keith stared at Rotor, feeling another institution crumbling down around him.

Rotor cringed, "I suppose you'll go spill your guts and make this place a living hell for everybody. Well, just remember this. If you do that you are putting your own ass on the line." Keith didn't know what to say. There wasn't anything to say. He felt a rage building. He needed to scream or cry, destroy something, someone, anything. Keith grabbed the water glass from the bedside cart and threw it at the door. What the hell was going on? Everything was out of control, everything was turning to shit. He tried to calm himself. Just say good-bye and get the fuck out of the room, he told himself. Before leaving, he had to get in a final jab, "No, you don't have to worry about me spilling my guts. I just wonder about the little speech you gave me about having it all together for the mission. The bit about lives depend upon what we are doing up there and all that crap." Rotor visibly shrunk back into the sheets. He sat silently for a second, "I was never high on a mission!" He looked a little sheepish now, almost apologetic, "I just took what I needed to get by and that's it!" It had always worked to justify it that way before; it worked for him. He looked at Keith like this should make sense to him. Keith turned to leave and spoke over his shoulder, "That sure makes everything else okay doesn't it?" He let the door slam behind him.

What was going on? Keith couldn't believe Rotor. How could he pull that kind of shit? Worse, how could Keith not have seen it before. It was all coming together now. Rotor must have been stoned when he jumped. How else could he have missed the speed of that helo and not seen the distance he was away from the water? Yeah, and that weekend in the Barrio when Keith had almost gotten married off, Rotor must have had some kind of a big drug deal to pull off. The fucking asshole! He preached about professionalism and doing a good job and the fuck head was on drugs the whole time. Keith headed for the NCO club to get something to settle his nerves.

✴   ✴   ✴   ✴

The next morning, Keith woke up feeling like the whole Polish army and all their tanks had driven over his head. Somehow the physical pain felt much better than the emotional pain he was currently experiencing.

Keith went to the chow hall, hoping a little food might give him the desire to live. He sat down beside Kimball who was wolfing down a plate of scrambled eggs covered with an oozing layer of ketchup. Keith pushed his plate of eggs back and sipped slowly at a cup of black coffee. Kimball was eating heartily when he stopped and looked over at Keith, "Little green around the gills, this morning are we?" Kimball finished his eggs and grabbed Keith's. He spoke between bites, "Hear about James out in Det 107?" Keith listened with one ear, and shook his head. Kimball kept on talking and eating at the same time, "He's going on emergency leave. His parents died, one day apart. Can you imagine? He may not even come back."

A light went on in Keith's head. Keith left his unfinished coffee and went straight to the personnel office. Keith was intent on volunteering to take James' place. He wanted out, out of the Philippines, away from Cyndi, away from Rotor, away from this stupid country.

He had been so impressed with Rotor. He'd been his best friend. He had showed him the ropes, made him feel safe, but now he had found out he was just as human as the rest of them, maybe less. There were no heros here. This was not a Western novel with macho men who relied only on their wits and their bare hands to solve their problems.

Cyndi was another story. She nagged at his morals. He was here to do a job, do what was ordered of him. She thought he actually had control over what was going on. It was all shit. He was fed up. He needed to get out, get away. He was sure they would accept him, as his present flight partner was in the hospital.

Keith was told to go back to work on Helo 45 and he would be notified if he would be going or not. Less than an hour later, Keith was ordered to get his bags packed. He was to leave on the 0700 aboard the first C-2 to the carrier. Keith felt relieved, he was going back to sea where he could do some good.

CHAPTER 38

▼

The COD caught the number two wire as it landed on board the U.S.S. Kitty Hawk. It was pulled to a sudden stop and Keith was pushed back into his seat. The rear cargo door opened up as the plane came to a stop beside the superstructure of the aircraft carrier, which all the sailors referred to as the island. Keith grabbed his gear when he got off the C-2 and saw one of the Big Mothers parked beside the island. Keith decided that he would just go over and wait inside the helo. He was sure there would be someone along sooner or later to direct him to the maintenance spaces where he would get a rack for the night. If nothing else, he would sleep inside the helo.

Keith was right, for just about two minutes later someone slid the back door of the helo open and climbed in. He looked at Keith and then pulled off his head gear and laughed a familiar laugh. Keith looked up and saw the big smiling face of Woody. The two old friends shook hands and patted each other on the back. "How've you been?" asked Woody looking closely at Keith. "Boy, long time no see! We've got a lot of catching up to do. Where are you headed now? My tour is about up and I'm due to head in. I've been out here almost sixty-five days now." Woody rattled on. Keith had a hard time getting a word in. Finally, Woody took a breath. Keith used this opportunity to convey his news, "I'm heading over to Det 107 to take James' place. I figured I could catch a ride on the Big Mother tomorrow." Woody sat down beside Keith, "Not tomorrow you won't. They just made a run today and won't be going back over for two more days. I guess you will just have to settle in on the carrier here for a while. This is great!" Woody looked so cheerful and Keith felt like shit. Maybe it would have been better if he had been trapped out on Det for sixty-five days. Woody wouldn't let Keith dampen his enthusiasm.

"Come on. Let's get you below to get you a rack. I'll take you by the maintenance spaces later so we can swap stories." He continued to chatter as they went below, "I heard Rotor was hurt pretty bad. What happened? Shouldn't you be watching out for your partner?" Keith turned a little red in the face, knowing that Woody was just trying to make conversation, but nonetheless it was scratching an open sore, "Rotor has to look out for himself. He's not my responsibility." Woody sobered just a little, sensing some hostility. If Rotor was a sore point with his old friend, he decided to make things right by pursuing another angle, "So how are you and Cyndi getting along? I heard you got to see her in Manila." Keith scowled again, "Can't we find something decent to talk about? Don't you have a life or something we can talk about?"

Woody cleared his throat, "They're serving hamburgers down in the forward galley, or does that piss you off too?" Woody waited for a reaction from Keith, who finally forced a weak smile and followed Woody down to the maintenance spaces. Det 110 worked twelve hours on and twelve hours off seven days a week. The guy's working day shift often slept in the racks that were just vacated by the evening shift, and vice versa. This was an old naval tradition know as 'hot racking', because the bed would still be warm from the former occupant. The group in the maintenance spaces Keith saw looked tired and he was glad he had been picked at the last minute to go to the Clementine Dets verses the Big Mother Dets.

The maintenance chief looked Keith over, "So, you're the guy who likes to land on Russian ships." Keith sighed, "I've almost done it, but don't think I'd like to make a habit of it." The chief smiled at this and asked Keith if he had any H-3 training. Keith smiled, "I trained with Petty Officer Wood here, chief, but was placed on Det 104 at the last minute." The chief scratched his head, "How would you like to help us out?" Keith shrugged his shoulders, "Be happy to if I can. Got no where else to go, nothing else to do."

The chief went on, "I'm really short of plane captains, I have a man in sick bay and I could really use someone to preflight Helo seven-six." Keith felt red flags going up and alarms going off in his head. He remembered his dream and the mention of seven-six brought it all back. He pushed these thoughts aside as he remembered the H-3 well, "Sure, no problem chief, I can help you out."

Helo seven-six was parked beside the island. Keith went up to do the preflight inspection. He checked all the oil levels, greased all the required lube points, checked all the hydraulic reservoirs, and inspected the rotor linkage. He inspected the tail rotor drive shaft, tail rotor gearboxes, and the tail rotor blades. He inspected the main rotor blades, the sponsons, the battery, and did every thing that was required for a preflight by a plane captain. He even cleaned up the inside of the helo and washed the pilot's windows. This one task took him six hours but he was glad to have something to do and was feeling useful for the first time since they went into the Philippines. When Keith finished his preflight he looked the helo over one last time and felt satisfied. He considered having one of the other plane captains just give it a quick look over since he had not done it for awhile, but thought to himself, "Hell, I used the book and I know I covered all the points. I would feel comfortable flying in her." With that Keith went down and signed off on the preflight inspection in the aircraft logbook for Helo seven-six.

After signing off, Keith attempted to go down to his rack. He got lost somewhere between the maintenance space and the berthing compartment, and ended up wandering around the ship for another hour until he finally found someone from HC-7 in the mess hall to give him directions. When he finally did get to his rack he was completely bushed and was asleep before his head hit the pillow. He was awakened by Woody shaking him, "Hey buddy, get up. I've got great news!" Keith sat up slowly, "It had better be good. I could sleep for another ten hours." Woody laughed, "You'll get up for this. I just got word that Ron is on his way out." Keith stood up, rubbing his eyes, "Ron Markel?" Woody leaned against the bulkhead, "Yeah, the one and only Ron from Atsugi. Boy, I still remember the first time we got him laid when we first got over to Japan."

Keith was fully awake now, "How in the hell did he manage that?" Woody shrugged, "Maybe he followed your advice and asked the skipper if he could come out. I remember after you told him about requesting this he thought about it long and hard." Keith was getting dressed, "Where is he now?" Woody stood up straight, "He's in Da Nang. We've got a Big Mother going in to get mail and some other passengers so I am sure he will ride out with them." Keith grabbed Woody by the arm and started walking down the passageway, "That's great! When will he get on board and what time is it now anyway?"

Woody looked at his watch, "It's 1300 hours, sleepy. That's why I woke you up. If we go and get some chow now, you should be in good shape when he gets aboard so we can visit a bit. He should be on board by 1500 hours, but sometimes these flights get delayed or rerouted."

Keith hurried down the passageways and up the ladders and soon Keith and Woody found themselves in the chow hall. Keith felt good to be back with Woody, "How's the corn coming along in Iowa?" Woody chuckled, "Should be a good year. This must be a safe subject, huh?" Keith smiled and finished his hamburger.

After chow Keith and Woody headed for HC-7's ready room to get the latest on when Ron would be aboard. They were told that Helo seven-six was rerouted and that they were not expected back until 1900 hours. Keith moaned at hearing this, as it would cut into the time he could spend with his old friend.

The ever optimistic Woody poked Keith in the arm, "At least they sent in a good bird to get him. Well, it should be in good shape anyway, unless you were sleeping during your preflight." Keith laughed good naturedly, starting to feel more relaxed again. Keith and Woody spent the next four hours talking about old times and what they were doing now. Woody was on standby, which meant he was on call. If an emergency should arise, he would have to run down and get aboard the standby helo and head out as directed. Keith kidded Woody about the soft carrier lifestyle.

"The ships I go on don't even have a ready room, much less one with plush captains chairs." Woody laughed his usual infectious laugh. Keith wanted to meet Ron on the flight deck so he and Woody headed up when they heard Big Mother seven-six was inbound. Keith stood back out of the way and watched as the helo came in on the port side of the carrier to make its final approach. The helo pulled into a hover on a course parallel with that of the ship with a nose up attitude.

It was about thirty yards off the port side of the ship, straight across from the island and about twenty yards higher than the flight deck when something seemed to go wrong. The helo changed directions, which was in itself unusual, and it also began losing altitude. The helo started spinning out of control as it plummeted towards the waves below.

Keith watched the scene as if it were in slow motion. In the back of his mind warning bells sounded as he ran over to the side of the carrier. It was part of his dream, only he wasn't on the helo, Ron was, and he couldn't do anything about it. He watched in shock as Helo seven-six hit the water and ever so slowly capsized. He watched the majestic helo as it slipped slowly beneath the waves. All around him was action but he stood frozen. The ship's one M.C. was blaring, "Helo in the water! Port side! Angel in the air." This meant that the ship was launching its own recovery helicopter to assist in the rescue. This was a standard practice while launching and recovering aircraft.

Keith couldn't move, praying that all aboard would get out. The numbers Seven-six kept appearing in his brain. In his dream he had been warned and he failed to heed the warning. He should have done something to keep that bird from going. He should have done something.

CHAPTER 39

▼

Helicopter seven six had thirteen passengers and twelve sacks of mail plus a crew of four on board. Keith watched over the next hour and a half while the two helicopters pulled up people and sacks of mail, occasionally coming back and landing on the ship to unload. As he waited, he sometimes would watch the sky, which was partially overcast. The sun seemed to tease him, now light, now dark, not unlike the rescue crew that picked the sailors at random from the waters. Sixteen people made it out alive and were rescued that day in the Tonkin Gulf. Only one went down with the helo. It was his first time to go to sea and he had only a week left to serve in the U.S. Navy. Ron Markel sank slowly to the bottom of the sea, still strapped in Helo seven six. It would be his final resting place.

Memorial services for Ron Markel were held on the hanger deck the next afternoon. Keith attended along with everyone else in HC-7. His flight to Det 107 was delayed because of the service and also because of the fact that he had signed off on the preflight inspection. Keith was sure they did not know what to do with him, not that he really cared. He was at the lowest point in his life. Those closest to him had become a disappointment, to put it lightly. Now, he may have just helped kill one of his best friends. If it hadn't all been so painfully true, he might have been able to laugh. It sounded more like a soap opera than real life, and it was all his.

After memorial services, Keith went out to sit on one of the sponsons outside of the hanger deck. It was one of the few places where Keith could be alone. He sat down and watched as the ordinance techs wheeled the thousand pound bombs by him and up to the flight deck. Keith thought, "Yeah, just another day in the fucking war." He sat watching and thinking and before long it was like he was no longer on the sponson but was standing above watching himself and all the activity going on around him. It occurred to him that something about this picture just wasn't right. He saw Woody coming out to where he was sitting. Woody began to shake his arm.

Keith looked up at Woody who was still shaking him, "Are you okay?" Woody asked. "Maybe you had better come with me." Keith shook his head, "No, I'll be all right. I just need a little time to sort some things out." Woody looked at Keith with concern, "I think you might need some help here, buddy. You don't look really good and you're acting kinda weird. Maybe we'd better go to sick bay. What do you think?"

Keith slowly turned his head as if he were in a daze. He looked at Woody and smiled a really slow lazy smile as if someone else were now in charge of his facial expressions, "I'll be fine. You worry too damn much. You should worry more about your corn and hogs and less about me." Woody sat down beside Keith. The two of them sat in silence for about ten minutes listening to the waves lapping against the side of the ship. Keith was the first to speak, "I wasn't sure when we got to Atsugi how I felt about the war; Ron made it all seem to come together for me. He made me feel like what we were doing was good. I was feeling pretty confident about that until Cyndi came along. Boy did she rock my boat. She made me look at things I didn't want to see." Keith took a deep breath, feeling responsible for all the failings of the world. Keith spoke again and Woody kept quiet thinking Keith needed to get some things off his chest, "I am no longer so sure that this war is right, Woody. If they would let the military fight the war, it would make a difference. But this is a fucking politicians' war, and you and I and about five million other people are caught right up in the middle of it. We are sitting here on the side of this ship doing what we are ordered to do, and for what? We are never going to win this thing." Woody stared somberly at the deck, knowing that for now what Keith needed was a good listener. Keith kept on, "I talked to some Marines back in Cubi, and they told me that we work for a week to take a hill and after we take it we retreat and let the enemy have it back. If we are here to fight then let's fight. We are out here playing fucking games. We are blowing innocent fishing boats out of the water. We almost blow our own airliners out of the air if they do not respond correctly. We are playing chicken with real live weapons, with the Russians no less, and when we can no longer deal with the insanity of watching our friends die for no good reason we turn to drugs to console ourselves. And after all that, when we've fought the big fight, we go home only to be spit on, to be called baby burners. What a crock." Keith lapsed into silence. Woody put his hand on his friend's shoulder and said nothing. There was nothing to dispute, and nothing to add. He just hoped he wasn't going to lose Keith too, but right now he wouldn't give even odds.

*   *   *   *

Keith was sent to Det. 107 the next day. They felt they had him close enough to question him if need be. The chief told him that they had pretty well figured that the reason for the failure of the helo was overloading.

A young sailor who had just come on board the U.S.S. Kitty Hawk was mystified with the flight operations and had taken pictures of everything he saw. He captured the helo as it went down. The tail rotor had quit and that is what caused the helo to start spinning. It was more than likely a tail rotor failure from too much fatigue.

Keith went over his inspection of the tail rotor in his mind. He reinspected each coupling and each section of tail rotor plus the gearboxes. He was sure he had done his job. Still, it was dark and all he had for light was his flashlight. No, he was sure he had not missed anything. But, what if he had? Well, if he had then he would have to live with it for the rest of his life. He would never know for sure.

*   *   *   *

His new flight partner was Hardon. He had picked up this nickname because of his condition whenever he hit the beach. They got along well enough, but Keith pretty much kept to himself these days. He was tagged as a loner by the rest of his crew, none of whom had known the old Keith. He did his job but no more. He began to question orders and when he was called on the carpet for it, he would argue with his superiors. The pilots on Det 107, Lt. Johnson and Ltjg. Bazer, were both pretty reasonable. Keith opened up on Ltjg. Bazer on a number of occasions and still the co-pilot stood by him through some of his tirades. Keith knew he would have to get a handle on this thing or he would end up in deep trouble.

Petty Officer First Class Harrison, the crew chief, came back to the maintenance space one day and told the crew that they were going to spread the blades on Clementine. Keith jumped up from his perch on the cruise box, questioning, "Why are we doing it again? We've got it down to under two minutes."

Petty Officer Harrison was quick to reply, "Because we can do better." Keith blew up and stormed off the flight deck walking right into Lt. Johnson. Keith stopped short and looked into the eyes of the Lieutenant who did not look happy, "Klein, I think it's time you and I had a little chat."

With that the Lieutenant led the way back to the fantail where they could be alone. The Lieutenant sat on the ship's sponson and looked at his crewman, "Klein, I know that you are feeling responsible for what happened to Helo seven-six over on the carrier. I also know you have some serious problems with the rightness of this war. How you feel about these two issues is none of my concern. What is of a concern to me is how these issues affect your performance when we are in the air. I think they are affecting your performance with the crew and you need to get this under control or it's going to affect you me and everyone else in this crew and it may end up costing some pilot his life." Keith stood with his head bowed, looking at the deck. He didn't think he could feel any worse if he tried. The Lieutenant continued, "If we need to go inland, I need a crewman I can rely on. I was asked if I wanted you on this Det. From the glowing recommendation I got from Bossman I jumped when I heard you had volunteered. To say I am disappointed is to put it mildly. I am not going to remove you from flight status, yet. Let's call this a conditioning period. I know you can do better and so do you. Petty Officer Klein, am I making myself understood?" Keith felt more than a little embarrassed, as the tips of his ears reddened. Yet it didn't really matter anymore. Nothing really mattered, did it? Keith finally managed to mutter, "Yes Sir."

The Lieutenant asked, "Is there anything I can do for you? Anything else you want to talk about?" A little voice nagged at him. At first he tried to brush it away. He heard Cyndi and her war-protesting friends questioning. "Sir, I heard that we shot a Vietnamese fishing boat up and sank it. I also heard that they fired first but I have only hearsay and I have not heard anything else. Usually things spread like wild fire. Do you know anything about it? The Pilot looked Keith square in the eye, "Maybe we should finish this conversation in my cabin."

CHAPTER 40

▼

After Keith left the Lieutenant's cabin he felt somewhat better. He felt as if one of many burdens had been lifted from his shoulders. He knew his question had an effect upon the Lieutenant. The Lieutenant said that the matter was still being investigated and that anything we said could and probably would hurt the investigation. It appeared to the Lieutenant that the matter was pretty straight-forward. The rules of engagement stated that if you were fired upon you had the right to fire back. Keith felt better talking about it and he knew Lt. Johnson was a square shooter. Keith went back and apologized to Petty Officer Harrison. They got back on track and soon were pushing Clem out on the deck.

Det 107 was a lot slower than Det 104 had been. There was a Big Mother on board every night and Keith was sure that their chances of being sent inland from here were quite slim. He was sure the Big Mother would go in first. Keith still stayed to himself but was gradually starting to notice life around him again. This was in a large part due to Ltjg. Bazer and his flight partner, Hardon. The more Keith got to know Hardon the better he liked him. Foremost in Keith's mind was that Hardon was definitely not on drugs. He was good to fly with and did not push too much. Keith felt comfortable with his flight crew. Ltjg. Bazer partici-pated in the flight much more than Keith was used to. Their rapport in the air was not overly friendly but was very cordial and professional.

Keith was on Det 107 for seventeen days when the first S.A.R. call came. Since the call came during the daylight hours, they were in the air in under a minute. They received their distances and vectors while they were in the air but were called back less than an hour into the flight. The Air Force Jolly Green Giants had already made the rescue. Clementine was less than ten minutes from her goal when the call came. Lt. Johnson muttered under his breath, "Damn Air Force."

After they landed and received more information they found out that the Air Force had intercepted the Navy's call and had gone in under their noses to get the pilots. The important thing to the Clementine crew was that they had been rescued. The important thing to the brass was that the Air Force had made the rescue. This sent some of the Navy admirals in a tizzy and ordered all ships supporting rescue operations to steam closer to shore.

"Typical, just fucking typical," were Keith's thoughts when he found out. "More games." In the morning they again woke up to Vietnamese fishing junks all around their ship. This was due to the fact that they were now practically sitting on the shore line. There were hundreds of the boats and it was impossible to tell one from the next. They had their families on board. Keith could see women and children as well as men pulling on the fishing nets. Keith thought, "This is the type of thing Ron had talked about seeing and now never would." Keith's thoughts switched in another direction and he wished he had not stormed out of the hotel in Manila as he had. Maybe he should have listened to what Cyndi had to say. But it was too late for that now, too. He started wondering if he had also been too hard on Rotor. He was beginning to understand a little better how someone might get caught up in drugs. In fact, Keith had seriously considered trying some drugs in order to get through his present situation, but did not know how to get his hands on any. His biggest regret, however, was the fact that he had told Ron to try and come out on Det. What kind of bullshit advice was that anyway? Keith seriously wondered if he was playing with a full deck. He wished this Det. wasn't so damn boring so he wouldn't have so much time to think. He was surely going to drive himself nuts.

It was on the evening of day twenty-five after the Big Mother had landed that Keith had found out that Rotor was out of the hospital and was back on flight status. He got this news from Woody who was with the Big Mother crew. Woody said he heard that Rotor was heading out to Det. 104 with Bossman. Keith felt his spirits lifting a little. He asked Woody if he wanted to take in the evening movie, something Keith had not yet done this time out to sea.

On day twenty-nine they had another daytime S.A.R. They launched and were receiving their distance and vectors from the ship when Keith felt a strange vibration in the back of the helo. He keyed his radio telling Lt. Johnson, better known as Big John, that he felt a bad vibration. Big John checked over the instrumentation and found they had lost hydraulic pressure on the main hydraulic pump. No problem, thought Keith, we still have two backups. Big John elected to continue with the mission. Clementine suddenly started getting very erratic. Big John keyed his radio, "We have just lost one of our secondary hydraulic pumps. I have taken the helo off of auto pilot in order to save our last pump."

Keith and Hardon inspected the outside of the helo aft to see if they were losing hydraulic fluid. Hardon reported that he saw a streak of red fluid running down the side of the helo.

"Damn," muttered Big John, "We get one call a month and we have to have problems every time." Big John lowered the landing gear and headed back to the U.S.S. Chicago. Keith did his best to talk Big John down but they were really having a hard time. The helo would not respond very well to the flight controls but the Lieutenant finally managed to set it down. He immediately shut down the helo and the crew ran out to inspect the damage. The problem was a ruptured hydraulic hose, which caused them to lose all the hydraulic fluid that the pumps use for lubrication. Loss of the lubrication caused the pumps themselves to go bad. Big John radioed over to the carrier and requested three new pumps, one new hose, and six gallons of hydraulic oil.

Clementine was down for the next two days awaiting parts. When the parts did arrive via Big Mother, all crew hands pitched in to flush the hydraulic system and put the new pumps on. The new hose was put on and the fluid was added. The Lieutenant requested a test flight the next morning, which was granted. Clementine was again ready for S.A.R.

On day thirty-one of this sea period, Keith and the rest of Det 107 cross decked to the U.S.S. Josephus Danials. The Danials was a lot like the Truxton in its shape and design. Two days after the cross deck, their twin detachment to the North, Det 104 got a S.A.R. call.

Big John called the flight crew together and told them that there was a lot of activity in Hiaphong Harbor and the carrier was doubling its flights to fight the new threat.

"We should be ready. There is a good possibility that there will be some S.A.R. activity through this period. Det 104 pulled two pilots from the drink last night." The next afternoon at 1500 hours, the next S.A.R. call came for Det 104. They were closest to Hiaphong Harbor. Big Mother was enroute to South S.A.R. at this time, and was rerouted to assist Clementine if needed.

Big John, who also wanted to get into the fray, had the helo crew standby on the flight deck. Keith and Hardon mounted the guns, just in case.

CHAPTER 41

▼

Aboard Det 104's Clementine, Rotor was also mounting the M60. They were en route to an area just southeast of Hiaphong. Two A-6 pilots had bailed out and were waiting to be rescued. The enemy was also looking for the pilots, so speed was essential. The helo pilot, Bossman, had Clem going for all she was worth to the last known position of the A-6. They were traveling at 165 knots and watching for signs of wreckage or the stranded men. Once they got in close enough, the downed pilots could either shoot off flares or radio them with their small hand-held radios. This was, of course, if the enemy was not too close.

Twenty-five minutes later Clementine one announced, "feet dry" which meant they had just gone inland and five minutes after that they were at the last known vectors of the downed A-6. Clem and her crew had just started the search pattern when Rotor saw a flare off the helo's port bow. Clem's pilots saw it also and headed in that direction.

Bossman could not see much because of the dense jungle, but circled the area warily looking for a landing place and the downed pilots. He saw a clearing and flew over to investigate. The area was large enough to land the helo, but they still had not sighted the A-6 pilots. The flare had been shot about fifty yards to the south. Bossman tried to raise the A-6 pilots on his radio, not knowing that a North Vietnamese regular had a handheld SAM missile aimed toward his exhaust pipe.

Bossman, trying to raise the A-6 pilots called, "Sea Devil 19 to Wolf Man or Axe Flyer. Do you read me? Over." They got their awaited reply from the A-6 crew, "We have you in sight, Sea Devil 19. This is Wolf Man." Bossman, smiled. "Roger, Wolf Man. Are you as American as apple pie or peach cobbler?" The response was the correct one, "That apple pie sounds good." Bossman looked at Rotor, "Sounds like we've got us some Americans. You be on your toes in case we start to draw enemy fire." To the A-6 crew he asked, "Are you injured, or can you run toward the helo?" The response was quick, "You land. We'll be there." Bossman spoke to the A-6 crew again, "We're going to set down now. Make your dash towards us."

Only when the helo began to shudder violently did Bossman realize that they had been hit. He yelled into his radio "May Day, May Day, Sea Devil 19 is hit and going down."

Bossman pulled up on the collective, but the helo would not respond. The collective felt as if it was bound up. He looked at his exhaust gas temperature, EGT, and saw that it read zero. This either meant that he had lost an engine or his gauge was defective. With a sinking feeling, he knew he had lost an engine. He tried to do an auto rotation by disengaging the rotors, but he was too close to the ground. Before he got the lever totally disengaged, the helo crashed to the ground and he lost consciousness with the sudden impact.

✳   ✳   ✳   ✳

Aboard the Danials, Clementine 2 had just been given orders to go in. Keith knew that some heavy shit must be going down. Never had he heard of them needing three helos for a rescue. He figured it had to have been a bird with lots of people on board, or maybe another fighter got shot down. Another possibility was that there was so much ground fire, they needed more cover. Keith felt his nerves tighten. He was scared and anxious, but was impatient to get going. This was why he was here, and he had a job to do. He was ready. His adrenaline was flowing and he felt the intensity of the moment, knowing that something dangerous lay ahead. The fear was there for the unknown but there was also anticipation.

Clementine 2 was in the air in under a minute. As they flew, radio reports were coming in rapidly, and it appeared that one of HC-7s helo's was down inland. Somehow in Keith's mind he knew that Rotor was onboard.

✳   ✳   ✳   ✳

Back at the crashed Clementine, Rotor was just regaining consciousness. He heard the whine of bullets as they were buzzing overhead. He looked out the open door and saw the gooks moving in. He grabbed the M-60 and started spraying the area. Bossman also came around about this time and got out his M-16. He helped Humper out from behind some armor plating where he had been pinned when the helo crashed. Humper had a graze that looked like a bullet had creased the side of his head. The second crewman, Little John, had been hit in the leg, but was also returning fire. It looked like they would be able to hold off the North Vietnamese for awhile, so Bossman tried to radio the two A-6 pilots again.

At precisely that moment, the two A-6 pilots, Wolf Man and Axe Flyer, came running into the clearing about twenty yards away from the crashed Clementine. One of them stumbled, as fire took him down at the knees. Bossman jumped out of the helo and raced toward the downed pilot who was being half drug by his partner, as the rest of the Clementine crew provided cover fire.

Back at the crashed helo once again, Bossman radioed out for help, "This is Sea Devil 19. We are down and drawing heavy ground fire. We have two A-6 pilots and a crew of four. Request immediate rescue."

*   *   *   *

Above them the Big Mother had just arrived and circled overhead. Big Mother's pilot surveyed the situation from the air, fearing the same fate that had befallen the Clementine.

The pilot ordered his rear gunner to spray down the area to the north of Clementine with his mini gun. The mini gun fired five thousand rounds every sixty seconds with every sixth round being a tracer round. The rear gunner was able to push back the North Vietnamese, much to the relief of the Clementine crew and the A-6 pilots below.

Big Mother was just going to settle down for a landing when the pilot saw the missile whiz by, narrowly missing the helo. The pilot immediately pulled up and cleared the area. She came back several seconds later and again sprayed the area with her mini gun. Big Mother would be able to hold down the gooks but would not be able to pick up the downed crew at the same time. The Big Mother pilot radioed to Clem 2 and hoped they were close. They needed help.

*   *   *   *

Clem 2 was less than five minutes out now. Keith had checked and rechecked the M-60 and all the small arms. They flew on until Big John spotted the Big Mother. He flew to the south of Big Mother who was still covering the North

Vietnamese with her mini gun. When Clem 2 was in position, Big Mother made an all out effort to spray the area to try to push the gooks back. Big John surveyed the situation and told Keith to open fire on the same position as the Big Mother, but to direct his fire in a wide pattern to keep any stray gooks from firing at them.

Keith was preparing to open fire when he heard the whine of bullets going through the cabin. Six perfectly round holes met his eyes as he looked over to where he had heard the wining sound. Keith froze. His face went white. This is it for sure, he thought. He heard Big John screaming orders, "Man your guns!"

The words from his dream sent chills down his spine, but Keith felt his fear being replaced by determination as his training took over. He knew the other crew was still alive and that they would have to get them out. Big John set the helo down less than twenty yards from Clem 1.

Keith held tightly onto the grips of his M-60 while showering down the jungle. Occasionally he could see gooks in green uniforms running towards shadows and hiding behind trees approximately fifty feet from the helicopter.

As soon as Clem 2 had set down, Hardon motioned for the entire Clementine 1 crew to come onboard. Rotor stayed to provide cover fire as everyone left. Hardon jumped out of Clem 2 to help carry the A-6 pilot into the helicopter. Humper and Little John helped each other across while Bossman continued to provide cover support with his M-16. Rotor looked and saw that everyone was close to boarding the helo. He decided that it was a good time to leave, abandoned the M-60 and grabbed an M-16 for the run to Clem 2.

As soon as Rotor ceased fire, Keith felt an increased pressure of fire power from the jungle. He heard the pilot yell at him, "Gooks on the ground! Ruskie, shoot, damn you, shoot! They're going to hit us if you don't keep them down."

Keith did his best to cover the entire area with his M-60, but the area was too large and he could see some of the gooks coming out. The crew from Clem 1 was only ten yards away now. All they had to do was get in the helo and they could get the hell out of here.

Keith watched the crew with one eye while covering the area with his other eye. Suddenly, Keith saw Rotor dash from the Clem 1 helicopter and watched him make the short sprint to Clem 2. The rest of the crew were just climbing aboard when Keith saw Rotor go down. Keith had to make a choice. He knew that Big John could not sit here much longer or none of them would leave. Keith turned his M-60 over to the A-6 pilot and jumped out of the helo, yelling, "Cover me!" as he raced towards Rotor. When he reached Rotor, he saw that Rotor had been hit in the legs, hip, and shoulder. He was still conscious, still had his M-16, and was still firing and swearing at the gooks.

Keith grabbed his old friend under one arm, while spraying the area with his M-16 in the other hand. Keith half drug, half carried Rotor toward the helo, watching in awe as it lifted off and headed out. They crouched in the rotor wash below, the blast of wind stinging their eyes and filling their mouths with sandy grit. Bullets were flying all around them. Both sailors laid flat on the ground and surveyed the area around them, watching as the shadows began to move in closer.

"Well, buddy, I think we're in some deep shit now," said Rotor. "I think we're about ready to cash in our chips." Rotor tried rolling over on his stomach to get a shot off at the gooks, but didn't have the strength. He lay back, closing his eyes as if resigned to his fate.

Keith tried to clear his head to think of a way out of their present situation. As he glanced around he focused on the downed Clem 1 and the M-60 seemed to shout at him. He surprised Rotor as he again grabbed him under his arm and started dragging him towards the helo. Rotor figured out what he was trying to do, "No, just leave me and go. You'll have a better chance." Keith yelled back, "Just shut up, and hang on." Keith had an odd and determined look on his face as he found strength he didn't know he had, "I'm not done with you yet, asshole. And believe me I deserve a chance to get even…for the fucking lousy things…" He continued his preaching as he tugged and grunted and pulled Rotor towards Clem 1. Rotor weakly smiled and tried to stumble along with Keith. Keith finally pushed his gun behind his back in order to support Rotor better. He had almost reached the helo when a gook jumped out from behind a tree less than fifteen yards away. The gook had his gun leveled at Keith and Rotor and was ready to shoot when Keith pulled his flare gun from his pocket and fired. The flare caught the North Vietnamese soldier in the stomach. A scream erupted from his lungs and Keith watched as the flare burned a six-inch hole through his body. The soldier threw his arms in the air before falling backwards.

"Yeah," Rotor muttered, "All the fucking lousy things, like how to use flares." Keith pushed Rotor inside behind the armor plating, grabbed the M-60, and started picking off gooks as they had gotten braver and were visibly running across the clearing. Rotor attempted to help, but was too weak to lift his M-16 so he helped feed ammo into the M60. When the ammo bucket was empty, Keith reached back for another, but there were no more. Keith and Rotor's eyes met briefly knowing that they were now in deeper trouble than before. Then suddenly, from their temporary shelter came a loud barrage of gunfire as Big Mother entered the clearing and landed twenty feet from Clem 1. Keith cast one look heavenward in a fleeting religious moment of "thank you" as he once again grabbed Rotor, this time throwing him over his shoulders, and began running toward the Big Mother. The numbers seven-seven seemed to jump out at him as he ran. He only had five feet to the Big Mother door when his legs went out from under him. He tried to get up but his legs would not respond. He felt a sharp pain in his left shoulder and something even stronger rip through his lower back. He felt hands grabbing and pulling him into the bird as they lifted off. He glanced quickly to his right to assure himself that Rotor was still at his side.

Keith leaned back against the bulkhead, breathing heavily. He had not gone far but it was like he had run ten miles. Keith suddenly felt light headed and it seemed as if he were having trouble moving. He tried to lift his legs but it was as if someone had tied them down, his arms were also very heavy. He was tired, so very tired. Maybe if he just closed his eyes for a moment.

CHAPTER 42

▼

When Keith opened his eyes all he could see was blackness. He was aware of movement under him and he felt as if he were in some kind of a machine. He knew he was still onboard the helicopter. He tried moving again and found that he could move his right arm out and back. He tried his left arm and it hit something solid. He moved his left leg and it to ran into something. Keith felt a wetness surrounding him, cold and sticky. It felt as if he were lying in a small wading pool. Consciousness began to fade again. He fought to stay awake, but it was no use.

*   *   *   *

It was semi-dark, and in the soft glow coming in from a window on the port side, Keith could make out two forms lying under blankets on the floor of the helo. He shook his head, trying to clear his thoughts, not knowing if he was back in his nightmare or if it had become a reality. He tried to reach out to the forms, which made pain streak down his left arm and then turn to numbness at his fingertips. Below was more numbness as he tried to move his legs with no results. With his right hand, he managed finally to reach over and lift the corner of the blanket off to disclose the face of the man nearest to him. It was Rotor, laying cold and still and unseeing. He lifted the blanket further. He saw the shoulder, the neck, and the chin, and finally recognized Woody's face. The semi-darkness closed in around Keith as he felt his body entering a vacuum, all light, all air being sucked away as he once again blissfully lost consciousness.

*   *   *   *

The next time Keith awoke, he saw he was still in the helo. He had been covered by a blanket…. He looked to his left and saw Rotor lying motionless. He looked for Woody, but there was no one else. He moved to shake Rotor, but his arms were so heavy he could not move them. He tried to kick him but his legs would not move. He yelled out Rotor's name but no one answered. Then he felt someone lifting him and again he fell into unconsciousness.

*   *   *   *

When Keith awoke this time it was to the quiet hum of machinery. Keith instantly identified the sound of a ship. He opened his eyes to see pipes and white overhead. He looked to his left and saw more racks, to his right was a bulkhead. He looked down toward his feet and saw more racks across the passageway from him. Two of the other racks were occupied. Keith tried to sit up but felt very weak. He was able to lift his arms but his legs felt very heavy and numb. He heard a voice coming from a great distance.

"Its good to see you awake. You've been out of it for some time now." Keith tried to talk but his mouth felt dry and sticky and the same time. He motioned for some water and a corpsman came over and poured him a glass and helped him sit up to drink it. Keith could not remember the last time a drink had tasted so good. He requested another. Suddenly the reality dawned on him and he grabbed the corpsman's shirt, "What about Rotor? Where's Woody. Are they okay?" The corpsman did not know who he was talking about. He took the glass away from Keith, "Settle down, buddy," said the Corpsman. "There is just this Petty Officer Seymore and Lt. Howard."

Keith tried the best he could to remain calm as he asked, "How is Petty Officer Seymore?" The corpsman promptly responded, "I'm not the least bit happy to report the asshole will live, unfortunately. We were not so sure about you though. It was nip and tuck for awhile there. You had lost a lot of blood and you're going to be very weak for awhile, but you should be okay too." Keith suddenly remembered Woody, "What about Woody? Petty Officer Charles Wood? Did he make it out alive?" The corpsman shrugged, "There's no one in sick bay by that name."

Keith laid back, knowing that if Woody wasn't in sick bay, it could only mean that he was dead. As he slipped into a deep sleep, he tried to figure out why

Woody had been on the helo. Woody shouldn't have been there in the first place. Another senseless mistake.

Keith was next awakened by someone shaking his arm. He looked up and saw what must be a Doctor taking his pulse, "How are we this morning Petty Officer Klein?" the man in the white frock asked.

Keith's mouth was very dry and he answered somewhat squeakily, "I am feeling much better, thanks, but I sure could use something to eat." Keith heard someone say, "Give the Boot camp a hot dog but make sure you fill it with mayonnaise." Keith laughed for the first time in a long time and it felt good, but it hurt at the same time. Rotor looked over at Keith, "Nice thing you did back there, Ruskie, but now I suppose you think I should thank you or something. Well, I appreciate you're saving my life and all, but you are still the Boot camp and don't forget it. Rotor paused for a moment, "It really was close and if you hadn't come for me, there'd have been nothing to come back for. It was that close. We just made it out of there by the hide on our assholes. I probably owe you big time for this one, but I'm sure not going to say thank you because you will never let me live it down." Rotor didn't seem like he would ever quit talking. Keith interrupted, "Gees, have I died and gone to hell? What are you doing here?" Rotor leaned up on his elbow, "Ah, you love me and you know it." Rotor pursed his lips for a kiss. Keith covered his eyes. Rotor continued babbling, "I think the pilots are going to put you in for a medal of some sort, but I think your whole crew will get one for this last rescue. It was the worst one I've ever seen. Those fucking gooks wanted our asses. Thanks to you guys they didn't get them. Keith sat up and looked at Rotor, "Why was Woody out there?" Rotor pulled back, "Woody? What you talking about?" Keith explained, "Woody was on the Big Mother." Rotor looked at Keith with a questioning expression, "The same one we were on? I knew the two crewmen on the Big Mother." Rotor scratched his head, "And Woody wasn't one of them." Rotor looked at the confusion on Keith's face and smiled, "You don't suppose he was the guy standing next to my friend all dressed in white, do you?"

Keith started looking hopeful, than started laughing, "You know, I bet you're right. I bet that was just a fucking dream. But I need to know for sure." Rotor persisted, "Hey, no dream, buddy. If it hadn't been for you and Mr. Clean, we'd both be dead." Keith laughed but it hurt, "Yeah, right." Keith looked around for a corpsman, "Corpsman, can you come here. I've got a question." The corpsman listened to Keith's inquiry and said he'd check it out. Keith looked back to Rotor, "So, how are you doing, Rotor? I mean, how are you really doing?" Rotor smiled a sheepish grin, "Fine buddy. Better than ever. Kicked the shit while I was in the hospital." Keith looked kind of surprised. Rotor's faced turned slightly pink as he continued, "They had a rehab and I figured, what the hell? If Boot camp can live without them…So what do you say, let's hit the barrio this time in!" Keith looked Rotor right in the eye, "Fuck you. But, then again, when is the next time in?" Rotor leaned back and put his hands behind his head, "We are on our way right now buddy. Tomorrow the Philippines Islands, the P.I. I can smell Shit River now."

It was at that moment that Woody walked into sick bay, and for the first time, Keith felt his eyes fill with tears as they clasped hands.

✻   ✻   ✻   ✻

The carrier Kitty Hawk, where the sailors had been recuperating, arrived in Cubi Point the next day and off loaded its cargo of injured personnel and damaged helos. Keith was transferred to the Subic Bay Naval Hospital where he was to finish the healing process. He was able to walk a little but was still very weak.

On his third day in the hospital, he was told he had a visitor. He was strongly expecting to see Rotor, and as he walked out to the visitor's area he was surprised to see Cyndi. His initial reaction was that he was excited to see her, but his second thought sobered him as he felt she had some explaining to do, "Well, look what the peace movement dumped in the visitor's lounge."

Cyndi smiled tentatively at him, not sure of the reception she was going to get, "Just thought I'd check and see if I could cash in on the life insurance policy yet. Looks like you're going to live to harass me another day." Keith did not smile, "I thought it was the other way around." Keith did not say anything else and a silence filled the room. Keith felt that an explanation was in order, Cyndi owed him that much. Cyndi finally walked over to Keith, "I never meant to hurt you, babe." She sat down on a chair in the waiting room but Keith continued to stand so she tugged on his hand forcing him down to her level. "My intention was not to break a confidence. I was using your examples of war experiences as typical of what was going on. I didn't realize they'd crucify the person and not the situation." Cyndi's eyes filled with tears. "I wasn't judging you. I could never have done the things you did. I could have never survived the things you have. I just want the war to stop before I lose any more." Cyndi looked searchingly into Keith's eyes. "I've lost you too haven't I?" Keith felt himself crumbling.

"No, pretty lady, not yet. I've got this reputation for being a little slow. Takes more than one cheap shot to scare me off." Cyndi smiled and Keith continued, "I know now that I'm doing the right thing. We may not be fighting for the right reasons but we're here and I feel we need to support our country. The people that are here need me; we need each other. That's where I am at. Take it or leave it."

Cyndi took Keith's arm, "Let me think about it for a bit. If you got killed in the line of duty it would be another loss and I don't know how many more I can take." Keith pulled Cyndi close for a healing kiss, and they started slowly down the hall, Cyndi supporting Keith as he leaned against her. They had only gone about ten feet when Cyndi replied, "I'll take it."

CHAPTER 43

▼

Keith was released from the hospital the next week, and assigned back to his squadron. He was in the personnel office on the third night of his release and was standing duty.

It was around 0330 hours when a call came in that there were three new men awaiting transportation at the air terminal. The Duty Officer looked over at Keith, "I want you to get in the duty truck, go down there and get those guys."

Keith was just due to be relieved and had been trying his best to keep from falling asleep. He got up from his chair, rubbed his days growth, and grumbled something about how late they always sent these guys in.

Keith threw on his ball cap and grabbed the keys to the truck. He half buttoned his shirt, starting with the wrong sequence, and sped off toward the air terminal. The old dodge pickup rattled and had a hole in the muffler, making it louder than the usual din. It seemed like all the vehicles on the damn base needed new mufflers.

As he approached the terminal, he saw what were obviously three raw recruits, standing uneasily on the corner, shuffling their feet and carrying their green canvas sea bags. He stopped the pickup beside them and yelled out the window, "You the three pukes going to HC-7?" They looked at each other, not sure that they wanted to go with this seedy-looking character. Keith was in a hurry, "Well don't just stand there. I ain't got all night. Throw your shit in the back and let's get you checked in, dozo. Just 'cause I got the duty don't mean that I want to sit here all night and baby sit a bunch of boot camps. So get your asses in this pickup and let's go."

The three young recruits nervously complied with Keith's instructions. One of the sailors reached out his hand to Keith, "My name's Dennis, and this is Larry and Dale. What's yours?"

Keith scratched the stubble on his chin and gave each of the men a quick firm hand shake, "The name is Ruskie. You probably already heard of me. That ain't my real name, of course. That's just what they call me." Keith shifted the old dodge into gear and popped the clutch, "Do you want to know why they call me that?" Keith didn't wait for the startled young men to respond; they were white knuckled from holding on to the door handles as Keith screeched around the corners going up the hill. He turned and looked at his three new recruits, "Cause I'm a legend in my own time, that's why." Keith looked at himself in the rearview mirror, "Yeah, that's me. A legend. Not only am I the only guy to try and land an American helicopter on a Russian ship, but I am probably the only enlisted man on record to be engaged to an Admiral's niece…You sure you ain't heard of me?"

THE END

978-0-595-38799-1
0-595-38799-3

Printed in the United Kingdom
by Lightning Source UK Ltd.
116860UKS00001B/235